OTHER BOOKS BY ANNABELLA MICHAELS

Souls of Chicago Series
Feeding the Soul, Book 1
Music of the Soul, Book 2
Protecting the Soul, Book 3
Renewing the Soul, Book 4

DEDICATION

This book is dedicated to all of Annabella's Sexy Souls. You are a unique group of wonderful, loving, caring and supportive friends. I love all of you and I'm so grateful to have you in my life.

PROLOGUE

Rocko

I FINISHED SHOVING MY CLOTHES IN MY SUITCASE AND ZIPPED IT shut, then pulled my long hair back into a loose ponytail. I'd listened quietly as my best friends and bandmates told me that they refused to stand by and watch me kill myself and that if I didn't go through rehab then I was out of the band. At first I was pissed that they were threatening my place as their drummer, but after giving it some thought, I realized that they'd only said those things because I'd scared them and because they cared about me. As soon as I was released from the hospital, I'd checked myself into a rehabilitation program.

The first several days had been pure hell as my body ridded itself of all the drugs and alcohol I'd poured into it. Detox was not for the faint of heart and I made a promise to myself that I would stay clean and sober from then on.

Since then I had spent countless hours attending daily group and private counseling sessions, as well as art therapy. I didn't have a clue how making a lopsided vase out of clay was supposed to help me, but I went along with it. The group counseling sessions were boring as fuck, but I was usually able to get through them without having to share too much.

The private sessions, on the other hand, were nothing less than an exercise in torture. Dr. Turner and I usually spent the hour staring at each other as he waited patiently for me to answer even the most basic questions. The truth was, I thought Dr. Turner was an alright guy and I wasn't trying to be a dick, but there were just some things from a person's past that were better left alone.

Finally, after two months, I'd completed the program and I couldn't wait to get home. I'd texted Landon, our band manager, and he said he'd arrange for a car to pick me up. I glanced around the room, lifting the blankets on the bed and checking the closet one last time to make sure I hadn't forgotten anything. Satisfied that I wasn't leaving anything behind, I picked up my suitcase and walked out of my room.

Dr. Turner was waiting in the hallway. "I just wanted to congratulate you before you left. You should be proud of how far you've come and I wish you all the best."

"Thank you," I murmured, not quite sure what to say.

He held his hand out and I shook it. "Good luck, Rocko. Try to let more people in; you might be surprised to find that not everyone will let you down."

I watched him as he turned and made his way back down the hallway, his words running on a loop through my mind. I walked towards the front door, feeling a little nervous to be leaving the safe walls of the facility. A black Escalade was sitting at the curb with its engine running so I opened the door and headed down the sidewalk. It was dark out and I was relieved when nobody jumped out of the bushes to snap a picture of me as I left rehab.

The driver got out and I handed him my suitcase then climbed into the back seat. I was grateful that the privacy screen was up between myself and the driver because I didn't feel like talking to anyone. I scooted down in my seat and closed my eyes, taking a deep breath as the car began moving.

It had been easy to follow the program while I was in rehab because there were no temptations. No one offered me drugs, alcohol, or sex. Out in the real world was another story though, and my hands began to shake as I wondered whether I would be strong enough to refuse my old vices when I was faced with them. I knew what was at stake though, so I would fight hard to maintain my sobriety.

I drifted off to thoughts of seeing my friends and playing the drums again. I jerked awake when I felt the car slow to a stop and peered out the window, confused about where I was. I pushed the intercom button. "Excuse me, I thought you were taking me home. This isn't where I live." Before the driver could respond, my door swung open. I climbed out of the car, ready to apologize to whoever lived there and explain that some mistake had been made, but I stopped short when I saw the person standing there.

"Hello, Rocko. I'm glad you're here," Lachlan Edwards said stiffly.

"Where are we?" I asked in confusion.

"This is my home. Please, come inside. We have some things to discuss."

Fuck! This can't be good. I clenched my jaw as he turned and started to walk away. I'd done everything the guys in the band had asked, including going through the rehab program and getting clean, so that I could keep my position as the drummer for Carter's Creed, but Lachlan owned Golden Entertainment Studios which held our contract; ultimately the decision of whether I was fired or not was up to him.

"I didn't know you had a place in the Chicago area," I said, trying to keep the nervousness out of my voice as I followed him up the drive. The man was easily the wealthiest person I knew and probably had homes all around the world, but no one had ever mentioned him living so close to the rest of us.

"I just purchased it recently," he supplied vaguely.

I looked around for the first time and my jaw dropped open. I had been to a lot of parties thrown by very wealthy people since the band had hit it big, but nothing compared to the enormous mansion Lachlan Edwards called home. The front porch was deep and there were three intricately carved wooden doors leading inside. The windows and doors were all arched and delicate looking chandeliers hung across the entryway and from the balcony overhead, their glow giving the place a warm and welcoming feel.

"Nice purchase," I mumbled. "Is that a garage?" I pointed at the large building which sat off to the side of the main house.

"That's the pool house. The garage is over there." He sounded almost embarrassed when he gestured to the gigantic structure to the left. The garage looked like it could easily hold more than twenty cars and I let out a low whistle of appreciation.

There was no more time to look around as Lachlan led me through one of the front doors and up a wide staircase. The hallway at the top stretched out in either direction and I followed Lachlan as he turned to the one on the right.

The door was opened at the last room and he stopped in front of it. "You can have this room. It's been a long day and I'm sure you are quite tired. We'll talk more in the morning."

"Wait, you want me to stay here? Overnight? I thought you brought me here to talk." I felt like I'd suddenly stepped into *The Twilight Zone* because I had no clue what was going on.

"We will talk, but you need your rest. Please, make yourself at home and I'll see you in the morning." He spoke quickly and then turned on his heel and headed back down the long hallway. I watched him as he went to the room at the complete opposite end and shut the door behind him.

"Goodnight to you too," I grumbled to myself, shaking my head. I wasn't sure why I couldn't have slept in my own home and met with him the next day, but I was too tired to argue. I yawned loudly as I went into the room and shut the door. My eyes felt scratchy and my body ached with exhaustion. It had been like that ever since I went through withdrawal. My doctor explained that it would take some time for my body to recover from all of the things that I had put it through and allowing myself time to rest was an important part of my recovery. I didn't even bother to change out of my clothes as I collapsed face first onto the bed; my eyes shutting as soon as my head hit the pillow.

CHAPTER
One

Rocko

I ROLLED OVER AND TRIED TO GET COMFORTABLE ENOUGH TO fall back asleep, but my clothes were bunched around me. I hated sleeping in clothes, usually preferring to wear nothing instead. I kicked off my shoes and let them fall to the floor with a thud then tried to wriggle out of my clothes, but by the time I had pulled my shirt off and worked my jeans down my hips, I was wide awake.

I rubbed a hand over my eyes tiredly, knowing that I should probably get up soon if I was going to have time for a cup of coffee before I had to sit through another mind-numbing group therapy session. In fact, I was surprised that I hadn't already been woken by the sounds of other patients as they started their day.

I blinked my eyes open and then sat up quickly when I realized I wasn't in rehab anymore. The events of the previous night washed over me and I groaned. Lachlan Edwards brought me to his home because he wanted to talk to me. My stomach churned. Whatever he had to say would make the difference between whether I would get to stay in the band or not. The thought of not being a part of Carter's Creed sliced through me like a knife and it had nothing to do with the money or the fame. The truth was, I didn't want to lose the other members of the band. They were my best friends and the only family I had.

There was a time when they would have fought Lachlan if he tried to fire me, but after all of the shit I'd put them through, I wouldn't blame them if they were already looking for a replacement drummer. Carter's Creed had been put on the fast track and they didn't need a screw-up like me bringing them down.

Carter, Tyler, and Kalia had visited me a couple of times in re-hab, but so far, I hadn't heard anything from Steve. While I was close with all of my bandmates, I was closest to Steve. Kalia and Tyler were in a relationship so when we weren't on tour, they preferred to spend their time alone, just the two of them. Carter was an awesome friend who always made time for me if I needed him, but between his fian-cé, Ryan, and his huge family, Carter didn't have much time for any-thing else and I didn't want to be a burden.

That left Steve. We became friends pretty quickly after we met, which had been a surprise to me; I'd never really had any friends be-fore and I had trouble trusting people, but I trusted Steve immediate-ly. He didn't push me to talk about my past and he never seemed to mind when I would show up at his door unannounced and spend the night playing video games or watching movies with him; in fact, he'd given me my own key to his place so I could come and go whenever I wanted. He had a girlfriend who I knew he was crazy about, but she was a photographer and travelled frequently with her job so he was alone a lot of the time.

Steve was on the shy side and while he was an outstanding gui-tarist, he preferred to have the audience's attention focused on Carter when we were on stage. I often wondered if it was Steve's calm, un-flappable demeanor that drew me to him. My life had been nothing but chaos and upheaval since the day I was born, but when I was around my best friend, all of that disappeared and I felt like I was able to breathe.

I couldn't remember most of the events that had led up to me being rushed to the hospital, but my friends filled in the missing pieces as much as possible. Apparently, I'd been in a hotel room partying with a group of people. When Steve hadn't heard from me in a couple of days, he went looking and found me passed out in the hotel bathtub where the others had left me before taking off. I was completely unresponsive and actually died twice on the way to the hospital. Carter told me that Steve just needed some time after the scare I'd put him through, but I had to wonder if maybe I'd finally fucked up enough for him to call it quits. Not that I'd blame him, there were times when I wished I could walk away from myself.

I'd originally agreed to go to rehab because my friends had told me in no uncertain terms that if I didn't get clean, they were going to kick me out of the band. Somewhere along the way though, I made the decision to remain in the program *for me*. I always had to depend on myself for everything growing up, but at some point, I'd lost that focus; letting sex, drugs, and alcohol take over until I was barely able to recognize myself. I felt guilty for the pain I'd put my friends through and I knew it would be a long time before they would trust me again, but I was determined to prove to them—and myself—that I was ready for a change. I just needed to find a way to convince Lachlan; if it wasn't already too late.

I sighed as I threw the covers off of me and climbed out of bed. After taking a quick shower, I brushed my teeth, then grabbed my clothes from the suitcase that someone must have brought to my room while I was sleeping. I got dressed and pulled my hair back into a loose ponytail, then took a deep breath and made myself open the door. I would have to live with whatever Lachlan decided, so I might as well get it over with. The sooner our little meeting was over, the sooner I could get back to my own place and start the work of repairing my relationships with the only people who had ever cared about me.

I stepped out of the room and peered down the long hallway. The door Lachlan had disappeared behind the night before was closed, but I had no idea if he was still in there or not. I made my way downstairs and stood at the bottom step, unsure which direction I should go. The place was massive, bigger than most luxury hotels, and I wondered why Lachlan needed that much space when it was only him living there. Unless it wasn't just him. I'd seen the man several times since we'd signed with his record label, but I knew very little about him. I hadn't even known he had a home in Chicago, so for all I knew, he could be married with children.

"May I help you, sir?" The voice, spoken in a crisp British accent, startled me and I whipped around to see a gentleman dressed in a suit. He looked to be around seventy years old and was tall and thin, but not frail.

"Fuck, you scared me. I didn't even hear you creeping up behind me," I said, placing my hand over my chest.

His mouth turned down in a frown. "I assure you, sir. I never creep anywhere." His demeanor was cold and I stared at him blankly as I tried to figure out how I could have offended him within seconds of meeting him. That was a new record, even for me.

"Sorry, man, I didn't mean anything by that. I'm Rocko." I extended my hand towards him.

He looked down at my offered hand then back at me. He dipped his head at me, but kept his hands firmly behind his back. "Benjamin Appleton. It's a pleasure," he said drolly, making it very clear that meeting me was the complete opposite. "Follow me, please. You may enjoy your morning meal and then I will show you to Mr. Edwards's study. He's been waiting for you." Without waiting for a response, he strode past me.

I turned and stared at his retreating back in disbelief. I wondered if he treated all of Lachlan's guests like that or if I was special somehow. After a few seconds, I realized he wasn't going to wait for me so I hurried to catch up, glancing around at my surroundings as much as possible as we went. *He sure moves fast for an old guy.* He led me through a living room which was decorated in blues and creams. The furniture looked modern and luxurious, but the best part was the floor-to-ceiling windows that made up the entire back wall.

Through the windows, I could see a large patio, complete with outdoor kitchen and a pool that could put Hugh Hefner's to shame. I could only imagine the parties Lachlan would be able to throw, but then I shook my head to clear the unwanted image from my head. I needed to stay away from parties of any kind until I became stronger in my sobriety. Not that I would ever be invited to a party Lachlan threw anyway. I was sure his friends were all very posh and sophisticated; not words anyone would ever use to describe me.

Next, we walked through a dining room with a table long enough to seat at least thirty people and I wondered if he invited friends over very often for formal dinners. I didn't even know thirty people well enough to have them over for dinner, so the idea seemed ridiculous to me. Benjamin turned a corner and led me through a swinging door and into a spacious kitchen.

An older woman was pulling something out of the oven as we entered and when I saw the freshly baked cinnamon rolls in her hands my mouth began to water. The smell of the cinnamon, combined with the rich aroma of brewed coffee, made my stomach grumble embarrassingly and she looked up at me with a smile.

"This is Ms. Lynwood. I will leave you to your breakfast and return for you in a bit." I raised my brows in amusement as he retreated from the room quickly. I turned back to Ms. Lynwood who was watching the swinging door with a look of confusion.

"Friendly guy," I muttered. "Hi, I'm Rocko." I offered my hand for the second time, but that time it was accepted. Her hand was delicate and soft and my own engulfed it when we shook.

"It's a pleasure to meet you, Rocko. Please, call me Kerry." She smiled at me warmly then ushered me over to the round wooden table in the corner. "I hope you're hungry; I just made a fresh batch of cinnamon rolls."

"I'm starving," I told her as she rushed around the kitchen, pouring coffee into a mug and filling a plate before placing both of them in front of me. I picked up my fork and took a big bite of cinnamon roll, groaning with pleasure when the warm, gooey sweetness melted on my tongue.

I opened my eyes and saw Kerry smiling at me, her eyes sparkling with amusement. "Do you like them, dear?"

"Hell yeah," I responded enthusiastically. My eyes widened when I realized what I'd said. "I'm sorry, I shouldn't have said that in front of you."

"Nonsense," she said with a tinkling laugh. "My father owned a pub when I was a young girl and I used to go there after school to help out. I've heard much worse than what you just said, dear." She sat down and patted my hand gently.

"These may very well be the best things I've ever eaten," I told her sincerely, before taking another big bite.

"My cinnamon rolls have always been Lachlan's favorite as well," she said proudly.

"Have you worked for him very long?" I asked.

"I've known Lachlan since he was a baby. I was hired by his parents right after he was born and when he grew up, I began working for him. I've thought about retiring a few times, but I don't have any family other than my sister and her husband and Lachlan's always been like a son to me, so here I am. Besides, after everything that happened, I just thought it would be best if I stayed with him a little longer." I wanted to ask her what had happened, but figured it was none of my business so I asked her something else instead.

"What was he like as a boy?" I wasn't sure why I was so curious about the man who was probably about to shatter my world, but I couldn't stop the question from forming.

Kerry's eyes took on a distant look, but she wore a soft smile on her face as she spoke. "He was always a sweet boy. He was very quiet and shy but also thoughtful and caring, even as a young child." I smiled at her even though I had trouble reconciling the self-assured Lachlan I knew with the boy she had described. I'd been expecting her to describe him as more of a pampered rich kid. Maybe there was more to Lachlan Edwards than I'd realized. I laid down my fork and had just finished drinking my coffee when Benjamin strode back into the room.

"Are you quite finished, sir? We shouldn't keep Mr. Edwards waiting, he is an extremely busy man after all," he huffed.

I rolled my eyes then stood and thanked Kerry for the wonderful breakfast. She beamed at me and promised to make them for me again very soon. She looked so happy that I didn't have the heart to remind her that I would be leaving after my meeting with Lachlan and most likely would never return.

I followed Benjamin down yet another hallway. I would surely get lost in the place if I was ever left to find my own way around. He slowed as he neared a set of wooden doors and knocked once.

"Come in," I heard Lachlan say.

Benjamin opened the door and led me into a spacious office. Lachlan was seated behind an enormous mahogany desk and held up a finger as he wrapped up a phone call. The room was comfortable and inviting, decorated in warm earth tones and over-sized leather furniture. Too many rich people bought furniture to impress others whether it was actually comfortable to sit on or not. Lachlan obviously believed in making his home both classy and functional and I found myself even more curious about the man who lived there.

I wandered over to a small round table in the corner and picked up the framed picture displayed there. I recognized a much younger version of Lachlan, probably about ten or twelve years old, with his arm thrown over the shoulder of a boy who looked a few years younger. They looked enough alike that I assumed they were related, perhaps brothers, and they each wore matching smiles. Lachlan's eyes shone with happiness and I felt my own lips curving up into a grin. It was a good look on him, one that I hadn't seen very often on the adult version.

Someone cleared their throat behind me. I glanced over my shoulder and was met with Benjamin's hard stare. He looked pissed off, but for the life of me I couldn't figure out what I had done to put that look on his face. *Dude seriously needs to remove the stick out of his ass.*

I set the picture back on the table and walked over to the desk, sitting down in one of the seats across from Lachlan. I slouched down in the chair and crossed my ankle up onto my knee, trying to appear much more casual than I felt. The truth was, I was nervous as hell. It was do or die time. When I left that room I either would or would not be a member of Carter's Creed and the fact that my future was in the hands of someone else both scared and frustrated me. I wanted to get our meeting over with because the not knowing was turning me into a nervous wreck.

Lachlan ended the call and gave me a small smile. "That was a business call I needed to take, but I apologize for making you wait."

"No problem," I said easily as if I didn't have a care in the world. If he was about to take away the one good thing in my life, I refused to give him the satisfaction of seeing how badly it would hurt me.

"Lachlan, would you like me to bring you anything?" Benjamin asked and I did a double take when I saw the warm, almost affectionate smile he gave his employer.

"No, thank you, Benjamin. That will be all," Lachlan told him.

The older man nodded at him then he turned to me and his eyes hardened. "Sir?" His tone with me was polite but his mouth pursed tightly.

"Nah, I'm good. Thanks for your hospitality though, Benji." I bit my tongue to keep from laughing as his eyes bugged out at the nickname. Too bad I wouldn't be staying, I had a feeling I could have a lot of fun with the old guy. Lord knew he needed someone to help take the starch out of his boxers. With a huff, he marched over to the door and shut it firmly behind him. I chuckled at his reaction and then turned my attention to Lachlan who was staring at me with a bewildered expression on his face.

"What?" I asked innocently.

Lachlan shook his head. "Nothing. Let's get started, shall we?" As simple as that, my humor was replaced with dread.

CHAPTER
Two

Lachlan

I TOOK A MOMENT TO LOOK OVER THE MAN IN FRONT OF ME. THE first time I laid eyes on Rylie Anderson, had been when I went to watch Carter's Creed perform at a local bar in their hometown of Chicago. I trusted my assistant's recommendation for new talent, but I still insisted on hearing the bands play for myself and seeing how they interacted with their fans before making a final decision as to whether or not I would sign them on to my record label.

I'd been impressed with the talent the band possessed and the easy way in which they blended the sounds of their various instruments, but what captured my attention the most was the band's drummer. He was dressed simply in a tight black t-shirt and worn jeans and he had long silky raven-colored hair that hung well past his shoulders and colorful tattoos down each of his muscular arms.

When he'd first stepped onto the stage, he'd played up to the fans, winking at some of them or smiling at others, but there was also a guarded look behind those bright blue eyes, one that suggested there was much more to him than what he let us all see.

I was curious so I immediately sorted through the files my assistant had put together until I found his. Rylie Anderson, known only as Rocko to everyone else in the world, was twenty-eight years old, with no known relatives. His parents, whose names were not listed, had given up their rights to him the minute he was born and it appeared that he had spent his entire childhood bouncing from one foster home to another. My chest felt tight as I closed the file and looked back towards the stage. I wasn't sure what it was, but something about the man grabbed ahold of me and refused to let go.

I'd signed Carter's Creed on with Golden Entertainment Studios the very next day and I'd been pleased with their progress ever since. They shot to the top of the music charts, just as I'd expected them to, but unfortunately Rylie started to unravel shortly after they hit the road for their first concert tour. I'd kept a close eye on him and asked the band's manager, Landon to inform me of any new developments regarding the drummer. The call I'd received telling me that Rylie had been rushed to the hospital after an apparent overdose, jolted me into action and I'd immediately put a plan in place.

When he'd arrived at my house the previous night, I'd been shocked at his physical appearance. His long hair had lost its shine, his skin was pale, and his once vibrant blue eyes looked dull and lifeless. It sent a chill down my spine and I said a silent prayer that it wasn't too late. To be honest, I wasn't sure why I was getting so involved. I'd represented many rock stars over the years and had seen more than my fair share of them sink to the bottom, once endless amounts of money and drugs were introduced into their lives.

I supposed the reason didn't matter all that much. The important thing was making sure Rylie got better. I knew he wasn't going to be happy about my plan, but I was determined to do whatever it took to save him from himself.

He crossed his ankle over his knee and looked at me with a bored expression. I could tell he was trying to appear casual, but the way his fingers constantly tapped out a rhythm along his leg and the tiny movement of his jaw as his teeth clenched, spoke volumes about the nerves running through him. Normally, I would have tried to put him at ease, but in his particular case, fear would work in my favor.

"Are you going to fire me?" he asked boldly.

"Should I?" I tilted my head at him.

"Yes. But I really hope you won't." I stared for a moment without speaking, surprised at his honesty. Most people would have presented me with a list of reasons why they deserved another opportunity. Rylie admitted that he didn't deserve a second chance, but was asking for one anyway.

"Why?" My eyes narrowed as I waited to see what he would come up with.

"It's everything to me. The band, my friends. I can't lose them." I watched as a portion of the wall came down within his eyes and I sucked in a quiet breath at the vulnerability I saw there. There was no doubt that he was being sincere, but I couldn't let it deter me.

"If it means that much to you then you won't mind fighting for it, correct?"

"What do you mean?" he asked cautiously.

"I mean that your stay in rehab was just the beginning. You need to fight your way back and prove to me, your band mates, and most importantly to yourself that you can handle living the life of a famous musician." I stood and made my way around the desk until I was in front of him again. He eyed me warily as I sat on the edge of the desk and crossed my arms over my chest.

"I've seen far too many people in your position that have lost everything because they let drugs and alcohol take over. I don't want to see the same thing happen to you, Rylie." He visibly flinched at the sound of his name and his eyes shot up to glare at me.

"It's Rocko," he corrected sharply.

I had apparently touched a nerve by using his given name, but I pushed on. "If you hope to get better then you need to quit hiding behind your rock star persona and get back in touch with who you truly are. Therefore, while you are in my home, I will refer to you as Rylie."

"I guess it's a good thing I'm leaving soon then, isn't it?" he hissed. His body nearly vibrated with anger, but I was reassured by the spark it brought to his eyes. If he was still capable of feeling anger, then perhaps he would be able to tap into his other feelings too and work his way through them. I was getting ahead of myself though, I still had to get him to agree to stay first.

"That's where you're wrong; at least I hope."

"What do you mean?" His anger was quickly replaced with confusion.

I unfolded my arms and placed my hands on the edge of the desk, leaning a bit closer to him. "What I mean is that you will be staying here while you recover."

Rylie's eyes widened. "For how long?"

"Until I feel that you are strong enough to face the rest of the world on your own and not end up in the hospital again or worse, the morgue." He grimaced as my words struck their intended target. I didn't like being so cold, but he needed to realize the gravity of the situation and as much as I hated to think about it, the morgue was probably where he'd end up if he didn't get himself sorted out.

I leaned back to avoid being knocked over as he stood quickly and headed for the door. "Thanks, but I don't need you to babysit me. If I need someone, I'll stay with Steve."

"I'm not sure Steve's an option right now." My words stopped him cold and I watched as his shoulders slumped and his head dropped down. I hated everything I was saying. It was never my intention to hurt him, but sometimes being tough with someone was the only way to reach them.

"Besides," I continued. "Your friends and I have spoken about it and we've all agreed that having you stay here would be the best course of action."

"They knew you were bringing me here?" he asked, whipping around to face me.

"They agreed that you needed more care than the rehab facility could provide," I answered carefully. The look of betrayal on his face made my heart squeeze. "They care about you, Rylie, and they want you to get better. They know that if you stay here, you'll be able to take the time to concentrate on yourself without all of the distractions of the outside world."

"So, what exactly am I going to be doing while I'm here? Yoga? Meditation?" he asked sarcastically.

Rylie folded his arms over his chest and I tried not to pay attention to the way his biceps bulged, stretching the sleeves of his t-shirt. I was supposed to be helping my client get his life back on track, not ogling him. I walked back around my desk and sat down, gesturing for him to take a seat as well. He stared at me stubbornly, but after a few moments he rolled his eyes and reluctantly sat back down. I had to bite my lip to keep from laughing at his petulant behavior.

"For the most part, you are free to do whatever you'd like. However, I have rules."

"Such as?" Rylie said through gritted teeth.

"First and foremost, there will be no drugs or alcohol of any kind. If I catch you with any of that, you will have to leave and your contract with Golden Entertainment with be null and void." He opened his mouth to object, but I held a hand up to stop him. "I will not permit anyone who represents my company to be chemically dependent. That's non-negotiable."

"I know you don't believe me, but I'm done with that stuff."

"Prove it," I told him. My words came out as more of a plea than a demand and I saw something flash in his eyes. I cleared my throat and continued. "You may not leave the house alone. If you want to go somewhere, then either my driver or I will accompany you."

"This is starting to sound like a prison," he grumbled.

"Not at all," I retorted. "You are free to leave anytime you'd like, but if you do, your contract ends. I'm doing this for your own good, Rylie."

"What else?" His fingers had begun tapping out a furious rhythm on his leg as his agitation grew and I realized I was walking a very fine line. He needed to understand how serious I was, but if I pushed too hard he may very well walk away and then there would be no stopping him from going right back to the lifestyle he'd been leading up to that point.

"I don't want any visitors here other than your bandmates. You don't need any outside distractions while you recover."

Rylie's jaw dropped and he stared at me like I'd just said the most ridiculous thing ever. "Hold on, if I can't leave without a babysitter," he sneered that last part. "And no one can come here other than my friends, then what the hell am I supposed to do about sex? I *need* sex, man."

My cock perked up when the word sex was spoken in his smooth, deep voice. What the hell was wrong with me? I had never reacted to another client that way. I was only trying to get him straightened out so the band could continue their rise to the top. It was strictly business, so why the hell was my body reacting to him that way?

"I suppose you'll just have to take care of things yourself for a while." I regretted my words when a mental image of the gorgeous man taking himself in hand popped into my mind, unbidden and I felt my cock begin to plump. *Seriously, WTF?*

Rylie's eyelids lowered and he wore a sexy smirk that I was sure had won him many sexual favors in the past. "Is that what you do in this big old mansion of yours? Tell me, Lachlan, what kind of porn do you watch while you jerk off?"

I knew he was just trying to get a rise out of me and I cursed the blush that heated my face, giving away the fact that his words affected me. His eyes travelled over my body slowly and then darted up to me as if shocked by something. I decided it would be best to ignore his taunting and get the conversation back on track.

"You will meet regularly with a therapist who will decide when he thinks you will be ready to be on your own again."

"Wait a damn minute," Rylie interrupted, the smirk suddenly gone from his face. "You're going to make me see a shrink?"

"I'm not *making* you do anything. As I said before, you can leave anytime you want to. The choice is yours, but you know my conditions." We eyed each other for several seconds and when it was clear he wasn't going to say anything else, I continued. "Dr. Hudson Westley is a friend of mine and also one of the best therapists in the country. He's in very high demand, but he has graciously agreed to come here to talk with you."

"And what if I don't want to talk to him?" Rylie asked stubbornly.

"I can't force you to talk to him, Rylie. I do hope you'll give him a chance though. You may be surprised by how much he can help," I told him.

"Is there anything else?"

"That's all. Are you willing to follow those rules?" I waited to see what his decision would be. I would be very disappointed if he decided to walk away, but there was nothing else I could do. I'd presented an opportunity for him to recover and heal whatever wounds had led him to drink and do drugs in the first place, but whether he wanted to take advantage of my offering was completely up to him. He was a grown man and needed to make the decision for himself.

His face gave away none of his thoughts as he stared at me, running his hand over the scruff on his face. Finally, he drew in a deep breath and sat up in his seat. "Fine. I'll jump through your hoops and prove to you that I intend to stay clean from now on." My shoulders slumped in relief.

"Regardless of what you think, you're not a prisoner, Rylie. I want you to consider this your home while you're here. Feel free to wander around and become familiar with the layout of the property. You're welcome to use anything here."

He gave me a wary look as he stood and began to leave the office. He opened the door then turned to me with a curious look. "Why are you really doing all of this?" he asked.

It took a few moments to figure out how to respond because I really didn't know the answer to that question. In the past, if a client had addiction problems, I would put them up in the best treatment facilities in the world. I'd never even thought of bringing one into my home. From the very first time I saw him, I'd thought he was gorgeous, but I spent my life around beautiful people so I knew it wasn't that. There was just something about Rylie that spoke to me and I needed to see it through personally. I wasn't about to admit any of that to him though, so I went with the safest and most believable answer I could think of.

"I've spent a great deal of time and money on Carter's Creed and I know the sky's the limit for you guys if you keep your heads on straight. I'm just trying to protect my investment." If I hadn't been watching him so closely, I might have missed the slight tightening around his eyes. He nodded silently and then walked out, shutting the door behind him.

I let out a long, slow breath and ran my hands down my face. I was glad that he had decided to stay and I hoped that by doing so, he could begin healing. I knew there were things in his past that must have hurt him deeply and I would bet money those things played a huge part in his addictions. I just hoped I was doing the right thing.

CHAPTER
Three

Rylie/Rocko

I LEFT LACHLAN'S OFFICE AND AFTER GETTING LOST TWICE, finally found my way back to my room. I was irritated as hell and just wanted to be left alone, so I locked the door behind me before collapsing on the bed. I rubbed my hands over my face and released a frustrated groan.

I replayed the conversation with Lachlan in my head. I supposed all things considered it had gone well. After all, I was still in the band and that's what I'd been the most worried about losing. As long as I got to keep being the drummer for Carter's Creed and stay with my friends, I could handle all the rest. Even if most of his rules seemed completely ridiculous to me; particularly the ones that kept me from going anywhere alone or having anyone over. How the hell was I supposed to go an indefinite amount of time without having sex?

I was a touchy-feely person, always had been. I figured it probably came from my growing up in foster care. I never had any parents or siblings to show me affection and most of the foster parents I'd been placed with never gave a damn about anything but the check they received for putting up with me. As I got older, I'd learned to get affection in other ways, mainly through sex. I'd never been in a serious relationship, but I'd never had a problem finding someone to hook up with.

I'd known from an early age that I was bisexual, but I usually preferred sex with men. Men just really did it for me, however they rarely wanted to hang around after the deed was done. The women I'd been with however, enjoyed it when I'd stay and cuddle with them and I craved that from them in return. If I could create the perfect person for me, it would be a man that I could fuck hard or who would fuck me into the mattress, but who also liked to spend the night wrapped up in each other's arms. So far, I hadn't found anyone close to that description though and it didn't look like I would have any opportunity in the near future with Lachlan's fucking rules in place.

I dreaded the thought of having to go through more therapy. The group sessions I was forced to attend in rehab were torture, pure and simple. People droning on and on about every little thing that had ever gone wrong in their lives and blaming their parents for it. Didn't they know how fucking lucky they were to even have parents? I'd sit quietly like a good little boy, but the whole time I just wanted to stand up and scream how pointless the whole thing was because when it came down to it, no one else could fix what was wrong with your life and the only person you could count on in this crazy world was yourself.

All I'd wanted was to get through the program as quickly as possible and get back to my life, so I kept my opinions to myself and suffered through each session. I'd hoped when I left rehab that therapy would be behind me, but apparently, Lachlan had other plans. I hoped that Dr. Westley wasn't a pain in the ass, but I already knew it was going to be harder to get away with not talking when the sessions were one on one. I'd have to figure something out though, because there were parts of my past that were off limits, plain and simple. I'd never talked about it with another person and there was no reason to; it wasn't like talking about it would erase what had happened, so why bring all of that shit up?

I wanted to move forward and forget all about my past and I'd done a pretty good job of it up until then. My closest friends didn't even know what my life was like before I met them and I preferred it that way. Then Lachlan came along and got his minions to dig around until they'd found something. It had been a shock to hear someone call me Rylie after so many years and I'd felt the flush of humiliation as I wondered what else he might have uncovered in his search.

I sat up and yanked the hairband out of my hair, running my fingers through my long locks. I could feel a headache forming in the base of my neck from stress and I let my head drop and used my fingers to try and massage away the tension. My hands shook as the familiar cravings kicked in. I knew that just one line of coke would help take the edge off and I wouldn't have to worry about rules and needing to prove myself to everyone. I could forget about how I had fucked up everything good in my life and just float away.

It was those kinds of thoughts that had landed me in that mess in the first place though, and I refused to go down that same path. Being drunk off my ass or high might have helped me forget about my problems for a little while, but it also left me weak and vulnerable; those were two things I never wanted to be again.

I stood up with a moan and checked to be sure my phone was in my pocket. I needed to get some fresh air and I wanted to have a little talk with Carter and find out why none of my friends had bothered to tell me about Lachlan's plan to hold me hostage.

I didn't know my way around Lachlan's home well enough to not get lost, so I headed for the door I'd come through the night before and stepped outside. The sun was shining and it warmed my skin as I walked down the long driveway. If I'd been in a better mood, I probably would have enjoyed what a beautiful day it was, but all I wanted at that moment was answers. I stopped walking when I got near the large fountain in the center of the driveway and pulled my phone from my pocket. I brought up my contacts and clicked on Carter's name then began pacing as I waited for him to pick up.

"Hey, man, what's up?" Carter answered after a couple of rings.

"That's what I want to know," I growled at him.

"What are you talking about?" he asked hesitantly.

"I'm talking about the fact that while I was in rehab—doing exactly what you guys said you wanted me to do—you all were out here plotting with Lachlan about locking me away for a few more months once I got out," I fumed.

"Rocko, it wasn't…" He started to explain, but I cut him off.

"And the worst part was that none of you thought it would be a good idea to give me a heads-up about it. You just let Lachlan drag me to his place where I'm now being held prisoner until he decides I'm trustworthy enough to be on my own." I stopped to catch my breath. I knew I was being dramatic, but I was pissed.

"Hold on a minute," Carter cut in. "You're at *Lachlan's* place?" I paused my pacing when I heard the genuine confusion in his voice.

"Yeah, he had me brought here as soon as I left the facility."

"Huh," Carter responded.

"What's that supposed to mean?" I demanded.

"Look, I'm sorry we didn't tell you, it was probably wrong to blindside you like that, but we were afraid you wouldn't go and we just want you to get better. Rehab was a great start and they helped you through the withdrawal, but you need something more that will help you work through your demons."

"I…"

"And don't say you don't have any because we all know there's stuff from your past you haven't told us about." He said that last part quietly and I could hear the concern in his voice. My throat felt thick and I suddenly had trouble swallowing. The anger rushed out of me and was replaced with gratitude for my friends. I knew how fortunate I was to have them in my life and after all the shit I'd put them through, I was lucky they hadn't walked away a long time ago. Although, maybe one of them had.

"Have you talked to Steve?" I held my breath as I waited for his response.

I heard him sigh through the phone and my stomach clenched. "I've talked to him a couple of times. He hasn't been around too much, been going with Lindsay on her job assignments." I smiled sadly. I was glad Steve wasn't alone and that he was travelling with his girlfriend, Lindsay, but I missed him terribly.

I cleared my throat. "That's good. I'm glad he's good."

Carter's voice was gentle when he spoke. "He'll come around eventually, don't give up hope, okay?"

"Yeah," I whispered.

"You scared all of us really bad, but Steve got the worst of it. He was the one that found you in that tub and called nine-one-one. He was there when the EMTs said they'd lost you twice on the way to the hospital. He needs time to recover from all of that. But he will and then he'll come around because he loves you just as much as the rest of us do."

"I hope you're right. Do you think you guys will ever be able to forgive me?" I was almost afraid to ask, but I needed to know the answer.

"I can't speak for everyone else, you know that. But as far as I'm concerned, it's not about forgiveness. I just want my friend back. I want you to be healthy and happy and if you can do that, then I'll be happy." I fought back the tears that threatened to spill down my face, but I couldn't hold back the tiny sob that left my lips. I knew he'd heard it, but I didn't care. Carter had already seen me at my worst and miraculously he hadn't given up on me. I didn't deserve a friend like him.

"We rarely get time to just shut out the rest of the world and focus on ourselves, but Lachlan's offering you that exact thing. Take advantage of it, okay?" he pleaded. Carter was right, I knew he was.

"I will, man. I promise." I hoped he could hear the sincerity in my voice because I meant every word.

"Good, now go out there and catch some waves, I hear it's good for the body and the mind," Carter said and I knew he was trying to lighten the mood.

"Waves? What are you talking about?" I asked.

"You said you were in California, right?"

"No, I'm in Chicago." I spoke slowly as if I were explaining something to a three-year-old.

"Okay, now I'm confused."

"I told you already, Lachlan brought me to his house right after I left rehab. You guys planned the whole thing together so what are you confused about?" I chuckled.

"That's just it, though, it's not what we planned at all. Lachlan said he was going to take you somewhere so you could recover, he never told us he was taking you to his house. Besides, I didn't even know he had a house in Chicago," Carter explained.

The smile left my face as his words sank in. "Yeah, he said it was a recent purchase. Look, man, I've got to go, but thanks for the talk."

"No problem. Take care of yourself, okay, Rocko? And don't worry about Steve. He'll come around. He loves you, we all do."

"Thanks, Carter." I wanted to tell him I loved them back because I did, but just like always, the words got stuck in my throat. "Come see me sometime?" I asked instead.

"I will and I'll bring you some of Caleb's manicotti."

"Oh, man, you know that's my favorite," I groaned. Carter's twin brother, Caleb, worked as a chef at the restaurant he owned with his husband, Giovanni, and he made the best manicotti I'd ever tasted. It had been months since I'd had any and my mouth watered at the thought of it.

"Yes, I know. You tell him that every time you see him. Well, that and that you'd love to fuck him, which gives me all kinds of heebie-jeebies. Seriously, man, he's my brother and you're like a brother to me. That shit's got to stop," he whined.

I laughed at the distress in his voice. I only said those things to get under Carter's skin. Not that Caleb wasn't sexy as hell and if he were anyone else I'd have already put the moves on him, but he wasn't anyone else. He was Carter's twin and there was no way I was going to jeopardize my relationship with Carter by messing with his brother. Besides, I was pretty sure Caleb's husband would break both of my legs if I tried.

"Mmmm…maybe I could eat manicotti, naked in bed with Caleb. Do you think he'd cook it, wearing nothing but an apron?" I teased.

"Oh God, that's it. I'm hanging up, asshole," Carter cried.

I couldn't hold back my laughter any longer. "Fine, I'll settle for just the manicotti."

"We'll see. I'm not sure you deserve any now," he grumbled.

"Okay, okay, I'll be good," I chuckled.

"I don't think you know the definition of good," he joked. "I'll see you soon."

We hung up and I stared down at my phone for a long time, my head spinning with everything Carter had told me. I pushed thoughts of Steve out of my mind for the time being. It was too painful to think about the hell I'd put my best friend through. Instead my thoughts drifted to Lachlan. Why hadn't he told my friends that he was bringing me to his place when they were putting their plan together, and why hadn't he mentioned to them that he'd bought a home in Chicago? The man was definitely a puzzle.

All I knew for sure was that instead of firing me, Lachlan brought me into his home so that I could heal and get my life put back in order and I had acted like a spoiled brat instead of thanking him for it. I shook my head and slid my phone in my pocket as I walked back up to the house. If I was going to win my friends back and keep my job as their drummer, then I needed to get my head out of my ass and start working for it.

CHAPTER
Four

Lachlan

"I'LL BE STAYING IN CHICAGO FOR A WHILE SO ANY MEETINGS that I have scheduled will need to be done electronically."

"Would you prefer to have Mr. Danvers conduct the meetings in your place?" Carolyn asked.

I considered her offer for about a second before I refused. It wasn't that I thought Tyrone Danvers, my chief operating officer, couldn't handle running the company in my absence, he was more than qualified and had proven his capabilities time and time again. The fact was, I built my company from the ground up and had worked tirelessly to ensure that Golden Entertainment Studios made it all the way to the top, knocking out the previous leaders in the music industry until all of the top artists wanted to sign with us. I'd always preferred to have a hand in each and every project and that wasn't going to change just because I was far away from my office.

"No, thank you. Just set everything up electronically and I'll handle it from my home office," I told her.

"Yes, sir, I'll take care of it," Carolyn responded. "When do you expect to return to L.A.?"

My thoughts turned to Rylie and the way he looked when he first arrived at my home. His usually arrogant swagger had disappeared, replaced with slumped shoulders and eyes that reflected a bone-deep weariness. I was going to do everything in my power to bring him back to the cocky, fun-loving man I'd first met.

"I'm not quite sure exactly, but not until my business here has been taken care of." I didn't mention anything about Rylie and Carolyn was professional enough not to ask.

I had just ended the call when my cell phone rang again. I glanced at the screen and smiled when I saw who it was.

"Micah! How are you?"

"I'm good, how are you?" Micah's deep voice sounded through the phone and brought with it a feeling of warmth and comfort.

Micah and I had become friends under terrible circumstances; when he came to tell me that my brother had been killed. Spencer, along with Micah and several others, had been taken hostage by insurgents in Afghanistan while they each were serving for their respective military units; Micah for the U.S. Navy and Spencer for the Royal Air force. They'd been beaten, tortured, and starved. Micah and Spencer became a lifeline of sorts to each other until the day that the insurgents carried Spencer out of his prison cell and killed him.

They made a pact with each other that if the worst were to happen to one of them that the other would tell their family. Micah held true to their pact, showing up at my door and letting me know as gently as possible what had happened to my brother. I know he'd spared me many of the more gruesome details of what they'd been through, but his words gave me a closure that I might have never had if he hadn't been such an honorable man.

At first, I was just so grateful to Micah for being there for my brother, so that he didn't have to die completely alone, that I tried to shower him with expensive gifts, which he politely but firmly refused. Over time though, we became close friends and formed a bond of our own which I valued more than anything. No one could ever replace Spencer in my heart, but Micah came in very close, often feeling more like a brother to me than a friend.

"I'm well. How is your fiancé? I haven't spoken to Landon in a while," I told him.

"He's great…amazing." I smiled when I heard the happiness in my friend's voice when he spoke of his fiancé. Landon Greene was the manager for Carter's Creed and was the older brother of Carter Greene. Landon and Micah had gotten close when I hired Micah to head up the security team for the band as they toured. Micah started out protecting Carter from a crazed stalker, but things had taken an ugly turn and he ended up needing to save Landon's life instead. In the process, the two fell madly in love and had since become engaged.

"So, I take it you're still in love," I teased.

"Am I that obvious?" he asked with a chuckle.

"Just a little," I replied. "It's good to hear you sounding so happy, Micah."

"Well, I can honestly say that I've never been happier in my life. Things with Landon are even better than I imagined, Hamilton Security has really taken off and it is so nice to have finally settled down and not have to travel so much." A smile spread across my face as I listened to him. I was thrilled for Micah that he had found his soulmate. Landon was a wonderful man and I trusted him not to hurt my friend.

"Enough about me though. I actually called for a reason," Micah continued.

"Which was?" I asked, curiously.

"Landon told me that you have Rocko staying with you, is that right?" The smile slid from my face as I heard the seriousness of his tone.

"Yes, that is correct," I said cautiously.

"Why?" Micah asked.

"Because he needed more help than the rehabilitation facility could provide. His bandmates and I agreed that he should get further treatment once he left there to make sure that he got set on the right path again," I answered stiffly.

"Yes, that's what Landon told me, but what I really want to know is why are you taking this on all by yourself? There are plenty of facilities you could have sent him to which have professionals specially trained to deal with a person in Rocko's situation."

"I'm not dealing with it all by myself," I explained. "I know I'm not qualified to give Rocko the help he needs. That's why I've hired Hudson to come in a few times each week and work with him."

"I'm relieved to hear that. If anyone can help him, it's Hudson," Micah admitted. When I had first told Micah that I was seeing a therapist to help me deal with Spencer's death, he'd insisted on meeting the man himself. One meeting with the doctor and Micah agreed that I was in very capable hands.

"But you still haven't told me why you decided to take him to your home instead of a facility and why didn't you tell me you had a house in Chicago?" I paused as I tried to figure out how to respond to his questions, especially when I wasn't sure of the answers myself. I started with the easiest first.

"I was going to tell you about the house, I promise. It was just a spur of the moment thing and I hadn't had an opportunity to speak with you about it yet. Besides, I thought you would be happy to have me living closer. Was I wrong?" I hoped my teasing would lighten the mood, but there was a lengthy pause as I waited for Micah to speak.

"Of course, you're not wrong. You know I've always wished you lived closer so I could help keep an eye on you, but I still want to know why you would choose to invite Rocko into your own home instead of sending him away to some other treatment center."

"I can't explain it, Micah. It was just something I felt I needed to do," I said with a sigh. I was confused enough about my reasons, so how was I supposed to explain it to my best friend?

"You can't save everyone else, just because you lost Spencer," Micah said gently. "I know, because I've tried."

"My bringing Rocko here had nothing to do with Spencer," I explained calmly.

"What's it about then? Because I know you've had other clients in the past that you've helped get clean, but I've never known you to take such a personal interest in them. Why Rocko?" he asked, sounding genuinely perplexed. I understood that Micah's words came from a place of love and concern, but something about the way he'd said it caused me to bristle.

"Why not Rocko?" I countered. Micah was quiet for several moments and I knew he was surprised by the sharpness in my tone. We had never argued before, not that what was happening between us really counted as an argument, but I was sure he could tell that he had struck a nerve.

"I didn't mean anything bad. I don't even really know that much about Rocko, other than the fact that he's the wild child of the band," he explained. "I was simply asking why you chose Rocko in particular?" I tried to come up with a reasonable explanation, but Micah continued before I could think of anything.

"Promise me you'll be careful, okay, Lachlan?" he pleaded. "You are one of the sweetest, most loving people I've ever known and I don't want to see you get hurt."

"I'm not sure what you think is going on, but this is purely business," I insisted stubbornly. "I have a lot of money invested in Carter's Creed and I don't need some drummer tearing apart the band's reputation just as they've reached the top." I hated lying to my best friend, but I wasn't about to admit that I felt something different for Rylie when I didn't even understand what that difference was yet.

"Some drummer, huh?" Micah said and my shoulders slumped as I realized Micah hadn't bought my flimsy excuse. "Okay, if that's what you want to go with."

"It is," I insisted stubbornly. After a few seconds, I heard Micah laugh softly through the phone and I chuckled too at the ridiculousness of our conversation. The earlier tension seeped out of my body. "Look, Micah, the truth is that I don't have all of the answers myself. I just know that this is something I need to do and it would make it a lot easier if I had your support." His response was quick and sincere.

"You're a brother to me, Lachlan, and I won't apologize for being protective of you because that's never going to stop. But you will always have my support, even if I have concerns about what you're doing."

"Thank you, Micah. You're my brother as well. I think Spencer would be very happy to know we've become so close." My eyes burned and my throat felt tight.

"I think so too," he whispered. When I'd first met Micah, he'd been shattered by what had happened to himself and Spencer and he'd built a protective wall around himself that seemed impenetrable. He'd allowed me inside because of my connection with Spencer, but he still held nearly everyone else at arm's length. It was only after he met and began falling in love with Landon that I saw the wall start to crumble until it had virtually disappeared. Landon was just what Micah needed in his life and the easy way in which he was able to show affection for others was a testament to how far he'd come.

I was smiling as I hung up the phone. It had taken a while for me to get used to Micah's somewhat overbearing need to protect me, but I'd soon learned that it came from a place of love. His words filled me with a warm feeling that I hadn't experienced with anyone except Spencer, Kerry and Benjamin. If I had to name the feeling, I supposed it would be *family*; and family was something I'd learned to never take for granted.

I heard the sound of Kerry singing softly to herself coming from the kitchen as I neared the door and it brought a smile to my face. She and Benjamin had practically raised me and Spencer. Our parents were socialites and preferred attending parties and travelling the world over raising their two boys. I'd often wondered why they'd even bothered to have children at all if they didn't want to spend any time with us.

Whether it was because she'd never had children of her own or because she felt sorry for us, I wasn't sure, but Kerry made sure we always had supper on the table each night and cared for us when we were ill. Benjamin taught us how to throw a ball and change the oil in an automobile. They'd each attended countless rugby and football matches over the years, cheering us on right alongside the other parents and when I finally got up the nerve to tell someone other than Spencer that I was gay, it was Kerry and Benjamin that I went to instead of my own parents.

She turned when she heard the door swoosh shut behind me and a tender smile spread across her weathered face. "There you are. I was just about to set supper out on the table and I thought I'd have to come pull you away from your study."

"I just finished a conference call and thought I would get a bite to eat before I start the next. Here, let me get that for you. You shouldn't be lifting such heavy things," I told her as I gently slid passed her and retrieved a platter of food from the counter and carried it to the table. I smiled to myself when I heard her delicate huff behind me. Kerry had never liked being coddled, but I liked taking care of her after everything she'd done for me over the years.

"You work too much, Lachlan. You should be out, enjoying your youth and finding a man to spend your life with. You'll never meet anyone hiding in your study or hanging around with us old people all of the time," she said.

"Old people?" Benjamin asked as he walked in. "I don't know any old people. I still feel like a spring chicken, and you, Miss Kerry, are just as beautiful as the day I first met you." I watched as a blush spread across Kerry's cheeks and she bit her lip before turning her back to us and going to get a pitcher of water from the refrigerator.

Benjamin stared after her retreating form with a pleased smile on his face and I tilted my head as I wondered what exactly was going on between the two of them. They'd always been close friends, but recently I'd noticed signs that perhaps things between them were becoming more than that. I didn't want to embarrass either one of them though, so I acted as if I hadn't noticed.

"I meet plenty of people through my work so there's no reason to worry about me," I assured her.

"That's not what I meant and you know it," Kerry scolded gently as she set the pitcher on the table. "I've seen you when you're working and you're very focused on the job. That's wonderful for business, but it'll never help you find a man. You should get out, go to one of those clubs like on that television show…what's it called? You know, the one we like to watch on Netflix, Benjamin." She looked to him for an answer and I raised a brow in question. *Since when did they spend time watching Netflix together?*

"Queer as Folk," he supplied.

"Yes, that's the one. I just love that Brian, although he needs to get his head out of his arse and show Justin how much he loves him before he loses him for good. Have you seen it before, Lachlan?"

"Yes, I've seen it," I murmured as I grabbed the silverware and began setting the table.

"Then you know that they go to clubs to meet men. That's what you need to do. Go to a club, relax, have a few drinks, dance with someone perhaps," she suggested.

"They also spend some time in bathhouses. Maybe Lachlan

should go to one of those." My back straightened when I heard Rylie's voice behind me and my fingers tightened around the forks in my hand.

"There is a lady present, young man. You would do well to remember that," Benjamin retorted.

"I apologize, Kerry. I didn't mean any disrespect," Rylie said, but I could still detect the humor in his voice.

"I already told you that I've probably seen and heard more than you, Rocko. Don't pay Benjamin any mind, he's just being cranky." Benjamin snorted, but didn't say anything as he began filling our glasses with water.

I noticed that there was some sort of tension between the two men, but I wasn't sure what had caused it. I made a mental note to speak to Benjamin about it privately. After we'd all taken our seats and said grace, I began serving the meal. Kerry had outdone herself with a delicious pork roast, perfectly seasoned hassel back potatoes, and fresh green beans.

"This is very good," Rylie said as he tasted the food and Kerry beamed at him as if he'd just told her she was next in line for the crown.

"I'm so happy that you like it. You look like you need a good feeding or two; a little something to help bring the color back to your cheeks," she said. I couldn't help the laugh that escaped when I saw him blush. His eyes darted up and locked with mine. The look in those crystal blue orbs had me freezing with my fork halfway to my mouth. I couldn't tell what he was thinking, but his gaze held me captive and I found myself unable to look away. It was exhilarating and unnerving all at once and I felt my pulse race under his watchful stare.

The sound of Benjamin clearing his throat startled me and I nearly dropped my fork. My eyes darted to the two other people in the room. Benjamin wore a surprising scowl on his face while Kerry seemed pleased as she looked back and forth between Rylie and myself. I barely managed to lower my head before I rolled my eyes.

Kerry was a hopeless romantic and I knew nothing would make her happier than to see me find my soulmate, but she was completely off the mark if she thought that someone would be Rylie. Not only did we have very little in common, but Rylie didn't strike me as the relationship type. I'd heard all of the rumors about his sexual escapades and I already knew that if I was fortunate enough to fall in love with someone then I would never be willing to share him with anyone else.

We finished eating in an awkward silence with Benjamin frowning in Rylie's direction, me trying to avoid Rylie's darting glances, and Kerry smiling smugly like she'd just solved a puzzle. The whole thing was mentally exhausting and I was ready to bolt from my chair by the time I finished my last bite. I thanked Kerry for the meal and returned to the sanctuary of my office. Getting lost in my work would help rid me of the unnerving feelings that always occurred whenever I was around Rylie.

CHAPTER
Five

Rylie/Rocko

I STOOD IN THE SHOWER, LETTING THE WATER CHASE AWAY THE last remnants of sleep from my body. I'd slept for nearly twelve hours, but as usual it was a fitful sleep and so I woke exhausted. I knew it was worry that kept me from getting a good night's rest. Worry about my position with the band, but also worry over my relationship with Steve. The fact that he still hadn't contacted me hung over me like a dark cloud.

Then there was Lachlan. When I'd heard his laughter at dinner a few nights before, I'd been surprised. He'd always seemed so serious and reserved whenever I'd been around him that it had been a shock to hear the deep rumble coming from his chest. I'd looked up quickly, but when I caught his stare, I froze. Goose bumps broke out across my skin and I felt cold and hot all at the same time. I'd never experienced anything like it before and I had no idea what it meant, but I was pretty sure it couldn't be good.

No matter how gorgeous he was or how warm his honey-colored eyes were, I knew that nothing good could come from me having the hots for my boss. The thought hit me like a sledgehammer. *Fuck! I can't have a stiffy for Lachlan.* I just needed to get laid, that was all. I hadn't had sex since that night in the hotel and I'd been so drugged out of my mind, I could barely remember any of it.

With a loud sigh, I shut the water off and reached for a towel. I was only there because Lachlan wanted me to recover so that I could perform at the highest level when I returned to the band. Protecting his investment is what he'd called it and I needed to keep that in mind.

I dried off quickly then stood in front of the bathroom mirror and took inventory of my appearance. My skin had regained a lot of its natural color and the dark rings had nearly disappeared from under my eyes, despite the lack of sleep. I could still see my ribs sticking out from under my skin, but I was sure a few more of Kerry's delicious meals would take care of that. My beard had grown in thicker than I preferred and would need to be trimmed soon, but I just couldn't find the energy to deal with it.

I leaned in closer and looked at my eyes. I'd always heard that the eyes were a window to a person's soul, but if that were the case, I must have completely lost mine. I saw nothing but a dark void when I looked at my reflection; someone who was unloved and unlovable. I squeezed my eyes shut, not wanting to look at myself for another second. A small cry escaped my lips and I had to grip onto the edge of the sink to keep myself from falling. My fingers dug into the porcelain and I wished I could take something to numb the familiar ache that spread through me. I should have been used to it, but after hiding behind drugs and alcohol for so many years, the pain had come back with a vengeance and was almost unbearable.

My hands were shaking as I leaned over the sink and splashed cold water on my face. When I'd calmed down a bit, I stood and brushed my teeth, carefully avoiding my reflection in the mirror. I ran a comb through my hair and decided to let it air dry. I usually took great pride in how my hair looked, but I figured there was no point since all I'd be doing that day was hiding up in my room again. Well, I would after I had my first session with Dr. Westley anyway.

I rolled my eyes as I walked into the bedroom, grabbing a pair of old jeans and pulling them on. *Dr. Westley.* Even his name sounded pretentious. He was probably the type that wore wool jackets and bowties every day. Not that a bowtie couldn't be sexy as hell, but on the old, stodgy guy that I had envisioned the doctor to be, it was laughable.

I'd been staying at the mansion for a week and as the days dragged on, I'd almost begun to hope that Lachlan had changed his mind about that rule, but then he'd informed me at dinner the night before that my session was scheduled for the following day. It was the first time in days that Lachlan had spoken to me directly other than to ask me to pass the salt. At first I was surprised, but then dread settled in my gut like a lead balloon and I'd suddenly lost my appetite.

I pulled a t-shirt over my head and then looked at the clock on the bedside table. I couldn't put it off any longer. With a resigned sigh, I stepped out into the hall and shut the door behind me. I would attend each session just like Lachlan wanted me to and I would be polite to the good doctor, but Lachlan was sadly mistaken if he thought I was going to talk about my childhood with someone I'd just met. Even my best friends didn't know the secrets I carried with me and I intended to keep it that way. Lachlan may have been hoping that Dr. Westley would be able to fix me, but I already knew that was impossible. Some things were just broken beyond repair.

I stood at the glass doors which led to the patio and stared out at the enormous pool. The sun glinted off the crystal-clear water and I wished I could spend my day stretched out on one of the many lounge chairs lined up along the sides instead of being cooped up indoors with a man who wanted to dig into my head and pull out all the darkness that lurked inside.

I could hear Lachlan's voice as he greeted someone at the door and my stomach clenched with nerves. The deep baritone voice that answered back didn't match the one I'd pictured the therapist having at all and I turned around, curious to see what the man looked like. My jaw dropped as they walked into the living room and I got my first look at Dr. Hudson Westley.

He was taller than me, probably around six-four and had broad shoulders that made me wonder if he'd been a linebacker before becoming a therapist. He had beautiful mocha-colored skin and deep brown eyes that lit up as he laughed at something Lachlan said. His head was shaved and he had a neatly trimmed goatee. The shock of seeing what he actually looked like, compared to what I'd imagined, had me fighting back a laugh and I felt my nerves settle down.

My eyes darted between Lachlan and Dr. Westley. They seemed very comfortable around each other, almost like old friends and I wondered how well they knew each other. They turned to face me and Lachlan introduced the two of us.

"Rocko, this is Dr. Westley." I narrowed my eyes at Lachlan. I still hated it when he called me Rylie, but I'd been prepared for him to introduce me that way. The fact that he hadn't, threw me for a loop. I stuck my hand out instead of questioning him about it and shook Dr. Westley's hand.

"It's nice to meet you. Please, call me Hudson," he said, then tilted his head in Lachlan's direction. "I've told him that about a million times, not that he ever listens," he chuckled.

"Hey," I mumbled lamely.

"Alright then, I have some things to take care of," Lachlan said.

"You are welcome to use my office if you'd like, that way you'll have complete privacy. Would you like me to ask Benjamin to bring either of you something to drink?"

"No, thank you," Hudson said with a warm smile. Lachlan returned the smile and then looked at me.

"Nah, I'm good," I answered quietly. Lachlan held my gaze for a few seconds. He looked like he wanted to say something to me, but then he nodded and left the room.

My nerves returned as soon as I was left alone with Hudson and I began tapping my fingers against my thigh. Just because he looked like a much cooler dude than I had imagined, didn't change the fact that I wasn't going to talk about my past with him. In fact, it almost made it harder to open up to him because there was no way a guy that looked like him could relate to someone like me. He looked like the type that had been the captain of his football team, surrounded by friends, and invited to every party. I was sure his parents had cheered him on from the stands almost as loudly as his girlfriend cheered with the rest of the pep squad.

I showed Hudson to the office, giving myself a mental pat on the back when I managed to find my way without getting lost. I looked around, not sure where to sit or what to do. Luckily Hudson made the decision for me.

"Why don't we take a seat and we can get to know each other," he said as he rearranged the two chairs in front of Lachlan's desk so that they were further apart than before and sat facing each other.

I sat across from him and slouched down in my seat with my arms folded over my chest. Hudson crossed his legs in a casual manner and looked at me with a friendly smile which I did not return. He was a very good-looking man and normally I would have been admiring the view, but I had gone into self-protection mode as soon as Lachlan left the two of us alone. We stared at each other for a long time, each waiting for the other to begin. I smirked when I saw him cave, just as I knew he would.

"You don't want to be here," he said, breaking the silence. It was a statement more than a question and I was sure my body language was answer enough.

"No, I don't," I stated. My smirk disappeared.

"Is it that you don't want to be here with me or you don't want to be in this house?" he pressed.

"Both," I responded honestly.

"So, why are you?" he asked, not seeming offended in the slightest. "I mean, you're a grown man. You have your own home and could leave if you wanted. Why stay if you don't want to?" My eyes narrowed as I looked him over, trying to figure out what his angle was. His eyes darted down to where my fingers had begun tapping out a rhythm against my bicep and I forced them to be still.

"I'm staying here because it's one of the conditions Lachlan laid out if I want to stay in the band. He's the boss, he gets to make the rules," I explained, shrugging my shoulders. Hudson uncrossed his legs and leaned forward, placing his forearms on his knees.

"You know, Rocko, I've heard you play. I attended one of your concerts in L.A. and I know just how talented you are. You could play for any band, get signed on by any record label. So, my question remains; why are you staying if you don't want to be here?" He spoke very gently for such a giant of a man and I felt myself relaxing around him even though I didn't want to.

"Because Carter's Creed isn't just any band. We're a family and I'm not going to just walk away from that. I'll do my time here, make Lachlan happy, and get back to my friends," I admitted.

"Fair enough," Hudson said, setting his pen and paper aside.

"That's it?" I asked in surprise. Was he really going to give up that easily?

"Look, I get that you don't want to talk to me; a lot of people don't. Therapy can be pretty brutal sometimes. It takes a lot of guts to open yourself up and look at your past, seeing how it shaped who you've become." He paused for a moment, studying me intently.

"Rocko, do you like who you are?" The question was spoken so quietly and with such sincerity that I responded before I could stop myself.

"No." A cold chill swept through me and I felt exposed. I couldn't believe that I had just admitted that to him. I never let anyone see the real me. It was easier to hide behind the party-boy, rock and roll image than to let anyone else see the ugly truths I held inside. Truths that I had fought tooth and nail to try and block from my own memory.

Hudson gave me a small smile; his look full of understanding. "Aren't you tired of carrying the heavy weight of your past around with you, Rocko? You've tried to deal with it all on your own. You've kept your secrets locked up tight inside of you and it nearly killed you. In fact, it did, twice. Wouldn't it feel good to have someone who could help lighten the load, even just a little bit? Maybe get you to a place where the next time someone asks you if you like yourself, the answer could be yes?"

I clenched my jaw and swallowed hard around the knot of emotion. What he was offering sounded like a dream come true, but I'd learned the hard way not to trust too easily. *What if he really could help though?* My thoughts were still swirling as Hudson stood up. I peered up at him, his tall frame towering over me.

"Come on, let's take a walk. I don't know about you, but I could use some fresh air," he said with an easy smile.

I let the breath I'd been holding whoosh out of me and my shoulders relaxed ever so slightly. "Fresh air sounds good," I replied.

"Great, let's go," Hudson said with a chuckle. I surprised myself when I felt my lips lift into a grin. I wasn't ready to open up to him yet and I honestly didn't know if I ever would be, but I supposed it wouldn't hurt to take a walk with him.

I felt restless. I'd been there over a week and I was tired of staring at the same four walls every day. Besides, my head was still a twisted mess after my session with Hudson. Once we'd left Lachlan's office, we'd headed out to the expansive backyard and walked slowly through the colorful gardens. I was relieved when he didn't immediately start prying into my past or asking questions about my drug and alcohol abuse. Instead, we'd talked about more neutral topics such as what it was like touring with Carter's Creed and which country had been my favorite to visit.

Hudson told me a little about himself, explaining that he'd grown up in Chicago, but then left for L.A. not long after high school where he attended college. After obtaining his doctorate in psychology with a focus on drug and alcohol addictions, he began working with a group of doctors in a private practice. The previous year he had made the decision to move back to Chicago to be closer to his sister and her son. He'd gone through all the proper channels and become licensed to practice in the state of Illinois and was in the process of opening his own private practice.

We'd talked for a long time, but Hudson had such an easy-going personality that I found myself feeling like I was talking to an old friend more than a therapist. I still wasn't ready to bare my soul to him, and I wasn't sure I ever would be, but Hudson had assured me that we would go at my pace and that I could share as little or as much as I wanted to.

As comfortable as I had felt with him, I knew that he would continue working to get me to open up more and more each time we met and that scared the crap out of me. As far as I was concerned, the things that had happened in my past should stay there, never to be talked about again, but Hudson had already been able to peel some of my layers away, exposing the way I felt about myself after just one session. At that rate, he would probably have me spilling all my secrets within a month.

My stomach clenched at the thought of sharing the more

sordid details of my past; things that I had never told another soul. Shameful things that were too painful to even think about, much less talk about. My heart began racing as some of the darker memories tried to creep into the edges of my mind and suddenly I was hit with an overwhelming urge to get high. Cocaine was my drug of choice and my body nearly vibrated with the need to pick up the phone and call one of my old buddies to hook me up. I pulled my phone from my pocket. That was all it would take to escape the pain and fear that riddled my body, just one phone call.

"Stop it! You're stronger than this," I muttered to myself. Sweat dotted my forehead as I fought the insane craving. I needed to get out of there. I needed to do something to work off the myriad of emotions that were swirling through me and making me weak.

I tossed my phone onto the bed and crossed the room quickly, nearly jerking the door off its hinges. I raced down the steps and out the front door like the hounds of hell were chasing me, which wasn't too far from the truth. I paused when I got outside, not sure where to go. Lachlan had said that I was welcome to use any part of his house that I wanted to, but so far, I had kept to either my room or the kitchen.

My eyes settled on what Lachlan had told me was the pool house located at the side of the main house. A swim sounded like the perfect way to work off the tension that flowed through me. The counselors at the rehab facility had urged me to channel my energy into something productive whenever I felt a craving hit and since I was experiencing a whopper of a craving, it looked like I would need to swim a lot of laps.

Having found something that I thought might help, I stalked determinedly over to the large building. I wondered if Lachlan kept it stocked with extra swimwear for guests. I was sure he did, he had always struck me as the type of person to plan everything out. If not, I guessed I'd be putting on a show for the gardeners and any other person who happened to walk by the pool. I needed to swim and I wasn't going to let a lack of clothing stop me.

I opened the door and let out a low whistle; it was no ordinary pool house. The building itself was the size of an average home and was set up as more of a guest house than a place to change your clothes. The floors were white marble with swirls of gray throughout which matched the color of the walls perfectly. There was a full kitchen with granite countertops and darker gray cabinets that I was sure had been custom made and resembled the type of weathered wood you might find in an old barn. The furniture was made of a soft, luxurious white material and I wondered idly how it stayed so clean with people coming in and sitting on it, still wet from the pool.

I made my way down a hallway with doors on either side and opened the first one I came to. It was a spacious bedroom that could easily be a master bedroom in the finest home, complete with a California King-sized sleigh bed, walk-in closet, and en suite bathroom.

I rolled my eyes at the extravagance of the place. Lachlan was obviously extremely wealthy, but I just couldn't understand why he'd want to waste that much money on a place that guests only used to change their clothes. Of course, my own salary had raised to an astronomical height since signing on with Golden Entertainment Studios, but I still couldn't imagine blowing through so much cash on something that was rarely used.

Most people would probably be shocked to learn that I didn't lead the typical rock and roll lifestyle. The press had labeled me as Carter's Creed's wild child; constantly throwing lavish parties and buying expensive cars. While I had attended several parties thrown by the rich and famous, I was never the one to host them and I didn't even own a car, preferring to call an Uber driver whenever I wanted to go somewhere that wasn't within walking distance.

The biggest purchase I had made with my money was my condo. While some people complained about the noise of a big city, I found it comforting to be surrounded by the sounds of other people; it made me feel less alone. The rest of my money, other than what had been used on drugs and alcohol, had been invested. I'd spent my entire life just barely scraping by and so, as soon as I'd signed the contract with Golden Entertainment, I'd hired the best investment banker in Chicago to handle my money. He'd since tripled my net worth and assured me that it was growing steadily. I never would have dreamed that I'd end up a multi-millionaire, but I was going to be smart with my money because I was never going to allow myself to be put in the position of having to beg for food again.

I would have even more money since I wouldn't be blowing it on drugs or alcohol anymore and I'd already made up my mind that I wanted to use that money for something good. Something that would help LGBTQ kids that were facing some of the same struggles that I had been through as a kid. I made a mental note to talk to Carter about my idea. I vaguely remembered him talking about some sort of place that he and his family liked to volunteer at.

I yanked open the top drawer of the dresser and smiled when I found several bathing suits and swim trunks inside. I chose a skimpy pair of bright blue trunks and tossed them onto the bed. It would've been fun to strut around the pool completely naked, but I guessed those would have to do. I quickly peeled my clothes off and slid the tight spandex up over my hips. I chuckled as I pictured how red Benjamin's face would get if he saw me. I had no idea why the old geezer despised me so much, but I sure did like to rile him up until that vein popped out on his forehead.

I stepped into the large bathroom and stood in front of the mirror. I turned around slowly, looking over my shoulder at my reflection. I could still stand to gain a little more weight and I needed to rebuild the muscle mass that I had lost during my stay at the hospital and in rehab, but I already looked much better than I had when I'd first arrived. I should have probably thanked Kerry more for all of the delicious food she prepared that was helping to put me back together. It was odd having someone mother me because I'd never had that before, but it felt good too.

Satisfied that my ass looked good, I grabbed a towel and headed out to the pool. It was hot outside and the sun beat down on me, quickly warming my shoulders. It probably would do me some good to be outside and soak up a little vitamin D for a while. I glanced around, not seeing anyone in the pool area so I tossed my towel onto the nearest chaise lounge and stepped closer to the pool. The water was crystal clear and looked very inviting so I dove in, relishing the feel of the cool water against my heated skin.

CHAPTER
Six

Lachlan

I ENDED THE CONFERENCE CALL I'D BEEN ON FOR THE PAST HOUR and stood up from my desk. My neck and back were pinched from sitting prone for such a long period of time and I twisted and turned, trying to loosen up the stiff muscles. I yawned loudly, reminding myself of how little sleep I'd gotten the night before. I had never been the type to require eight hours of sleep, usually functioning quite well after only four or five hours, and when I did go to bed, I usually fell asleep without much difficulty. Recently however, I'd found myself tossing and turning as images of a certain drummer invaded my sleep. The way he'd looked the first time I'd seen him on stage; full of confidence and swagger, to the way he'd looked when he'd arrived at my home.

I had felt an instant attraction to him that first night and when

I'd seen him climb behind his drum set and flip his long raven-colored hair over his shoulder, my dick had stirred to life. I'd refused to acknowledge the attraction though, given that he was a client and had done a fairly good job of not letting anyone see the feelings he evoked within me.

Then Landon had called to let me know that Rylie was starting to unravel. I flew out immediately to where they were touring under the pretense of checking in on my clients, but really, I had just needed to see how Rylie was for myself. I'd stood at the side of the stage as I talked with Landon about how the band was doing, but I kept my eyes trained on Rylie, my heart thumping wildly in my chest at the knowledge that he was so near.

I had followed the band's progress daily through various social media sites and had felt something resembling jealousy each time pictures of Rylie showed up with his arm thrown around some random man or woman. I had no delusions that he was a virgin, but it bothered me to see the faces of the people he was hooking up with. I'd been in a few relationships before and I'd cared a great deal for some of them, but I had never felt the level of attraction for any of them that I felt for Rylie.

I didn't understand the strong hold he had on me and I'd fought it as hard as I could, but it was getting harder and harder with him living under the same roof as me. I knew when I had made the decision to bring him to my home that it would be difficult being around him and acting like his presence didn't affect me in any way, but I never once regretted my decision to help him. More than anything, even more than my desire to be with him, I wanted to see the spark come back into his eyes that I had seen that first night. If I was able to achieve that goal, then I would be satisfied; even when it came time to watch him leave.

With a sigh, I grabbed my favorite mug off of my desk and headed out of my office and towards the kitchen in search of coffee. I would need some caffeine if I was going to make it through the next meeting. I was walking through the living room when a movement out of the corner of my eye caught my attention. I turned and looked out the glass doors and my breath caught in my throat when I saw Rylie swimming laps in the pool.

Without any conscious thought, I changed course and headed in the direction of the pool. Setting my mug down on a side table, I slid the heavy door open and stepped outside. The sun was bright and I was momentarily blinded. I waited for my eyes to adjust to the light and could hear the rhythmic slapping of Rylie's arms as they sliced through the water. My vision cleared and I was finally able to see him again. He hadn't noticed me yet and so I stayed back a little so I could observe him unnoticed.

He looked like a man on a mission as he reached the end of the pool and pushed off the side, heading back in the opposite direction without pausing for a breath. He looked healthier than he had when he'd arrived, but he still held the signs of a person who needed to recover from an illness which is exactly what his situation was.

A lot of people seemed to think that addiction was simply a selfish choice that a person made and that if they really wanted to stop then they would. But I'd done a lot of research and had known my share of addicts throughout my career and I knew that addiction was in fact an illness which held its victim in such a powerful vise that they had to struggle day to day, sometimes even minute to minute to resist its seductive call. Recovering addicts weren't weak, in fact they were probably the strongest people among us because they fought their demons every day and had the battle scars to prove it.

The sudden lack of movement and sound pulled me from my thoughts and my eyes widened when I saw Rylie watching me from the far end of the pool. He looked surprised to see me standing there and I scrambled to come up with an excuse as to why I had been staring at him as he swam closer to where I stood. When he was in front of me he leaned against the side and crossed his arms, propping himself up along the side of the pool.

I tried not to stare at the brightly colored tattoos that covered his arms and shoulders. I'd always had a thing for tattoos on men and on Rylie in particular, but up until that moment I'd only seen the ones that were visible under the sleeves of his t-shirts.

"I hope it was okay that I helped myself to the pool. I needed to get out of my room for a while and you said before that I should make myself at home," he said, sounding unsure. His deep voice rolled through me, causing goose bumps to appear on my skin and I prayed he didn't notice the shiver that wracked my body.

"Of course," I assured him, trying to keep my voice neutral. "I want you to feel comfortable and to treat my home as your own while you're here."

"Thanks," he replied. I stood there for a minute, but couldn't come up with anything else to say so I simply nodded and turned to head back inside. The sound of his voice had me whipping back around. "I'm surprised to see you out here. I was starting to think you never left your cave."

Was I imagining the touch of sadness in his voice? I knew his friends hadn't come to see him yet because Carter had called to let me know that they were going to give him time to adjust before they stopped by so they wouldn't overwhelm him, but I wondered if it had made him feel abandoned instead. And I was sure I hadn't helped the situation by bringing him there and then avoiding him for days on end. Suddenly I felt like a selfish arsehole. I'd only been thinking of myself and how I needed to keep my distance instead of considering how he would feel being left all alone in a strange place, especially after just leaving rehab. I made a promise to myself that I would spend more time with him while he was there; I'd just have to work harder to hide my feelings for him.

I cleared my throat. "I was actually just on my way to get coffee between meetings and I saw you swimming," I explained lamely. "I figured I'd come out and say hello."

He pulled away from the side and made his way over to the

ladder. My eyes widened and I nearly swallowed my tongue as he gripped the railing and hoisted himself out of the pool. Water flowed from his long black hair and in the sunlight, I noticed some natural auburn highlights throughout his thick tresses. The water ran over his skin in rivulets, cutting paths over his sculpted body. I knew he had large biceps, thanks to the hours he spent playing the drums, but the tight-fitting clothes he usually wore had somehow managed to hide just how utterly perfect his body was.

While his arms were covered in a full sleeve of tattoos, his chest was bare, showing off his firm pecs. *Oh, dear God, his nipples are pierced.* My tongue darted out to wet my lips as my eyes traveled further south over rippling abs, to a thin dark line of hair. My attention snagged on another tattoo on his hipbone, but I couldn't make out what it was because it disappeared beneath the skimpy swim trunks that matched the blue of his eyes perfectly. I had to bite back a moan when I caught sight of the outline of his dick and something else underneath the wet material. *Is he pierced there too?* All the blood in my body rushed to my groin and I felt my cock lengthening within my briefs, leaving me wishing I'd worn something other than the thin dress slack I was wearing, which hid nothing.

I heard his quick intake of breath and my eyes darted up to his. He was staring at my groin and I couldn't tell if it was the heat of the sun or a blush that had my face feeling so warm. I knew that he had seen the evidence of my arousal when he looked back up at me with questions in his eyes. I stood there at a loss for words as I waited for what seemed like hours to see if he would get angry or mock me for even thinking of him in a sexual way. Instead, his eyes softened and his lips turned up into a flirtatious grin.

"Thanks for the swim trunks," he said with a wink.

"Yeah, uh…they look um…you're welcome," I stuttered. I was mortified by my inability to articulate, but he didn't seem to care as he brushed by me, leaving a trail of fire where his body touched my own. I watched his retreating form, as he sauntered back towards the pool house. My knees felt weak as he bent over to pick up a towel from a chair and I got the perfect view of his rounded arse.

My eyes followed him until he disappeared into the pool house and then I let out a lungful of air I hadn't even realized I'd been holding. *So much for hiding my feelings from him,* I thought as I rolled my eyes and turned to go back into the house. There were no two ways about it, I was good and truly fucked.

Rylie looked surprised when I walked into the kitchen and sat down for dinner. Our eyes met briefly, but then I quickly looked away. I was still embarrassed by my obvious display earlier, but I needed to find a way to get over it and move on. He was my client and we would have to interact with each other on a regular basis, so the sooner I faced him, the sooner we could hopefully move past any awkwardness.

I sank down into my seat and looked up at Benjamin who was busy darting glances between Rylie and myself, his expression unreadable. He placed a pan of lasagna on a hot pad in the middle of the table then sat down without a word. Kerry turned from the counter, holding a large bowl of salad, and a smile lit up her face when she saw me.

"Lachlan, I'm so glad you decided to join us for dinner. I've missed seeing your face at the table." I knew that Kerry hadn't meant anything by the remark, but I still felt guilty. She had always been more like a mother to me than my own mother and it hadn't occurred to me that by trying to avoid Rylie, I was distancing myself from her and Benjamin as well.

"I'm sorry, I've had a lot of work to catch up on lately," I replied softly.

She set the bowl of salad down with a huff. "You work too much if you ask me," she scolded as she joined us at the table.

"You need to get out more, be around people." I opened my mouth to protest, but she cut me off, anticipating my usual response. "And not just your business associates; I mean real people." That wasn't the first time she'd voiced her opinion on my lack of a social life and I was positive it wouldn't be the last. I rolled my eyes heavenward and raised my glass of water to my lips, hoping she was finished so we could enjoy our meal. She usually stopped there, satisfied that she'd made her point so I never saw the curveball she was about to throw.

"When's the last time you went out on an actual date?" she asked.

Suddenly the water I'd been drinking went down the wrong way. I quickly grabbed a napkin and covered my mouth as my eyes watered and I began choking loudly. I heard a deep chuckle coming from Rylie and I tried to glare at him, but it lacked the fierce effect that I had intended when it was combined with my very real struggle to breathe.

"Are you alright, dear? What happened?" Kerry asked innocently. I gave her an incredulous look as I wiped the tears that had run down my cheeks during my fit.

"My drink just went down the wrong pipe, I suppose," I answered. It was easier than arguing with her.

"I know it's not a date, but I was going to ask if you wanted to watch a movie or something after dinner," Rylie said quietly. I was surprised I hadn't hurt my neck with the speed in which my head swiveled in his direction. "You know, if you feel like getting out of the office for a while."

He shrugged his shoulders nonchalantly as if my answer wouldn't affect him either way, but something in his eyes told me to tread carefully. I had the feeling that he didn't leave himself open to the possibility of rejection very often, but he shouldn't have worried because the thought of rejecting him was the furthest thing from my mind.

"Yes, thank you. I suppose I could take a break for one night," I told him, trying to appear casual. My brain tried to remind itself that his offer had probably only come because he was bored, but my heart was too busy doing flips inside my chest to heed the warning. A small smile spread across his face and his eyes held a glimmer of the spark that had been missing for way too long.

I started to smile back, but then Benjamin stood abruptly, his chair scraping against the floor, causing us all to turn our attention toward him. I narrowed my eyes when I saw the fierce scowl he wore, wondering what had caused it and why he seemed to be directing it at Rylie.

"Benjamin, are you alright?" I asked. He turned his gaze on me and straightened as if he realized he'd been behaving strangely.

"Yes, I'm fine. Thank you," he replied with a nod before turning his attention to the lasagna where he began cutting it and serving it onto our plates.

"Kerry, you might want to cut back on the amount of starch you're using in old Benji's tighty whities. Something seems to be chafing him," Rylie drawled.

"My undergarments are none of your concern, I assure you," Benjamin retorted primly. His face turned red and he pursed his lips as Kerry and I tried to hide our amusement. I'd never seen anyone ruffle Benjamin's feathers the way Rylie was able to.

"Excuse me, sir. I was simply trying to help a chap out," Rylie said in a nearly perfect rendition of a British accent. Benjamin raised his eyes to the ceiling as if he were praying for strength, but he lowered himself back into his seat and we all began eating.

I glanced over at Kerry who was grinning smugly at me and Rylie, I could almost hear her thoughts as she congratulated herself on a job well done for setting up the scene in which Rylie invited me to watch a movie.

Don't get too excited, it's only a movie. It wasn't like anything was going to come from spending one evening together. Other than our encounter at the pool earlier, Rylie had never shown any real indication that he was attracted to me. Sure, he'd sized me up in my office on his first day at my home, but he'd done that more to try and rile me up because he was pissed that I was laying out my rules for him.

Besides, even if he were attracted to me, I'd heard all of the rumors about him. Rylie didn't do relationships; he flitted around from one hook-up to the next. I, on the other hand, preferred something a little deeper and more meaningful than that. I didn't necessarily need a commitment, but I wanted to know that the person I was having sex with cared about me and wasn't sleeping with anyone else at the same time. Some people may have considered that old fashioned, but that was the way my heart worked.

Regardless of what happened, I was looking forward to getting to know him better. Perhaps we'd even be able to forge a friendship, which was something I could use more of and I had the feeling the same could be said for Rylie.

After dinner, Kerry shooed us from the kitchen, saying that she didn't need any help cleaning up, but it was obvious that she was anxious for Rylie and me to spend time together. I smiled when I saw Benjamin roll up his sleeves and pick up a stack of dishes to take to the sink. The two of them had been spending a lot more time together lately and I needed to remember to ask him about it.

The door swung shut behind us and Rylie turned to me with a nervous expression, his hands shoved deep into the pockets of his jeans. It was such a contrast to who he was on stage or the way the media portrayed him, but I felt a slight tugging inside my chest as I realized that I was finally getting to see the *real* Rylie Anderson. I was sure that not many people could say that they'd seen that part of him before and I felt honored to be one of them. That wasn't something I took lightly and I wanted more of it.

"We don't have to watch a movie if you've got stuff to do. I know you're really busy," he said, working his bottom lip with his teeth.

"I am very busy," I told him. He nodded his head in understanding and turned to walk away, but I grabbed his arm before he could leave. My fingers burned where they touched his bare skin and he glanced down at my hand and then back up again. From our close range, I could see the black that ringed the ice-cold blue of his irises. His jaw held just the right amount of scruff and I wondered if it would feel soft or scratchy against my cheek. He really was an extraordinarily handsome man.

"I am always busy," I repeated once I'd found my voice. "But there's nothing that can't wait for one night. I would like to watch a movie with you very much, Rylie." I was relieved when he didn't flinch when I used his given name, but smiled instead. His whole face seemed to light up with that grin and I had to remind myself to hold on to my heart. It would be far too easy to hand it over to him.

"Just give me a minute to call my office manager and then I'll be ready," I told him.

"No problem. I'm just gonna run and change," he said, hooking his thumb over his shoulder in the direction of the stairs. My eyes flickered down to the jeans he had on and then my own button-up shirt and slacks.

"I think I'd like to get more comfortable as well," I agreed. "I'll meet you back down here in about ten minutes?"

"Sure, okay." He gave me one more quick smile and then turned and walked away.

I watched him until he disappeared around the corner then let out a sigh. How was I going to make it through an entire evening of sitting in a darkened room next to Rylie without touching him, when all I wanted to do was feel his skin against mine?

CHAPTER
Seven

Lachlan

I CALLED CAROLYN AND ASKED HER TO CANCEL MY MEETINGS FOR the rest of the evening. I tried not to take offense by the surprised sound in her voice. Was I really that much of a workaholic that she couldn't imagine me taking an evening for myself? Between Kerry's gentle scolding at dinner and Carolyn's reaction, the answer to that question was glaringly obvious.

I hadn't always been like that. Sure, I'd worked hard; you had to when you were building a business from the ground up. But I would also find time to go out, have fun, and even date occasionally. Then Spencer was taken from me and the whole world just seemed like a colder and darker place. I lost interest in dating and had no desire to socialize other than the obligatory social events that I attended as the CEO of Golden Entertainment Studios. I focused on my job and stopped leaving my home, unless it was work related.

My sessions with Hudson had helped tremendously. He diagnosed me with depression and began treating me with a combination of medicine and counseling. My friendship with Micah, of course, had a big impact too. He was afraid that I would resent him or blame him in some way for making it out of that situation alive when my brother hadn't, but I'd never felt that way. Micah was my last link to Spencer, the last person to talk to him and hear his thoughts. The fact that he was there to comfort my brother through the worst time in his life was precious to me and I would forever be indebted to him.

After a lot of time, I had been able to cut back on my medication and no longer felt like the world was hopeless. I still didn't go out much with friends and I couldn't remember the last time I went on a date, but I knew how much progress I'd made. Apparently though, I still needed some help learning to spend more time away from my office.

I checked my watch, realizing what time it was and hurried out of my office and up to my room so I could get changed. My stomach fluttered as I thought about spending the evening with Rylie. *It's not a date, you fool*, I reminded myself. I rushed around my room, tossing my clothes into the hamper and pulling a black pair of soft cotton lounge pants and a t-shirt out of my closet. I yanked them on and went to the bathroom where I decided it couldn't hurt to brush my teeth.

After brushing and flossing, I messed with my hair a bit and then stood back to observe myself. I was surprised to see the brightness in my eyes and the faint flush to my cheeks. It took me a moment to recognize what it was I was seeing; it was excitement. I smiled at my reflection. Sitting at home, watching a movie with Rylie may not be considered a date, but it was still the most excited I had felt about anything in a very long time and it felt good; it felt like living again.

By the time I made it downstairs, Rylie was already waiting for me in the living room. He was sitting in a chair and scrolling through his phone so he hadn't noticed my arrival. My eyes widened when I saw the gray sweats he wore and the thin white t-shirt that stretched over his broad chest. He had removed the rubber band from his head and his long black hair hung softly on either side of him, blocking my view of his gorgeous face. As if hearing my thoughts, he reached up and smoothed it back behind his ear on the side closest to me. I wondered if he had any idea how beautiful he was. Somehow, I doubted it.

I didn't want to get caught ogling him again so I cleared my throat, alerting him to my presence. He looked up, his eyes raking over me and smirked. I glanced down quickly, making sure I hadn't forgotten my pants or anything embarrassing like that, but everything looked in order.

"What is it?" I asked, looking back up. He stood and my pulse quickened as he walked closer to me, his sweatpants barley hiding the impressive bulge underneath.

"I just hadn't expected to see you wearing something so casual," he explained.

"Is there something wrong with what I'm wearing?" I questioned.

"Not at all," he said. "I just had this image in my mind of what you wear to bed and it wasn't that." My eyebrows shot to my hairline and his eyes rounded as he realized how his words sounded.

"Not that I've been picturing you in or out of your clothes…or in your bed or… Ah, hell!" he stammered. He threw his head back and looked up at the ceiling with his hands on his hips. I couldn't help the chuckle that escaped at seeing him all flustered like that.

"I think I understand. You thought I'd be wearing something stuffy like an old-timey dressing gown and cap perhaps?" I grinned at him.

"Well, not exactly," he replied. "More like a pair of starched and pressed pajamas that button up to your neck," he teased.

"Really?" I said, arching one eyebrow. I stepped closer towards him, close enough that I could see how long his lashes were and the way they outlined his ice-blue eyes. "I guess you'd be shocked then to learn that I sleep without a stitch of clothes on, wouldn't you, Rylie?" I wasn't sure what had possessed me to behave so boldly, but I was glad that I had when I heard his swift intake of breath. I became aware of the heat radiating from his body and soaking through my thin t-shirt and I wished that there was nothing between us.

"I have to admit, Lachlan. You just gave me one hell of a visual." His voice sounded strained and inside I was pumping my fist in the air. We stared at each other for a long minute, the electricity surging between us enough to light a small village. I watched as his pupils dilated and his tongue darted out to wet his lips. He was as turned on as I was and I felt myself leaning in closer.

"Excuse me," someone cut in, startling us both. I stepped back quickly and turned to see Benjamin standing in the doorway, holding a tray with two glasses and a pitcher of lemonade. He didn't look very happy, but to be honest, I wasn't all that thrilled at the moment either. My cock was throbbing and I turned slightly, trying to hide the evidence since my pants clearly hid nothing.

"Was there something you needed, Benjamin?" I asked, my voice sounding gruff.

"Kerry thought you might like some lemonade," he explained. "Would you like for me to take it to the media room?"

"Ahh, yes, please. Thank you," I replied. Benjamin nodded stiffly then turned to leave.

"Thanks for the lemonade, Benji. And as always, your timing was impeccable," Rylie quipped. Benjamin shot him a look over his shoulder, but then turned and left without a word.

I knew Rylie was being sarcastic, but he wasn't exactly wrong. While I'd hated to stop whatever it was that was happening between us, a part of me was thankful for Benjamin's interruption because it gave me the time needed to clear my head. I wasn't sure what had come over me, but I needed to remember who I was dealing with. Not only because of Rylie's playboy reputation, but there was also a lot of things he still needed to work through. I should be helping him focus on his recovery, not trying to get him naked.

"Shall we go watch the movie?" My words sounded as stilted and awkward as I felt.

"Yeah, sure," Rylie answered. He avoided my gaze and I wondered if he'd been as thrown off balance as I had been by the level of attraction between us.

"Holy shit! Look at this place," Rylie blurted out as I opened the door to the media room. He walked in a slow circle as he looked around.

"Is this the first time that you've been in here?" I asked.

"Yeah," he answered distractedly as he made his way over to the large media cabinet that took up one entire wall.

"Why?" I questioned. "I told you to make yourself at home while you're here."

"Too easy to get lost," he said with a shrug. "Besides, I didn't want to get in the way any more than I already had. Just easier to stay in my room." He opened one of the doors of the cabinet and began browsing the hundreds of movies contained inside.

I felt a pang in my chest and I wasn't sure if it was because he hadn't felt welcomed in my home and had hidden himself away or if it was the fact that he just seemed to accept that he would be in the way, almost as if that were a normal occurrence in his life. I supposed growing up in the foster care system could leave a person feeling as if they didn't really belong anywhere, but it still hurt me to think of him feeling that way.

"So, Hudson said your first session went well," I told him. I walked to the tray that Benjamin had left on the table and began pouring glasses of lemonade, more to give my hands something to focus on so I wouldn't reach for him and wrap him into a hug.

"What else did Hudson say?" he asked sharply. Rylie shot me a look over his shoulder and I realized how my words could have been misconstrued.

"Don't worry. Hudson would never betray your confidence," I rushed to assure him. "He takes his profession very seriously; you can trust him implicitly. I simply saw him as he was leaving and asked him if everything was alright. He answered yes and that he looked forward to getting to know you better." I was glad when his shoulders relaxed slightly. He turned to face me, his head cocked to the side.

"Why did you introduce me to Hudson as Rocko? I mean, not that I'm complaining, but I thought one of your rules was that I was supposed to go by Rylie while I was staying here."

"I only said that I would refer to you as Rylie. I figured that it should be your decision who you choose to share that part of your-self with," I explained. I picked up the full glasses and carefully made my way over to the couch where I set them down on the coffee table.

"You had no problem making that decision for me when you de-cided to have your minions snoop around, digging up dirt from my past," he interjected. His eyes were narrowed and I could tell he was still angry about that.

"That was different. That was just…" I started to explain, but he cut me off.

"Business. Yeah, I know, this is all a business transaction for you," he muttered as he turned back towards the cabinet.

I wanted to correct him, to tell him that nothing about my deci-sion to bring him there had ever been just business, no matter how much I'd tried to convince myself otherwise. The words wouldn't come though. What would he possibly think if he found out that I had been holding a secret desire for him ever since the first time I saw him or that there was nothing in the world I wanted more than to get to know him and see if the wild chemistry between us could turn into something more, something lasting?

In the end, I said nothing because I couldn't risk having him run away. If he discovered my thoughts and decided to leave, then he wouldn't get the help he needed. Him becoming whole again completely outweighed my own selfish desires. Luckily, I didn't have to come up with an answer because he'd already found a distraction.

"No way, you have an original NES?" he shouted excitedly. I walked up behind him as he pulled the gaming system out of the cabinet and began digging around for the games that went with it. "Aww, man. This is awesome! You have all the best games," Rylie said as he spread them out on the floor in front of him.

"Those were actually mine from when I was a kid," I told him. "Would you like to play?"

"Are you serious? Yeah, I want to." He looked up at me with a wide grin that was so boyish and full of joy that it left me breathless. He jumped up from the floor, but then hesitated. "Oh, but wait. What about the movie?"

"We can watch a movie any night, right?" I really didn't care what we did, as long as I got to spend time with him and it put a smile like that on his face.

"Does that mean you might come out of your cave more often?" he asked, laying his hand on his chest. I couldn't help the laugh that came out of my mouth as his eyes opened wide and his jaw dropped in mock surprise. The playful side of Rylie was new and I loved it. In fact, I hadn't seen a side of him that I didn't care for; even the lost and broken one.

"I'm not that bad, am I?" I teased. Rylie cocked his head to one side and studied me as if he were giving my question a lot of thought.

"Well, you don't quite have the stick up your ass that old Benji does, but..." he trailed off with a laugh, ducking quickly as I grabbed a pillow from the couch and tossed it at his head.

"What's going on between the two of you anyway?" I questioned as I dropped down onto the couch.

"I have no idea, dude just hates me for some reason," he said with a shrug.

"I can't imagine why. You've always been so charming around him," I deadpanned. Rylie threw back his head with a laugh and it was the best sound I'd ever heard. Deep and throaty, and one hundred percent carefree.

"I'm just giving it as good as I get it. Mario or Donkey Kong?" He held both games up so I pointed to one without really looking. I was too distracted by his words and the questions that they brought to mind, such as, was Rylie a top or bottom? Or was he a switch like me?

I grabbed my lemonade and took a long drink, trying to slow the blood rushing to my cock as visions popped into my head of Rylie bent over the coffee table as I prepared him for my dick or of him taking me from behind as he tossed me over the back of the couch. I heard the familiar sounds of the game and quickly grabbed a pillow to place in my lap so Rylie wouldn't see the erection that threatened to rip through the front of my lounge pants. He plopped down on the cushion next to me and handed me a remote. There was barely any space between us and my skin burned where his bare arm brushed mine.

"You okay?" he asked.

"Yes, I'm fine," I answered as evenly as possible. "Would you like to be Mario or Luigi?" I kept my eyes on the television screen, but I could see him looking at me out of the corner of my eye. A blush crept up my neck as I realized that clutching a pillow in front of my crotch probably had the opposite effect and instead of hiding the problem had shined a glaring light onto it.

"Everyone knows that Luigi's the best," he finally said, letting me off the hook and turning to face the screen. We started the game and played in silence for several minutes. It became obvious rather quickly that Rylie was a much better player of video games than me.

"You're very good. You must have played this a lot as a kid," I said with a laugh as I caused Luigi to die for the third time.

"Nah, the places they put me in didn't spend that kind of money on something for the kids. They did it for one reason only, a pay-check." His fingers never stopped moving over the game controller, but I could feel his body tense ever so slightly beside mine.

I was quiet for a moment, stunned that he had willingly shared something about his childhood with me and knowing that how I responded could make the difference of if he ever opened up to me again. He was testing me and I prayed that I wouldn't fail. I knew him well enough to know that any further questioning on my part would cause him to retreat. I also knew that if I showed any signs of pity, the conversation, and perhaps our evening together, would come to an immediate halt.

"Not everyone should be allowed to become a parent, that's for damn sure." I watched him out of the corner of my eye and was relieved when I saw his shoulders relax.

"No, they shouldn't," he replied. He was quiet for a few seconds, the only sounds in the room came from the game dinging as our characters collected coins. I wasn't sure what to say next, so I waited for him to decide. Dealing with Rylie was like dealing with a skittish horse; one wrong move and he'd bolt. Finally, he spoke.

"I'd listen to the kids at school talking about the newest video games they'd bought and making plans to go to each other's houses and play. It always sounded like so much fun." While Rylie hadn't said any of that like it bothered him, I knew it had to have been hard for him to always be on the outside looking in and my heart ached for the little boy he once was.

"Anyway, it was Steve that taught me how to play video games. One night, not long after we met, I showed up at his house and he was in the middle of a game. I watched him for a while and then I gave it a try. I sucked almost as bad as you that first time," he joked and I jabbed him in the side with my elbow, making him laugh.

"You and Steve seem pretty close," I stated.

"Yeah, we are. Or at least we were," he replied. "Until I fucked everything up."

"Hey, he'll forgive you," I told him, bumping his shoulder with my own. "You just scared him pretty bad, but he wouldn't have gotten so upset if he didn't care about you, right?"

"Yeah, I hope so," he said quietly. He sounded so sad that I had to ask.

"How close are you? I mean, did you guys ever..." My words trailed off and I felt my gut clench as I waited for his answer. I'd never heard about anything going on between the two bandmates, but long hours spent on the road could lead to some lonely nights. If there was something happening there, then I needed to know right away and perhaps it would help put my crazy thoughts to bed once and for all because I would never even consider being with someone who was involved with someone else.

Rylie looked over at me as if I'd grown two heads. "Oh, hell no, it's nothing like that. Steve's my best friend. He's the closest thing to family I've ever had." I smiled at him.

"I'm glad you have that. Everyone needs a person they can count on."

"Who do you count on, Lachlan?" he asked.

"Micah," I answered immediately. Rylie paused the game and turned his whole body to face me.

"Micah, as in Landon's fiancé, Micah?" I chuckled at his shocked expression.

"Yes. Micah is my best friend." He shook his head as if trying to clear it.

"Okay, I've got to hear this story. What in the world could a British music mogul and an ex-Navy SEAL have in common?"

"It seems strange, doesn't it?" I gave a little laugh, but my heart felt the familiar heaviness I usually felt when I thought of how Micah and I had become friends. It didn't hurt as badly as it used to, but it was still difficult to think of those first few days after he told me about Spencer.

"My younger brother, Spencer, served in the Royal Air Force. He and Micah met when each of their platoons were captured by insurgents and held prisoners of war." Rylie drew in a deep breath and he reached out and placed his hand on my leg. I looked up at him in surprise and he started to pull away, but I grabbed his wrist and held on until he relaxed and let his hand rest on my leg again. I hadn't been touched by anyone in a long time and it was comforting.

"They were held there for several weeks. Many of the soldiers didn't survive the torture or the beatings. Spencer was one of them." I heard Rylie's quiet gasp and he turned his hand over in a silent offering. I thread my fingers through his without giving it another thought and it felt right; like my hand belonged in his.

"Anyway, Micah and Spencer had made a pact with each other that if one of them didn't make it, the other would tell their family what had happened. That's how Micah and I met." Rylie blew out a breath between his pursed lips.

"I'm sorry. I had no idea or I wouldn't have brought it up." The look on his face was sorrowful.

"Don't be," I said with a small smile. "It's hard to think about the manner in which he died, but knowing that he had someone there to care for him makes it easier."

"Was Spencer the kid I saw in the photo in your office?" he asked.

I smiled fondly. "Yeah, that was him. He was three years younger than me and my very best friend in the world." I laughed as memories of the two of us as kids sifted through my mind. "We did everything together. Video games, hiking in the woods behind our house, riding our bikes. We each had a fondness for music though and as soon as I got my driver's license, we went to as many concerts as we could. In fact, I still have most of the ticket stubs from the concerts we attended stashed away somewhere."

Rylie smiled at me. "Is that why you started Golden Entertainment?"

"Yes," I admitted sheepishly. "It was such a happy memory from my childhood that I guess I just couldn't let go of it as an adult."

"Well, I think you ended up doing pretty well for yourself," he teased, gesturing around the spacious room with his hand.

"Thank you," I said shyly.

"What about your parents? Do they still live in England?"

"Yes, they do." I sighed and Rylie looked at me curiously. "My parents never should have had children. I'm sure they probably loved us in their own unique way, but they were too busy attending parties and other social events to be bothered with two young sons. Kerry and Benjamin practically raised me and Spencer."

"It sounds like we both drew the short straw on shitty parents, huh?" Rylie said and I burst out an unexpected laugh.

"Yes, I suppose that is correct," I agreed. I was glad that I had told him about Spencer. It was nice to have someone to talk to and it felt good to remember the fun things that my brother and I used to do. I hadn't done that in a long time because it was easier to push the memories aside than to risk letting the pain from his death seep back in.

"I still have one question." Rylie's forehead was scrunched up like he was truly puzzled.

"What's that?" I asked.

"If you and your brother used to play video games all the time then why are you so terrible at it?" he said with a laugh.

"Shut up, it's been a really long time since I played. You just wait until I get back into the swing of things, I'll be kicking your arse then," I boasted.

"Oh, God, I love your accent. Arse!" That caused Rylie to laugh even harder.

"What's wrong with the word arse?" I asked with false indignation, which I was sure was ruined by the grin I wore.

"Nothing," he replied. "It just sounded funny coming out of your proper British mouth."

"I think you'd be surprised at how very improper my mouth can be at times," I joked, but he didn't laugh.

"That's good to know," he said and I felt a chill race up my spine from the way he was looking at me. I knew I should pull away. I should make some excuse and leave the room, but my need to taste him was more powerful than my sense of right and wrong at that moment and I felt myself leaning towards him.

CHAPTER
Eight

Rylie/Rocko

As soon as Lachlan started talking about his improper mouth, my mind went straight to the gutter and my dick got rock hard as I pictured that mouth stretched around the broad head of my cock. Lachlan Edwards was nothing like the people I usually hooked up with. Those were, more often than not, bar flies from wherever we happened to be playing that night or ever since we'd started touring and making a name for ourselves, groupies who just wanted to say that they'd slept with the band's drummer.

The women usually wore skin-tight, barely-there clothes and too much makeup while the men typically dressed in either very tight jeans and t-shirts or leather from head to toe. They flaunted their goods for everyone to see, leaving very little to the imagination.

Lachlan, on the other hand, was much more distinguished and conservative. While I had no problem with a person showing off their body and had enjoyed those bodies more times than I cared to admit, I found Lachlan's preppy clothes and perfectly styled hair to be sexy as fuck. There was something to be said for leaving things to the imagination and I had spent a lot of time lately imagining what he kept hidden.

At that moment, with Lachlan's words still ringing in my ear and my cock begging for some attention, all I wanted to do was peel him out of his clothes and find out if his body was as good as what I had conjured in my mind. He must have been sharing my thoughts because the next thing I knew, he was leaning towards me, his intentions clear within those hooded honey-colored eyes.

His lips pressed against mine, lightly at first, as if he were making sure I wasn't going to push him away. The thought never even crossed my mind. I urged him to open for me and when I finally felt his tongue sweep into my mouth, I gasped with pleasure. He tasted like lemons and sugar from his drink and something else that I'd never experienced before. It was both foreign and familiar to my body at the same time and I wanted to drink it in until I was drowning in the flavor of him.

The tension that had been building between us snapped and we were suddenly all over each other. My body ignited with the need to explore every single inch of him with my fingers and my tongue. I slid a hand behind his neck and another around his waist and pulled him towards me as my tongue continued to mate with his, dipping and swirling in an age-old rhythm.

His kisses were as urgent and demanding as mine and I growled deep in my throat when he threw his leg over my lap and straddled me. His hands tangled in my hair, rough at first, but it just added to the fire raging between us. I thrust my hips up and we both gasped at the first contact between our straining erections. It still wasn't enough though, so I reached between us and began tugging at the pull string of his lounge pants.

It took a few seconds for my sex-crazed brain to catch up with the fact that his hand was covering mine and he was no longer kissing me. I opened my eyes and looked at him. His skin was flushed and he was breathing heavily. His eyes were dark with desire but there was also something else and I recognized it well, because I'd seen the same look in the mirror many times after a night of binge drinking or getting high. It was the look of regret and it hit me like a bucket of ice water.

Lachlan scrambled off of my lap and stood, smoothing his hair down nervously as he looked everywhere but at me. My stomach filled with dread before the words ever left his mouth.

"I'm very sorry. I'm not quite sure what came over me, but I should have never done that. You are my client and I brought you here to get better, not for…that," he gestured to the couch with a shaky hand.

My body stiffened as I felt my walls go up. I should have never left myself vulnerable, I was smarter than that. I couldn't find any words to say as he walked quickly to the door. When he reached the doorway, he glanced over his shoulder at me.

"I'm terribly sorry, Rylie. I hope we can still be friends after what happened." I flinched at his use of my real name. I'd gotten used to him calling me that the longer I was at his house, but I felt too exposed at that moment so it came at me like a punch to the gut.

"Of course," I answered weakly.

He stared at me for a long moment and then gave me a single nod before walking out. I let my head fall to the back of the couch with a moan. What the hell had I been thinking? Lachlan had made it clear that I was only there as a client. So then why had he kissed me in the first place? With a frustrated sigh, I turned off the TV and stood up. Hopefully a good night's sleep would help me figure things out.

I watched Hudson with amusement as he tried to squeeze his large frame into the tiny two-seater sports car I had chosen to take out for a spin. He had discovered that I was more relaxed—and therefore more willing to talk—if I wasn't cooped up inside Lachlan's office, so he'd begun taking a more liberal approach to my therapy. Sometimes we would take a walk or sit along the side of the pool, it didn't really matter to me as long as I didn't have to have him staring at me the entire time we talked. It was easier to bare your soul when you didn't have to witness the judgement or condemnation in the other person's eyes. Not that I'd told him all that much, but I had definitely opened up more over the last few weeks.

When I'd woken that morning and seen the sunlight streaming in through the windows, I'd known exactly what I'd wanted to do during my session. I'd expected Lachlan to balk at the idea, but he'd agreed immediately, looking pleased that I had come to him with the request. It wasn't the first time we had spoken since the kiss, in fact we'd continued eating dinner together and occasionally watched movies afterward, but it wasn't the same as before. We kept a respectable distance from each other during those times and neither one of us talked about anything significant.

It was awkward and a bit awful after experiencing the closeness that had been developing before that night and I'd wondered if he'd been missing it too when I saw the way his eyes lit up as I asked to borrow one of his cars. He'd told me to choose whichever car I liked and so I'd set off for the garage like a kid in a candy store. Once inside, I'd walked through the rows of cars, trying not to drool on the hoods before finally settling on a raven black Koenigsegg with red leather interior. Even though I didn't own a car, and could never imagine spending the insane amount of money that I was sure Lachlan had spent on his collection, I had always enjoyed looking through car magazines and dreaming of driving one of the elite model sports cars someday. My heart raced as I realized that my dream was about to become a reality.

"Are you sure Lachlan's okay with you driving his car?" Hudson asked. He'd managed to maneuver his body into the confining space and was seated with his knees pressed tight against the dashboard. I couldn't hold back my laughter at the sight of him. "Go ahead, laugh it up," he said. "I'll just add your funny time to the rest of your bill." He glared at me which only made me laugh harder, but I saw the twitch of his lips that told me he wasn't really upset. When I'd finally gained control of myself, I answered his question.

"Yeah, I asked Lachlan and he told me I could pick any car I wanted."

"And this is the car you chose," Hudson said drolly and I chuckled.

"Sorry, I wasn't really thinking about how you'd fit in it. I was just thinking what a kickass car this is," I explained. "We can use another one if you'd rather. Lachlan has pretty much every car ever made. We might even be able to find a minivan in here somewhere that you can stretch out in," I teased.

"Just start driving before I lose all circulation to my lower half, would you?" Hudson rolled his eyes when I gave him my most brilliant smile.

"Okay, but only if you're sure," I said sweetly, but I was already backing out of the garage so he couldn't have changed his mind if he tried. I drove down the long driveway and then peeled out a little too fast onto the road, causing another car to swerve so they wouldn't hit me and lay on their horn angrily. Hudson grabbed onto the dash and I eased my foot off of the gas pedal slightly.

"How long has it been since you drove, man?" he screeched.

"A while," I admitted sheepishly. He shot me an incredulous look. "I don't own a car, never saw much need since I live in the city. I either walk wherever I need to go or call a cab or ask one of my friends for a ride if it's too far," I explained.

"Do you even have a license?" Hudson asked evenly. I looked at him like he was ridiculous.

"Why? Is that important?" I asked seriously. His eyes nearly bugged out of his head and I burst out laughing. He mumbled something that sounded like *jackass*, but I couldn't really hear him over the sounds of my own laughter.

"Don't worry, big guy. Of course, I have my license. I don't have my own car, but I've driven Steve's many times. I know what I'm doing, I'm just a little rusty is all and this car handles a lot differently than any other car I've ever driven."

"It's also probably a lot more expensive than any car you've ever driven," Hudson said sarcastically. "If you damage it, you're going to have to go on several more world tours to pay for it."

I nodded my head in agreement. He wasn't lying about the cost of the car, but I felt sure that I had things under control. Besides, I couldn't remember the last time I'd felt so relaxed and carefree without the aid of drugs and alcohol. I put the window down and took a deep breath of fresh air. I felt the tension in my body easing with each mile that passed.

After about thirty minutes, I pulled into the parking lot of a diner and parked the car. Hudson groaned as he climbed out and stretched his legs. I felt bad for having put him through such an uncomfortable ride. Next time, I would be more thoughtful to his needs. He really was a good guy and I was surprised to find that I had actually begun looking forward to my time with him. Of course, there were still some topics that I had kept off the table, but he always seemed to sense when he was about to push me too hard and he'd back off. I liked that about him and it made me feel like I could trust him, which I was sure was the whole point.

"You hungry?" I asked, eyeing the diner. It looked like the kind of place that would have been popular in the fifties, with a juke box playing in the corner and girls delivering food to the cars while wearing roller skates. However, new restaurants and food courts in the malls had probably lured away most of the customers, leaving only a couple of cars parked close to the building.

"Starving," Hudson replied and I chuckled when his stomach gave an answering rumble.

"Come on," I said. "I'll buy your lunch for being such a good sport about the ride."

"You owe me more than a burger and some fries for the near-death experience I just suffered through," he joked.

"Fine, I'll buy you a milkshake too. Are you happy?" I rolled my eyes dramatically and Hudson let out a rumbling laugh.

"Yes, that will make me happy. Thank you." We were still chuckling as we entered the diner. There were two people seated at the counter, talking to a waitress who was dressed in a pink, retro uniform. Although, given the dated look of everything around us, her uniform may not have been retro as much as authentic.

"Just sit wherever you want," the waitress said tiredly before resuming her conversation with the other customers.

I followed Hudson to the back of the restaurant and slid into the smooth, red booth seat. The Formica table that sat between us was cracked along the edges and weathered with age. We each grabbed a menu from the little silver holder on the table which also housed ketchup, salt and pepper shakers, and little packets of sugar. We were quiet as we looked over the food choices until the waitress sidled up alongside our table, pen and pad of paper in hand and a bored expression on her face.

"You boys know what you want?" She popped her gum loudly and began tapping her pen against the pad of paper. I glanced around the empty diner and wondered what exactly we could possibly be keeping her from. I shook my head and turned back to Hudson who smiled up at the waitress as he gave her his order. She looked at him warily at first, but when he glanced at her nametag and tacked on a "thank you very much, Beatrice," to his order, she became putty in his hands.

It was a struggle not to flip him off as he gave me a smug grin when Beatrice turned her head my way. I ordered the same as

Hudson, a burger with everything, fries, and a chocolate shake. She wrote it all down and then walked away, not sparing a smile for me.

"You're a suck-up," I accused him as soon as she was out of earshot.

"I believe it's called charm," Hudson replied, his eyes dancing with amusement.

"Yeah, whatever," I said with a laugh.

"So, what was all of this about today?" Hudson asked. He still wore a friendly smile, but he looked at me directly as he waited for my answer. I shrugged my shoulders at him.

"What do you mean? You know I like to get out of the house when we have our sessions."

"I know. There just seems to be something different about you today. You don't seem upset so I don't think anything bad happened, so what is it?" he prodded. I felt embarrassed, so I concentrated on where my fingers were picking at the cracked table. And avoided his eyes.

"Today's my birthday," I mumbled.

"What?" Hudson nearly shouted. "Why didn't you tell me? We could've gone somewhere nicer than this place," he said, whispering that last part.

"Nah, this is perfect. I never make a big deal out of it and nobody else knows." I enunciated that last part so he would pick up on my meaning. I didn't want him to run back and tell Lachlan who would feel like shit for not doing something special for me; that was just the kind of guy he was.

Growing up, I'd never had anyone that cared enough about me to want to celebrate my birthday, so one year, when I was around nine or ten, I decided that I would find something to do for myself. I was dirt poor, so it wasn't going to be anything extravagant. I remember, I walked down to the end of our block where Michaelson's Comic Book Store was.

Mr. Michaelson had the biggest and best collection of comic

books that I had ever seen. I could never afford to buy one, but he must have felt bad for me because he would let me stand in the store and read them as long as I wanted to. I'd always had a fascination with the colorful books and I could get lost in the pages for hours on end as I read and reread the stories of my favorite super heroes as they fought the bad guys and saved the day. A few weeks before my birthday, Mr. Michaelson was supposed to get a new shipment of comic books. I raced there after school before any of the kids could beat me to it and sifted through the stacks, searching for one in particular.

Suddenly, there it was. The X-Men were my favorite comic book characters of all time and I was determined to finally have one that was all mine. I'd held it up in my hand triumphantly and ran to the front of the store, breathless. Mr. Michaelson looked over the issue, nodding his satisfaction with my choice. With a smile, he placed it behind his counter and handed me a broom and dustpan. He'd already promised that when I found a comic book that was special enough, he would hold onto it for me and let me work off the money I owed.

I worked nearly every day after school, sweeping floors and stocking shelves and by my birthday, that comic book was mine, free and clear. That had been the happiest birthday I had ever had and I made myself a promise that from then on, I would find something special to do for myself each year on that day.

"Well, I'm glad you told me," Hudson said with a smile, pulling me from my memories. "So, is that why you decided to go for a joy ride?"

"Sort of. I felt like getting out of the house for a while anyway, but when I looked out the window this morning, I saw Lachlan's huge garage and I decided that a drive sounded like a fun thing to do." I smirked at him. "I also figured he'd have some kick-ass cars to choose from and I was right."

"I'm honored that you let me share your day with you, but next time could we take something with a little more leg room? I saw a few bad-ass muscle cars that I wouldn't mind taking a turn driving." I laughed at the longing on his face and agreed that next time he could choose the car.

We were interrupted when Beatrice delivered our food to us and then we dug in. The diner itself may have been run-down and forgotten, but the food was out of this world. Hudson and I continued to talk and laugh. We didn't delve into anything too deep, probably because he wanted to take it easy on me since it was my birthday. Whatever the reason, I ended up having a really good time.

Hudson left as soon as we got back to the house. I stood at the base of the steps, listening for any sounds inside the house. I felt a twinge of disappointment when it seemed as if everyone was gone. It had been nice getting to spend my birthday with a friend and I guess a part of me had been hoping that it could continue once I got back to the house.

Why would it when you never let anyone know that it was your birthday? I had no one to blame but myself, I thought as I climbed the stairs to my room.

The sound of someone knocking on my door pulled me away from the book I was reading. "It's open," I said, distractedly. I was at a pivotal part in the story and I didn't want to stop.

"Whatever you're reading must be very good, you've been up here for hours." I jerked my head up, surprised to find Lachlan standing beside my bed.

"Uh, yeah. It's a really good book," I replied. He reached down and lifted it from my hands, studying the cover.

"This looks hot," he said as he handed the book back to me. "I never would have thought you'd be the type to read romance books though."

"Have you ever read a gay romance novel before?" I asked.

"No, I haven't. I rarely have time to read anymore and when I do, it's usually a mystery novel."

"Oh, man, you're missing out," I told him. "When I was growing up, the only romance books I could find were about men and women, which was fine since I like that too. But I always wished there were books about boys falling in love with boys, you know? Luckily, as people's views on gays started to change and they became more aware and accepting, they seemed to realize that the equipment on a person doesn't matter; what matters is the love between two people." Lachlan nodded his head, looking at me intently, like he really cared about what I had to say. I shrugged my shoulders, suddenly feeling embarrassed for having rambled on. Lachlan must have thought I was a total nutcase.

"I agree with you," he said, sitting down on my bed. I could feel his warmth against my leg. "It would have been nice to have had books like that when I was growing up. It might have helped me to make sense of what was going on with me when all of my schoolmates were whispering about girls and I just didn't understand what the fuss was all about." I chuckled at the bewildered look on his face.

"Fortunately, there are tons of gay romance books out there these days, although I don't think I would recommend them for a young kid. Some of these books are hot enough to burn the pages. I follow some of the authors online and they, as well as their fans, are kinky as fuck. You should see some of the pictures they post. Dayum!" We both laughed at that.

"I'll have to check that out then. I could use some more heat in my life," Lachlan said offhandedly. His face turned a bright shade of red when he realized what he'd said.

"You let me know if I can help you out with that," I told him in a voice dripping with innuendo. I pressed my leg up against his side and his eyes shot to mine in surprise. "I'll be sure to give you some book recommendations," I teased.

Lachlan chuckled at my joke, but the flush on his skin remained and his gaze fell to my mouth. I wondered if he had thought about our kiss as much as I had. Neither one of us had mentioned it since the night it happened, but I'd thought about it and used the memory to jerk off more times than I cared to admit. He stood from the bed quickly and cleared his throat, looking around at everything except me.

"I almost forgot that I came in here for a reason which was to tell you that dinner is ready," he said in a rush as he backed up towards the door. "I'll wait for you downstairs, take your time." He slipped out the door without another word.

I smiled as I stood from the bed and went to the bathroom to wash my hands. I liked seeing Lachlan get all flustered. Before I'd come to his house, I'd only ever seen Lachlan as a businessman, a giant in the music industry. I never would have guessed that beneath that preppy exterior lay a sweet, funny and passionate man. The more time I spent with him, the more I got to see new and interesting layers of his personality. As each layer was revealed to me, I found myself liking him more and more and that was what scared the fuck out of me.

I washed quickly and then headed downstairs. Something smelled really good and my mouth watered even though I wasn't sure what it was yet. As I neared the kitchen, I saw Benjamin peeking out of the door at me and I eyed him warily. The old guy still seemed like he wasn't sure what to think of me most of the time, but he no longer acted like he hated my guts. Of course, I still enjoyed ruffling his feathers every chance I got, which probably hadn't helped him to warm up to me sooner, but it amused me so I kept it up.

"I'm touched, Benji. Have you been waiting on me?" I batted my eyelashes at him coyly.

"With bated breath," he answered dryly, without missing a beat. I laughed at his response. I'd gotten the feeling lately that he had a much better sense of humor than he let show. He turned his head to look in the kitchen and gave a nod to someone before turning back to me and holding the door open.

My laughter faded away and I was immediately on guard as my instincts warned me that he was up to something. I moved past him and stepped into the kitchen and then froze. Streamers and balloons hung from the ceiling and the table had been set with a tablecloth and fine china. Candles burned in the center of the table and on the counter, I saw a beautifully decorated cake.

My skin felt hot and a little too tight and I had to blink several times to try and push back the sudden wetness that was blurring my vision. I glanced at Lachlan who was chewing his bottom lip nervously and then to Kerry who looking at me with a radiant smile on her face.

"Happy Birthday, love," she announced excitedly. "I wasn't sure what your favorite food was, so I had Benjamin grill some steaks and I baked some potatoes. I figured every man likes meat and potatoes, right? I mean, unless you're a vegetarian, which I know you're not."

"Tha…" I had to stop and swallow down the lump in my throat. "That's perfect. Thank you."

I was overwhelmed and I wasn't sure what to do with myself so I sat down at the table. Lachlan sat next to me as Kerry and Benjamin moved around the kitchen, bringing the food to the table. I stared up at the streamers hanging in a beautiful design above my head and I felt a hand on my leg. Afraid that I would start crying if I looked at him, I reached down and covered Lachlan's hand with my own.

I didn't even care that he had probably found out about my birthday from the information his team had dug up on me. The only thought that kept swirling through my brain was that I was a twenty-nine-year-old man and this was the very first time someone had cared enough about me to throw me a birthday party. I squeezed Lachlan's hand as another thought popped into my head; how would I ever survive having to walk away from these people?

CHAPTER
Nine

Rylie/Rocko

I'D BEEN AT LACHLAN'S HOUSE A LITTLE OVER A MONTH AND things were going very well. After my birthday dinner, Lachlan had taken me down to his basement where he'd surprised me with a fully equipped recording studio. He told me that he'd figured I was probably missing my drum set so he'd designed a place where I could go and play whenever I felt like it. I'd tried to argue that it was too much, but Lachlan dismissed me with a wave of his hand.

I'd been so excited that I'd practically launched myself at him. He'd laughed in surprise, but then he'd hugged me back. I spent a lot of time since then in the studio, it felt good to take a break from my own thoughts for a while and just get lost in the music.

Lachlan and I had begun spending more time together and he'd convinced me to start running with him in the mornings. I'd never been much of a runner. My exercise routine usually revolved around strength training, making sure I looked good enough to be on stage in front of thousands of fans. Lachlan, being an avid runner was quick to point out the need for cardio workouts and wouldn't let up until I'd agreed to give it a try. I finally gave in and so there I was at six-fucking-o'clock in the morning dragging my ass out of bed to go running with Lachlan.

I stumbled bleary-eyed into the bathroom and went through my morning routine, then I pulled on a pair of shorts and a t-shirt, too tired to care if they even matched. I sat down in a chair and laced my shoes up while staring longingly at my bed. Maybe I could just crawl back between the sheets for a few more minutes without anyone noticing.

"Rise and shine, sleepyhead, let's get moving!" Lachlan yelled cheerfully from right outside my door. I groaned loudly and then glared at the door as I heard him laugh. He was annoyingly chipper for that time of the day.

I stomped down the stairs, not caring that I was acting like a spoiled child. I was tired and I hadn't even had any coffee yet. Lachlan gave me a broad grin and winked at me, nearly causing me to trip down the steps. What gave him the right to look so fucking gorgeous that early in the morning? He handed me a bottle of water.

"Are you ready? We need to get a move on if we're going to beat the sunrise," he said, putting his hands together with a loud clap. His enthusiasm matched that of a pep squad.

"If you don't tone it down a notch, the sunrise won't be the only thing I'll beat," I warned.

"Wow! You're not much of a morning person, are you?" he asked.

"I'm perfectly fine with morning when it happens around nine o'clock and is accompanied by a steaming mug of coffee," I retorted.

"I'm sorry," Lachlan said. However, the grin he was fighting told me otherwise. "I'll make you a deal. You get out there and run with me and when we're all done we'll come back here and have breakfast and you can drink all the coffee your heart desires. Sound fair?"

"Fine, let's get it over with," I grumbled. With a laugh, Lachlan headed out the front door with me trailing behind him reluctantly. He stopped when we reached the paved driveway and turned to me.

"This is your first time so we'll start out slow, but we need to get you stretched really well so you don't get hurt." He pulled one leg up behind him and began stretching his muscles.

"It's not my first time, but it has been a while so I appreciate the tenderness, sugar," I drawled. I grinned when he lost his balance and nearly toppled over. I knew he hadn't meant his words the way they'd sounded, but I couldn't stop myself from teasing him.

I loved watching him get all flustered and it made me feel good to know that I had some sort of effect on him, even if it wasn't the kind I would have liked. I had no doubt in my mind that Lachlan was attracted to me, the chemistry between us was off the charts. The problem was that he saw me as nothing more than a client and, considering the fact that he was a successful music executive and I was just a drummer who was also a recovering addict, I couldn't picture him ever wanting anything to do with me long-term.

Not that I was considering anything long-term anyway. I'd known since birth that no one would ever want me on a long-term basis. I was more of the fun-for-a-while type of guy and I was okay with that. Mostly. There were times lately, especially watching Carter find his soulmate and the way Tyler and Kalia loved each other, that I found myself wondering *what if?* But then I'd remind myself that what Carter had with Ryan and what Tyler and Kalia shared just wasn't in the cards for me.

"You know that's not what I meant," Lachlan sputtered. "Now get stretching before you pull something during our run." He gave me a no-nonsense look.

"Yes, Drill Sergeant, sir," I said. I winked at him playfully and turned around so that my back was to him. I bent down slowly and stretched my fingers to the ground, showing off my ass. I heard his quick intake of breath and smiled to myself. He may not want me for long, but he definitely wanted me then and I was determined to have fun with him for as long as it lasted.

"Okay, I think that's enough stretching," he said after a few more seconds of me showing off my assets. His voice sounded strained and I sneaked a glance at the bulge in his shorts. *That's going to hurt to run with.*

"Whatever you say, boss. I'm just following your lead here," I said amicably. He turned and stalked away from me, allowing himself time to cool off, I assumed. I used the elastic band around my wrist to pull my hair up into a loose knot and then started following him, suddenly very happy to be going on a run with him.

The sun was already peeking its head over the horizon by the time we reached the end of the driveway and set off at an easy jog. We ran in the opposite direction of traffic so we could see any cars coming our way. We were still jogging about a mile down the road when Lachlan suddenly veered to the right and crossed the road into the woods that ran alongside of it.

"Where are we going?" I asked as I checked for cars and then hurried to catch up with him. I found him waiting for me just inside the tree line.

"There's a path through the woods that I run on every morning," he answered. Sure enough, there was a well-laid path that cut between the large oaks and pines.

"How did you ever find this place?" I asked curiously.

"This is still my property," he responded.

"Of course, it is." I chuckled and shook my head. Only Lachlan would be able to run a mile down the road and still be on his property. Even though I was staying in his mega-mansion, I rarely thought about how rich he was. Not that I was exactly poor anymore after signing on with Golden Entertainment, but my income was a drop in the bucket compared to Lachlan's. He never flaunted his money though and most of the time, I forgot that we weren't just two ordinary guys hanging out and playing video games together.

"Alright, here we go," he said, clapping me on the shoulder and taking off at a run. "Try and keep up, if you can," he shouted over his shoulder. I could hear him laughing as he left me behind.

"Shit," I cursed, taking off after him before I could get lost.

He let me catch up with him after a few minutes and we began a steady pace. The path was wide enough for us to run side by side comfortably so we did. We ran for about thirty minutes until I was gasping for air and my legs felt like they were on fire. Lachlan was still breathing evenly beside me and looked like he could go at least another hour. I knew he was holding back from his usual routine for me and I felt both embarrassed and appreciative. I could definitely stand to get in better shape. He must have noticed the way I was wheezing beside him because he slowed our pace to a jog. After a few minutes of that, we slowed to a walk. He glanced at me as we continued along the path.

"Are you okay?" Instead of making fun of me for not being able to keep up, he seemed genuinely concerned.

"I'm pretty sure I lost my right lung back there on the trail somewhere, but other than that, I'll live," I told him. He stopped walking and faced me.

"You did great for your first time. If you'd like we can make this part of our daily routine," he offered.

"Thanks, but I know you were holding back for my sake. I don't want to be a burden."

"You have never been a burden," he insisted, taking a step towards me. We stared at each other for a long moment and I tried to make sense of what it was I saw in his eyes. He turned his head before I could figure anything out and looked off into the distance.

"Besides, it's nice to have the company," he said quietly.

"Why do you have such a large home when it's only you, Kerry, and Benjamin that stay here?" I asked hesitantly. I didn't want him to think I was judging him; I was simply curious. He shrugged his shoulders and his mouth twisted into a wry grin.

"Part of it was how I was raised. My parents always had to have the biggest and best of everything. I never cared about any of that and most of the time I hated it because it made it harder to figure out if the kids that came over to play were there because they liked me or because they liked the things I had, you know?"

"Yeah, I can imagine that would be hard," I said.

"Anyway, even though I don't do it to impress anyone, I suppose somewhere along the way, I picked up the habit of buying the best of everything. I hadn't even realized I was doing it until you mentioned it," he told me.

"Sorry, I didn't mean to offend you, I was just curious," I explained.

"No need to apologize and you didn't offend me in the slightest. I guess sometimes it takes someone looking from the outside in to see what's really going on," he replied.

"What's the other reason?" I asked suddenly.

"Excuse me?" He looked up at me, startled.

"You said that was part of the reason why you have that big mansion of yours. What's the other part?" His cheeks turned a pretty shade of pink and he stared at the ground, running his fingers through his thick brown hair. My hands itched to touch it and see if it felt as soft and luxurious as it looked.

"You'll probably laugh, but I've always dreamed of having a family of my own one day. I want it all, the husband that loves me and kids running around. Lots of kids," he chuckled. "So, I've always purchased large homes just in case that dream ever becomes a reality."

"Why would I laugh at that?" I asked him. "I think it's great that you want those things. I hope you get them someday." I made a big show of looking at my watch then and commented on the time, making the excuse that I needed to get a shower before Hudson showed up for our therapy session. Lachlan nodded his head and led the way to an opening in the trees. When we stepped out, I could see that we were at the very back of his property.

As we walked through the yard and up to the house, we made small talk. I tried to laugh at the appropriate moments, but I was pretty sure that he could tell something was wrong because I could see him giving me odd looks out of the corner of my eye. There was no way I was going to admit that he had just described everything that I'd ever wanted in my entire life. I especially couldn't tell him that I hated the thought of him getting married and having a family because picturing him with some other guy made me feel like I'd been punched in the gut. I needed to get away from him as quickly as possible and get my head on straight because no matter how badly I wanted those things, they were never going to happen.

"I'd like to talk more about your childhood today, Rylie," Hudson said.

My stomach knotted. I knew the time was coming when he would expect me to open up about my past. I'd finally told him what my real name was during our last session and he'd called it a real breakthrough. I suppose it was a big thing that I had willingly shared that information with someone, but the truth was, I'd just gotten used to hearing Lachlan call me that. I no longer associated it with the painful memories of my past because somewhere along the line, hearing my name being spoken from Lachlan's mouth had become something special. I should have realized though that sharing something about myself would only have Hudson asking for more. I just didn't know if I could do it.

I closed my eyes and drew in a deep breath through my nose. I could see the sunlight through the thin skin of my eyelids and for just a moment, I imagined that I were far away from there; somewhere all alone where nobody was asking questions and picking at old scars.

My eyes popped back open and I stared out over the gleaming water of the lake. We'd been walking for a long time and had finally reached a lake at the back of Lachlan's property. No matter how much I explored his home, it seemed that there were always new things to see. He should have really considered handing out maps at the front gate like they do at amusement parks. That way guests could find their way around more easily and not miss anything. I smiled a bit at the amusing thought, thankful for the brief reprieve from my building panic.

"Let's sit down for a little while, okay?" Hudson suggested. He pointed to a pair of Adirondack chairs that were seated near the edge of the lake a few feet away from us. I nodded my agreement. We sat down and Hudson stretched his legs out in front of him. I watched a pair of butterflies dipping and swirling along the edge of the water. They were so beautiful and carefree and I wished I could be like them.

"Did I ever explain the three R's to you, Rylie?" he asked.

"No," I answered, turning my head to look at him. He was dressed casually in a pair of light blue jeans and a salmon-colored polo that looked beautiful against his skin. It was hot out, but the trees behind us shaded us, offering a bit of relief as we sat.

"Well, there are three R's that I like to use when working with a client. They're kind of like checkpoints that a person works their way through during therapy and it helps me to evaluate where they're at. I thought if I told you about them that they might help you to look at how far you've come in your journey and what is left to work on," he explained.

"Okay, I'm listening," I told him.

"Good. The three R's stand for Recover, Redeem, and Renew, in that order. You can't pass on to the next checkpoint without completing the one before it. You've already completed the Recovery stage. You did that by purging the drugs and alcohol from your system and by allowing your body time to heal and become stronger. You'll have to fight cravings for the rest of your life, but the stronger you are in body and in spirit, the easier it will be to resist." I nodded my head. I knew there were going to be times where the cravings were stronger than others, but I already felt stronger and healthier than I had in years and I hoped that was enough to get me through the darker moments.

"Next is the Redeem stage, which is what you're in now. The Redeem stage is very complex and requires the most amount of work. I called it redeem because it's in this stage that you find that person inside of you, the one that got lost under all of the pain and turmoil of your past and you pull him out. You remember the good inside of him and the value he held and you make him a part of you again. It will take a lot of honesty and soul searching and it may be very painful at times, if it wasn't you would have never tried to hide him from the rest of the world. But I can promise that you don't have to go through any of this alone; I will be with you."

My hand was shaking as I lifted it and ran it through my hair. I stared out over the water as I turned Hudson's words over in my head. I'd not only kept my past from my friends, but I'd also spent years pushing the memories from my own mind. It was easier to ignore it and pretend it had never happened than to face the pain that those memories evoked. I knew I stood a chance of losing everyone I cared about and that scared the shit out of me. I had spent my entire childhood alone and I didn't want to do it again, but I was also tired—like down to my depths, bone-weary—of trying to fight everything by myself. I didn't want to be the person I was a few months ago, but I needed help.

"What's the last stage?" I turned to look at Hudson who sat quietly, allowing me time to think. His gaze was on the lake, but he turned to me with a grin when I spoke.

"The last stage is called Renew. That's the stage where you take everything you've discovered about yourself—the good the bad and the ugly—and you decide who you want to be from that point on.

Your world is a blank canvas at that point and you can choose what you want to do with the new life you've created."

"That sounds amazing, but is that really even possible?" I asked skeptically.

"It's absolutely possible. That's the beautiful thing about life, Rylie. It's constantly changing and we get to decide how we will let it mold and shape us. Even though you've tried to push your past away, you've never really been able to do so because it's always there, lurking in the shadows and holding power over you. So, my question for you is, are you willing to put in the work required to take that power back? To control your own destiny instead of letting it control you?" I stared at him for several minutes then took a deep breath before opening my mouth.

"Where do we start?"

CHAPTER
Ten

Lachlan

I STOOD UP FROM MY DESK AND STRETCHED. I'D BEEN IN MY office for the last several hours and I needed a break. I checked the time on my watch. Perhaps Rylie and I could have lunch together if he was finished with his session with Hudson. As usual, a smile spread across my face at the thought of spending time with Rylie.

I'd taken his words to heart and had been making a conscious effort to work less, handing some of the responsibilities over to my chief operating officer at the Los Angeles office. Tyrone had sounded surprised, but pleased, when I'd told him that he would now be heading up the entire west coast division in my absence. He'd assured me that he would handle everything and would let me know straight away if there were any issues. His response had shown me how tightly

I had been holding on to the reins and I conceded that perhaps Rylie, Kerry, and Benjamin had been correct in their worry over my work habits.

Ever since that point, I had scheduled all of my meetings during normal business hours so that by the time dinner was ready, I was done for the day. I had expected to feel worried that things were going to slip through the cracks if I wasn't there overseeing every minute detail, but I'd been surprised at how utterly freeing it was to not be chained to my desk for twenty hours each day.

Instead, I had time to enjoy things like swimming, playing video games with Rylie, or reading a good book. In fact, I'd even tried a couple of the books that he had recommended and I could see why he enjoyed them so much. Although, they did make it difficult to go to sleep sometimes after reading a particularly sexy scene.

Smiling, I went in search of Rylie. I climbed the stairs and poked my head into his bedroom, but it was empty. I went back downstairs and checked the media room and the pool, neither of which showed any signs of him before heading down to the recording studio in the basement. I peeked in the window of the soundproof room and my shoulders slumped in relief when I found him.

He was seated on a stool and was staring down at the drum set in front of him, tapping out a slow and steady rhythm. His hair hung loosely on either side of his face, blocking my view and my fingers itched to brush it back so that he couldn't hide himself from me. His head popped up when I opened the door and his blue eyes widened in surprise, but I could see the sadness in their depths. I wanted to know what had caused that look in his eyes so I could try and fix it, but I knew better than to push.

"Hi, I've been looking everywhere for you," I told him. The door shut behind me as I stepped inside the room.

"Oh, I'm sorry. I just needed a few minutes by myself after my session with Hudson. Did you need something?" he asked.

"No," I told him, waving him off with a hand. "I was just coming to see if you'd had lunch yet."

"Thanks, but I'm not very hungry," he told me. I nodded my head and turned to leave; I was disappointed not to get to spend any time with him, but if he needed some time alone then I would give him that. "Wait, where are you going?" he asked and I whipped back around.

"I thought you wanted to be alone," I responded. He was quiet as he stood, shaking his head slowly and stepped around the drum set. His eyes never strayed from my face as he began walking towards me. I could feel my heart beating furiously in my chest as he neared, until he stood directly in front of me.

"No, I don't want to be alone," he said huskily. "In fact, that's the last thing I want right now." Like a switch had been flipped inside of him, he no longer looked sad. Instead, he looked like a hunter stalking its prey and I suddenly felt a lot like Bambi. Although, I didn't recall Bambi ever wanting to be caught by the hunters the way I wanted to be captured by him.

My breathing became erratic as he slid one hand behind my neck and pulled me towards him. I went willingly and soon his lips were covering mine. The kiss was soft and unhurried and I felt myself melting into it. I slid my palms up between us, feeling the hard muscles of his chest through the thin material of his shirt. I slid my tongue along the seam of his lips, begging him to open for me so I could taste him like the last time, but he pulled away. I let out an embarrassing whimper as my fingers dug into his shirt, trying to stop his retreat. I hadn't even begun to have my fill of him yet. Instead of turning away from me though, he leaned his forehead against mine and I was happy to hear the sounds of his ragged breaths, proving that I wasn't the only one affected by our kiss.

"Look, Lachlan, I know the deal alright? I know that this is all just business to you, but please, I need someone right now. I don't want to be alone, please," he begged.

I squeezed my eyes shut. I hated that I had ever let him believe that he was nothing more than a business deal to me. The truth was that he was so much more; he was everything to me. Somewhere among all of the movies, video games and morning runs that we had shared, I had fallen in love with him and even though I was certain he would never return those feelings and only wanted someone who could take the pain away, I would give him whatever he needed because there was no way I could ever turn him away. I backed up until I could look into his eyes, which were guarded as if he were bracing himself for rejection.

"Take whatever you need, Rylie," I whispered shakily. The blue of his eyes darkened until they were nearly black and I gasped as his hands came up on either side of my face, locking me in place and his mouth descended on me. There was no gentleness, no hesitancy; only a passion that threatened to consume both of us.

He bit at my bottom lip, tugging it gently between his teeth, and I sighed from the pleasure. As his tongue swept into my mouth, I slid my hands around his waist and pulled him closer until there was no space left between our bodies. Rylie's body felt perfect next to mine; all of those hard edges and sleek muscles and I could feel his hard cock pressing against my own through the material of our pants.

Without stopping the kiss, he maneuvered us until my back was pressed against the door. His hips began a sensual rolling motion, lending friction to my swollen cock and my head dropped back against the hard wood as pleasure rushed through me. I moaned as he began nibbling at my jaw and licking a path down my throat. He stopped to suck on my Adam's apple, lighting every nerve ending and for the first time since I was a teenager, I was afraid I was going to come in my pants.

He backed up and let his eyes run over me hungrily as if he were trying to figure out what he wanted to do next. I held my breath as I waited for his decision, the anticipation causing me to tremble. He looked back up at me and smirked with a wicked glint in his eyes and my breath hitched in my throat.

"Take your clothes off for me, I want to see you." Without a word, I began undressing. I slowly undid the buttons of my shirt, unrolling the sleeves and working it down my arms. I let it drop to the floor beside me then reached for my belt, sliding it from its metal clasp.

It should have felt awkward with me getting undressed while he remained fully clothed, but as Rylie's half-lidded eyes stayed focused on each movement of my hands, I felt more emboldened and desirable. I slid the belt from its loops and dropped it with a clank on top of my shirt. I reached for the button on my pants, but before I could open it, Rylie dropped to his knees in front of me. I looked down in surprise as his hands shoved mine out of the way and made quick work of opening my pants. He peered up at me through his thick black lashes and gave me a naughty grin.

"You were taking too long and I decided I was hungry after all." The meaning of his words went straight to my cock, making it jump in front of his face, capturing his attention. He chuckled throatily. "It looks like your dick is on board with my plans."

"Oh yes, he's in total agreement," I told him, surprised that my brain was still working enough to form words.

"God, that accent," he groaned. "You have no idea what it does to me." *What? Since when?* My thoughts flew out the window as he reached behind me and slipped his hands underneath the thin material of my briefs then began sliding my pants down, his fingers leaving a trail of fire over my arse and down the back of my legs.

I kicked off the offensive material then stood there as his eyes feasted on me. My body shook with desire and my cock stood up proudly, just waiting for a proper introduction. A thin strand of moisture formed at the tip and dribbled down the side. Rylie flicked his tongue out, capturing the milky offering and a deep growl rumbled in his chest as he swallowed it down. It was the most erotic sound I'd ever heard in my life. He flattened his tongue and ran it up and down the length of my shaft, licking the pre-cum from my sensitive skin.

"Please, quit teasing me," I gasped. I couldn't take the torment any more, I needed to feel his mouth on me.

I didn't know if he was finally taking pity on me or if he just wanted it as much as I did, but I didn't really care either way as he leaned forward and swallowed my cock, not stopping until it hit the back of his throat and his lips were wrapped against the base. I wasn't exactly what you would call small, so I was rather impressed that he was able to handle all of me at once. He held there for a few seconds before sliding back off. He looked up at me with an almost drunken smile on his face.

"You taste so good," he whispered. He went back to work, his tongue circling the tip before plunging back down. His lips stretched wide as they slid over me and his cheeks curved inward as he increased his suction.

My fingers slid into his hair, enjoying the silky texture against my palms. I didn't use my hands to force his movements, but let him set the pace himself. My eyes rolled into the back of my head as we found a rhythm that was all our own with my hips undulating in perfect sync with the bobbing of his head. He moaned and I felt the reverberations along the entire length of my cock.

I forced my eyes open and looked down at him, wanting to commit the moment to memory. I gasped at the sight before me and I quickly pulled his hair back from his face so I could have a better look. Rylie's eyes were closed and his face looked serene as he licked over the veins of my cock. His lips were wet and red from sucking me. I could see his arm moving quickly and I knew from the movements that he was working his dick with his own hand. I was disappointed that I couldn't see his cock and that I wouldn't get to return the favor, but it was also erotic as hell that he was getting off on pleasuring me.

Sweat dotted my lip and my tongue swept over it, capturing the saltiness. I let myself imagine that it was the salty taste of his cum and that was all it took to push me over the edge. I pushed at his shoulder desperately in warning, but he was having none of it. I shouted as my orgasm tore through my body and cum spilled from me, filling his mouth and shooting down his throat. He swallowed quickly, but I could still see some of the white liquid, leaking out of the corner of his mouth. I slumped against the door weakly as my body was wracked with the aftershocks of the best orgasm of my life. I was still gasping for air as Rylie stood, already tucking in his cock and zipping his jeans.

I caught his eye and I thought I saw something there, but it was gone before I could be sure having been replaced with the same cocky look he wore when he was on stage and knew he was winning over the crowd. It spoke of a detached arrogance and even though I knew it was probably just a defense mechanism, I hated it all the same because it left me feeling cold and confused.

"See, boss, we can get off and it doesn't have to mean anything, right?" He held my gaze, almost like he was challenging me, but reality had begun to sink in, leaving me breathless.

I had known all along that Rylie wasn't the type to want more than to *get off*, as he'd described it, but hearing it spoken out loud was like a slap in the face. What in the world had I been thinking to assume that I could play along with his games without getting hurt? I knew myself better than that, but it seemed that I lost all sense of reason when it came to Rylie Anderson. I needed to gain control of myself so I nodded stiffly.

"Of course, not, but that still should have never happened." The lie tasted bitter on my tongue and I swallowed thickly around the sudden lump in my throat. I had to fight hard to keep my emotions from showing on my face. After what had just happened, there was no way I could let him see how I felt about him. It would strain our friendship and make working together very awkward if not impossible.

He stared at me for a few more seconds and I was surprised when he almost looked hurt. How could that be when it was my heart that felt like it was shattering? Finally, he turned away and walked to the other side of the room where he grabbed some tissues to clean his hand. I scooped my clothes up off the floor and began dressing as quickly as possible. I wasn't sure how much longer I would be able to hold myself together. As soon as I was finished I muttered an excuse about needing to get back to work and slipped out the door without looking back.

I raced up the stairs and to my office, slamming the door behind me and leaning against it. I rubbed my chest, trying to relax the tightness there. I had been a fool to let things go that far when I knew my feelings for Rylie were completely one-sided, but as bad as it hurt, I knew that given the opportunity, I would do it all over again.

A few days later, I was in my office going over some paperwork when the phone rang. I picked it up without bothering to check the caller id and was surprised to hear Carter Greene's voice on the other end.

"Hi, Lachlan, how are you?" he greeted me cheerfully.

"I'm good, Carter, and yourself?" I couldn't help the smile that spread across my face when I heard his happy-go-lucky voice. Carter was an amazing man and I was glad that we had become friends. He was happy, fun-loving, and easily one of the most talented musicians I'd ever had the pleasure of working with.

"I'm great!" he exclaimed.

"You sound very excited about something. What's going on?" I asked with a chuckle.

"I am excited. Ryan and I have finally set a date for the wedding," he announced and my smile grew with the news.

Carter and his fiancé had seen their fair share of ups and downs, having dealt with a long separation while the band was on tour as well as Ryan's close call when a fellow firefighter tried to murder him just because he was gay. Each of the experiences had tested their relationship, but their love for each other had only grown. I had never seen two people as crazy in love with each other as the two of them were and I was thrilled that they were finally going to make things official.

"That's terrific, Carter! When will it be and where?" I asked.

"Well, that's one of the reasons I wanted to talk to you before I told Rocko," he said, his voice taking on a more serious tone.

"Okay…" I said, confused.

"Well, I'm sure you know that we put aside our wedding until after the tour was over, but then all that stuff happened with Rocko and my sisters had their babies, plus I've been doing a lot of promotion for the band. Anyway, it seems like it's just been one thing after another and time is slipping by," he explained.

"And you're tired of putting it off, am I right?" I said with understanding. I could only imagine how hard it would be to have met the person you wanted to spend the rest of your life with, only to have to wait to begin your life together.

"Exactly," he said with a sigh. "I want Ryan to be my husband more than anything and I'm tired of waiting for that to happen."

"I understand. You and Ryan were meant to be together and it's great that you're finally putting yourselves first and getting married. I don't understand though why you needed to talk to me before Rocko though," I said.

"Because we've decided to get married this weekend," he stated carefully.

"Wow! That's quick, but I know how crazy your schedule is so I guess you have to take advantage of any break you can get," I responded. As the lead singer of one of the world's most popular rock and roll bands, he was busier than any of its other members. As the front man, he was the one that the fans and the press paid the most attention to and therefore most of the talk show interviews and magazine photo shoots fell on his shoulders.

"That's not all though," he said slowly. "We've decided to get married in Vegas." There was a long pause as I let what he was telling me run through my mind. I knew why Carter was so worried about talking to Rylie about his wedding and I had to admit that I was concerned as well. Rylie had come a very long way since he'd arrived at my house, but was he strong enough to resist all of the temptations that were on offer in Vegas? That wasn't something I readily had the answer for, but I knew who would be able to help.

"I appreciate your concern and I'm glad you called me first," I said. "Rocko's made a lot of progress and I think with all of his friends around him he'll be able to stay on track, but I'd feel a lot better if I could discuss it with his therapist first. Give me a chance to talk with him and I'll get back to you as soon as possible, alright?"

"That would be great, Lachlan. I appreciate it," he said sincerely.

"You're welcome and congratulations, Carter," I responded.

We ended the call and I leaned back in my chair, pinching the bridge of my nose between my thumb and forefinger. Rylie and I had been avoiding each other ever since our encounter in the studio a few days before, so I had no clue where his mind was at right then or how he was progressing with his therapy. I hadn't even found out what had upset him so much that day.

Once I'd gotten over the initial hurt his words had caused, I'd taken the time to really think things over. I'd gotten to know Rylie fairly well by that point and I'd learned that underneath all of his sarcasm and devil-may-care attitude was a kind, considerate, and sensitive man. The cold way he'd behaved after the intimacy we'd shared, didn't match up with the man I'd known him to be. If I'd been thinking with my head instead of my heart that day, I would have realized that he had been putting me through another one of his tests; a test which I had unfortunately failed. I'd only heard his words and not the meaning behind them so instead of telling him the truth about how I felt and what I wanted from him, I'd lied to him and agreed that it had meant nothing.

I'd been just as guilty as he was for staying away from each other, but I missed him terribly. I'd never realized just how much I looked forward to our times together until they were taken away. It wasn't even just my feelings for him that made me miss him; most of the time I simply missed my friend. In the time he'd been there, he had become the most important person in my life and I missed having him to talk to. The sound of someone knocking drew my attention to the doorway and I smiled when I saw Hudson standing there.

"Come in," I told him as I walked around the desk to greet him. We hugged and then I gestured for him to have a seat.

"I just finished up with Rylie and I wanted to stop in and check on you, see how things are going before I took off. Am I interrupting anything?" he asked as we sat across from each other.

"Of course not, I'm always happy to talk to you. Besides, I was just finishing up for the day," I told him. I rolled my eyes as he made a big production of looking at his watch and then gave me a shocked look. He smiled as I explained my decision to cut back on work.

"That's really terrific, Lachlan. You know I've wanted you to find a better balance for a long time. So, what finally caused you to make that change because I know it wasn't my begging and pleading," he teased. I chuckled, but then looked away shyly.

"Lachlan, you know you can tell me anything," Hudson said.

"I know, it's not that," I assured him quickly. "It's just...well, it has to do with Rylie."

"What about him?" Hudson asked, his head tilting to one side as he tried to figure out the direction of my thoughts. I swallowed hard. I wanted to talk with Hudson about my feelings for Rylie, but there wasn't much point since I was sure nothing else was going to happen between us.

"He just made me realize what all the rest of you had been say- ing and I decided that it was time to cut back some," I said instead. Hudson was quiet for a long moment and I began to squirm under his close scrutiny.

"I'm glad he was able to get through to you when no one else could, I'm just curious as to why that is," he said. I stared at the floor, unwilling to meet his eyes. My eyes darted up as he leaned forward, resting his forearms on his knees. "Is there something I should know, Lachlan?"

"It doesn't even matter," I mumbled.

"What doesn't matter?" he asked. He looked at me with concern and I felt guilty for making him worry over something that would probably never amount to anything, still I couldn't stop myself from asking him just in case. I stood up quickly and shut the door so that no one would hear what I was about to say, then I sat back down across from Hudson with my hands fisted in my lap.

"Would it be harmful to his recovery if Rylie were to start seeing someone?" I asked in a quick huff of air. Hudson gave me a thoughtful look as if he were weighing my words carefully and my heart pounded in my chest as I waited for him to answer.

"Most therapists would recommend that a person with Rylie's addictions wait until they are further in their recovery to begin a relationship." My shoulders slumped. "I however am a firm believer that no one makes it through this world alone," he continued.

"So, you think he could become involved with someone without it hindering his progress?" I asked hopefully.

"Perhaps," Hudson stated slowly. "Depending on the person he became involved with. It would have to be someone who was aware of his situation, someone who was willing to be patient and considerate of the fact that he needs to keep his primary focus on himself and not the relationship until he's recovered fully." I nodded my head in understanding. I could do all of those things.

"Is there someone particular you had I mind?" Hudson asked with a wry smile. I ducked my head to hide my grin.

"Yes," I confessed, "Me."

"I see. Does Rylie return your feelings?" I sucked in a deep breath and then blew it out between my pursed lips.

"I'm not sure. There are times that I think he does. We've become rather close since he's been here, but then there are other times where his walls go up and he won't let anyone near him." Hudson nodded his understanding.

"He does that with everyone, not just you. It's something we're working on and I hope you don't take it personally," he said kindly. I assured him that I would try not to. "This is a unique situation for me in that I'm not only Rylie's therapist, but yours as well. On the other hand, I also have a better understanding of who you each are as individuals. Rylie has made great strides in his recovery and while he still has a way to go, I think he'd also benefit from the reassurance that he won't be going through it alone; whether it's with a friend or someone more special."

I listened attentively. I had no idea if Rylie could ever feel about me the way I felt about him, but I knew how special he was and I wanted to be a part of his life in any way he would let me. The last few days without him had been miserable and I didn't want to avoid him anymore.

"You were devastated when Spencer died, understandably so, but I'm very pleased to see that you're ready to begin living again. I believe Spencer would have wanted that for you. You have one of the kindest and most giving hearts of anyone I've ever known and you deserve to find someone who will make you happy. Whether that someone is Rylie or not, who knows, but I think you could both be very good for each other."

"Thank you, Hudson." I couldn't hide the small smile that lifted the edges of my mouth. "There's something else I need to ask you about."

"Sure," he said. I explained my conversation with Carter and our concerns about Rylie going to Las Vegas. He nodded his head in understanding. "I can see why you're worried, but I've been very pleased with Rylie's progress. Not only is he stronger physically, but he's willingly offering me more information about his past because he really wants to get better mentally as well." I felt a surge of pride for Rylie as Hudson described how far he'd come.

"You know as well as I do that he will deal with his addictions for the rest of his life. There will be times when he can face his cravings with a strong attitude and others where he'll be more vulnerable to their calling. So far, he's been safe in rehab and in your home. The temptations have been minimal, but that's not real life. He will have to learn to deal with them eventually and, honestly, I would rather he learn to do that when he's surrounded by the people that care about him the most than when he's all alone. At least for the first few times."

"That makes sense. I just felt better checking with you first. I don't ever want to do anything that will hurt him," I said.

"I believe you," Hudson said with a warm smile. "I don't know what will happen between the two of you, but I would consider Rylie very lucky if he were to end up with you, Lachlan."

I shook my head. "No, I'd be the lucky one. He's a truly incredible person," I said quietly.

"You're right, he is," Hudson agreed. We both stood and he clapped me on the shoulder.

"Thank you for speaking with me," I said with a smile.

"Anytime. Just remember to take things at his pace, okay? He's still dealing with a lot," he warned.

"I will," I promised. I walked Hudson to the front door and watched him pull away. I had no idea if Rylie had ever considered dating someone or if he would consider me in particular, but I was tired of hiding my feelings for him. I knew that I had fallen in love with him and it was time to find out where we stood with one another. It was reassuring to know that Hudson was okay with it, I just needed to build up enough nerve to talk to Rylie. First things first though, we needed to make sure he survived a trip to Sin City.

CHAPTER
Eleven

Rylie/Rocko

I STARED OUT THE WINDOW OF LACHLAN'S PRIVATE PLANE, pretending to be very interested in the scenery below. In truth, I was avoiding the looks that he kept sending my way. I wanted to kick myself ever since I'd said those things to him because it had taken away any hope that I might have had that something could develop between the two of us.

Ever since the night that we first played video games together, Lachlan had been nothing but thoughtful and kind to me. The looks he would give me sometimes or the way he'd smile when I walked into the room, almost like he was excited to see me, had begun to give me hope. Despite the warning bells that were going off inside my head.

I should have listened to those warnings and stayed away from him, then maybe it wouldn't have hurt so badly when he'd confirmed that what had happened between us meant nothing to him. My entire life I'd been taught that it was useless to hope for anything better than what I already had, so why had I allowed myself to hope for more with Lachlan? He was funny and beautiful and everything that I had ever wanted, but had always known was too far out of my reach.

I couldn't blame him though; he had made it perfectly clear from day one that it was nothing but a business arrangement. I was the fool for thinking that the way he'd felt for me might have changed. So, I'd stood there, the taste of his cum still lingering on my tongue and challenged him to tell me that what was going on actually meant something to him, but instead he'd thrown the cold hard truth back in my face; his feelings hadn't changed and they never would.

The worst part was that I felt like I had lost my best friend. Even losing Steve hadn't hurt as bad as watching Lachlan pull away from me. Of course, the way I felt about Steve was completely different from the way I felt about Lachlan. Steve was like a brother to me, a person who I knew would always have my back, but who also had his own life completely separate from mine. Lachlan on the other hand, knew more about me than anyone else, other than Hudson, and still had never turned away from me. I cared about Lachlan and I believed he cared about me, even if for him it was only friendship. I also never wanted to rip Steve's clothes off and explore every single inch of his body with my tongue the way I wanted to with Lachlan. I drew in a deep breath at the thought.

Being with Lachlan had been a dream come true. He'd looked and tasted even better than I'd imagined and for just that small amount of time, he'd been all mine. But then reality had come crashing down around me and it was my fault, all because I had to open my damn mouth. If I would have just played along, then maybe more would have happened between us. Even if he hadn't felt anything for me, getting to be with him in that way was better than the cold distance that had developed after I'd ruined everything.

I let the breath out of my lungs slowly and tried to stop my fingers from the furious tapping I hadn't realized I'd begun along the arm of the seat. I needed to get my mind off of the situation with Lachlan and concentrate on the weekend ahead in Las Vegas. I knew that it was going to be tough being surrounded by all of the drugs and alcohol that was in a city like that and I'd be lying if I said I wasn't worried about how I would handle being faced with temptation for the first time. I'd already had to fight cravings that had threatened to drag me under and that had been at Lachlan's house where none of my vices were available. How in the hell was I going to resist those cravings when it was right in front of my face?

I was also nervous about seeing Steve again after all the time that had passed. I had no idea what kind of reception I would get from him, but the fact that he still hadn't called or come to visit me left me to assume that it wasn't going to be easy. Not that I deserved easy after the hell I'd put him through.

After the plane landed, a limousine was waiting to take us to the hotel. I leaned forward in my seat, gawking at the sights as we passed. I'd never been to Las Vegas before, although, I'd seen enough movies and pictures to have a pretty good idea of how bright it was, but none of those things had prepared me for seeing it live and in person. I couldn't believe how many hotels, restaurants, bars, and casinos were packed into one area that was only a little over three miles long. There was something for everyone, from high-end clothing stores to seedy strip clubs and I wondered how long it would take a person to explore everything being offered there.

I didn't have long to look though because all too soon, the limousine pulled into the circular drive of an enormous hotel that looked golden against the nighttime sky. The name Palazzo was written down the side of the building in bold white letters and three bellhops came rushing out of the hotel as soon as we pulled up to the curb, one opening the door of the limo for us while the other two retrieved our luggage from the trunk.

Despite Carter and Ryan's protests, Lachlan had insisted on paying for the hotel accommodations for the entire wedding party. His assistant had set everything up in advance so we didn't have to bother with checking in. Instead, the hotel manager led us straight to an elevator which sat separate from the rest and handed Lachlan two keycards. He explained that our party would be the only guests using that elevator and that our rooms were completely separated from everyone else, ensuring our total privacy when we wanted it.

Lachlan and I climbed into the elevator, riding it up the tall building in complete silence. The tension in the air was thick as I tried to pretend that he wasn't there, something that was nearly impossible with the smell of his cologne filling my senses and making my head spin. I made the mistake though of looking up only to catch him staring at me in the reflection of the mirrored doors. My heart slammed in my chest as we held each other's gazes. The look in his eyes almost resembled longing and regret, but I knew that couldn't be right so I quickly tamped down the hope that flared inside of me. I pursed my lips and looked back down at the floor for the remainder of the ride, letting my hair block him from my view. When the elevator finally stopped, I glanced up, surprised to see what floor we were staying on.

"What, no penthouse?" I asked sarcastically. His eyes widened in surprise as he looked at me, probably because those were the first words I had spoken to him in almost a week. I hated the anger in my voice because it spoke of how deeply he'd hurt me and I didn't want him to know the power he had over me, but I couldn't seem to stop it from coming through. I'd always found it difficult to hide my emotions from Lachlan which was another first for me. With everyone else, I'd nearly made hiding my feelings into an art form.

"I left that for the newlyweds," he explained quietly, making me immediately feel guilty. There he was being incredibly generous to my friends and I was acting like a spoiled brat, but instead of apologizing to him, it just pissed me off more.

"Can I have my keycard please," I asked stiffly, holding my hand out. I needed to get away from him so I could get my head on straight. He handed me a card and I stepped out of the elevator, quickly finding the room since there were only two doors to choose from on that floor. I assumed the other one was for Lachlan, but I didn't care as long as I was given my space.

I walked inside and felt my jaw drop at the extravagant surroundings. We had stayed in some very nice hotels when we were on tour, but nothing quite on the same level as the Palazzo. The marble floors were a warm cream color with swirls of gold throughout. The entryway led straight into a large living room which was furnished with a deep cushioned couch and chairs and a thick area rug that I longed to bury my toes in. The focal point of the room however was the large glass door leading out to a balcony that, even from where I was standing, I could tell offered an amazing view of the city.

Two hallways led off in either direction from the living room and I followed one to where it opened up into a spacious bedroom. A California king-sized bed, covered in a thick white comforter and more pillows than any one person needed sat in the center of the opulent room which also contained a large walk-in closet, a rich chaise lounge in the corner, and a fireplace complete with flat screen TV above the mantel. Another set of doors allowed guests to step out onto the balcony from their rooms and offered a view just as spectacular as the other.

The bathroom attached to the room was more luxurious than any other I'd ever seen in a hotel. It was decorated in cream-colored tiles to match the marble floors, with a giant whirlpool bath and a shower large enough to fit ten people in it. A large mirror hung above two sinks whose fixtures I could only assume were real gold. I shook my head at the overindulgence of the place. Although, I should have expected as much from Lachlan, considering his home was even more extravagant.

I walked back out to the living room and stopped when I saw

Lachlan standing on the balcony, looking out at the lights. I allowed myself just a moment to appreciate his beauty since he wasn't paying any attention to me. I'd noticed that he'd gotten his dark brown hair cut right before we left and it was styled perfectly with the sides cut shorter and just the right amount of thickness on top. He wore a light blue dress shirt with the sleeves rolled up, showing off the perfectly golden skin of his forearms which were covered in a light dusting of dark hair. His look was completed with a pair of khaki pants that fit him perfectly, accentuating the rounded curve of his ass. I had to force my eyes to look up as he turned and walked back into the room.

"What are you doing here?" I asked. He shoved his hands into his pockets and shrugged his shoulders casually, but the stiffness of his jaw suggested otherwise.

"We'll be sharing a room while we're here," he informed me. I must not have hidden the shock on my face very well, because he rushed to explain that he would be staying in the bedroom at the opposite end of the suite.

I wanted to ask him why he'd gotten a room for us to share when he could have easily afforded another one, but I stopped myself as the answer became glaringly obvious. Lachlan didn't trust me to be alone. He'd probably expected me to start drinking or getting high as soon as the plane landed. Well, I had news for him; he could go fuck himself. I glared at him, angrier than I could remember being in a long time.

"Good news, you get the night off from babysitting tonight because I'm going to find my friends and spend the evening with them," I spit out.

He looked genuinely surprised at my anger which only pissed me off more. How had he thought I'd take the fact that he expected me to fail? I knew that it was going to be difficult to face my old vices head on, but after all of the work I'd put into getting better and the time I'd spent with Hudson, I felt stronger than ever and was actually looking forward to proving to myself that I could do it. Lachlan wasn't even willing to give me that chance though and it hurt. I refused to show him that though, choosing to get angry instead.

Without waiting for his response, I strode over to the table inside the entryway and scooped up the keycard that I'd tossed there then I walked out, slamming the door behind me. I punched the button for the elevator and was relieved when it opened right away. I stepped inside and waited for the doors to shut before slumping against the wall. I had no idea where I was going, I just knew I needed to get far away from the man who held the power to destroy me.

Everyone laughed loudly as Landon's face turned a bright shade of red and he glared accusingly at Micah. It was funny seeing the ex-Navy SEAL nearly panic as he rushed to explain.

"I'm sorry," Micah said as he threw his arm around his fiancé. "You know I would have never intentionally told that story to anyone, it just accidentally slipped out."

"If it helps, it really was an accident," Micah's best friend, Giovanni, added. "We were at the gym together and some guy tripped on his shoelace and nearly fell. I started laughing and Micah told me to stop because he knew how embarrassing that could've been for the poor guy. Of course, I forced him to explain his comment and that's how it all came out."

"Of course, it was no accident when Gio raced home and shared the story with me," Caleb said with a cheeky grin.

"Or when Caleb called and told me what had happened and I passed it along to Ryan," Carter added with a laugh. Everyone laughed again as Landon hung his head in defeat; he clearly understood when he'd been bested. Everyone at the table now knew about the time that he had fallen off of a treadmill because he'd been too busy ogling Micah to pay attention to the moving machine. Micah pulled him closer, kissing the side of his head.

"I'm sorry that you're embarrassed, baby, but I won't ever be sorry that it happened. I've never had a man actually fall for me before that." Landon elbowed Micah in the side, but he soon joined in the laughter at his own expense.

That was just one of the many things I loved about the Greene family. They could make fun of each other, but nobody ever took it seriously or got their feelings hurt because they knew that it was all said in fun. Each member of their family, future spouses included, shared a bond with each other that could never be broken by something as insignificant as a few teasing words. That was something that I never had in my life and as wonderful as it was to see, it was equally as painful because it was a glaring reminder that I was an outcast.

I looked around the large table and saw that each person there was matched up with someone else; everyone but me. Every single one of them had found someone that they could call their own, but I'd never had that and probably never would. I hoped they understood how lucky they were, although the way they looked at their soulmates told me that they probably did.

My eyes swept over the crowded bar. Carter and Ryan had rented out the back room for our party, but from where I was sitting, I could see the crowded dance floor as well as the bartender who stood behind the long wooden bar, pouring someone a shot of whiskey. My mouth watered at the sight and my hands clenched in my lap. I took a deep breath through my nose and let it out slowly through my mouth, practicing one of the many tricks that Hudson had suggested I use to help me get through my cravings. Apparently, the flow of oxygen to the brain would help clear my mind, allowing me to think more clearly and therefore make better choices. I did that several times until I felt the craving begin to pass.

I made myself look away from the bar and my eyes landed on Steve who was sitting at the far end of the table. He was staring right at me and running his fingers through the condensation that dripped down the sides of his glass of water. I froze, surprised that he was looking at me, but he turned his head quickly as Lindsay whispered something in his ear. He'd been avoiding me ever since they'd walked into the bar and found our party sitting there. There'd been a moment of awkward silence as everyone's eyes darted back and forth between the two of us. I'd looked right at him, but he'd busied himself by pulling a chair out for Lindsay and then shaking hands with the two grooms.

It was the first time I'd seen him since I'd been in the hospital and while the dark smudges under his eyes and the deep-set lines that marred his forehead that night had disappeared, I still felt bad knowing that I was the cause of the tense set of his shoulders and the obvious reason he wasn't having any fun. Any other time, I would have gotten up and left so that he could enjoy the party, but I couldn't do that to Carter. Despite the tension between Steve and me, we were there to celebrate the wedding of one of our closest mutual friends and I wasn't going to let Carter down.

That was also the reason I remained seated when I saw Lachlan walk in the door. He looked absolutely delectable in his dark blue, button-fly jeans and black polo shirt which fit his tight, lithe body perfectly. Unfortunately, we were in a gay bar and there was more than just one head that turned as he approached our table. That only added to my irritation and I turned to the others, needing to distract myself before I did something stupid, like march over there and tell all of those mother fuckers that I'd had Lachlan first and therefore he was mine.

My eyes flicked back and forth between Carter and his twin, Caleb, and a devious smile spread across my lips. It had been too long since I'd done anything to rile Carter up, but that was about to change.

"So, tell the truth. Have you and Caleb ever invited someone to have a threesome with the two of you?" I had to fight hard to keep a straight face as Carter whipped his head over to look at me, his face conveying his disgust at the thought. Caleb, who was sitting across from him and had heard my question, looked at me with the exact same look as his twin.

"Dude, he's my twin," Carter said.

"So, have you?" I continued.

"He's. My. Brother," Carter said slowly as if he thought I had trouble comprehending. God, he was fun to pick on.

"You don't have to do anything to each other," I explained. "Just tag team the other guy. I bet it would be really hot."

"Would you want to watch your brother having sex?" Caleb asked incredulously.

"Don't know, I don't have a brother," I said with a shrug. The two of them looked at each other and I could almost hear the conversation they were sharing through their silent twin-speak. They both turned to look at me at the same time and it was more than I could take. My lips started trembling, giving me away and Carter's eyes narrowed right before he punched me in the arm.

"You did all of that on purpose, didn't you, asshole?" he asked, punching me again for good measure. I was probably going to have a bruise the next day, but it was worth it. The look on their faces had been priceless.

Carter rolled his eyes at me, muttering something about getting even with me, while Caleb continued to stare at me as if I'd grown two heads. I winked at him and his face turned bright red which made his husband chuckle. Apparently, Giovanni had been listening to the exchange as well and liked seeing his husband get so flustered.

I looked down the table and saw Lachlan watching me from where he was seated beside Carter's parents. My humor from moments before fled as I remembered what had happened to make me so angry with him in the first place. It was going to be a very long weekend if I didn't find some way to relieve some of my tension.

Dinner was delicious. The bar we were in was much fancier than the ones I'd hung out at in Chicago and therefore they served much better food than the usual bar menu allowed. I'd decided to splurge on a juicy steak, baked potato with everything on it, and green beans; I was on vacation after all.

We spent dinner talking about the wedding and reception that would follow. Carter's parents had rented a small chapel for the ceremony and a larger conference hall for the reception. Carter's brother-in-law Jason, spoke up, wondering if there would be an Elvis impersonator there to perform the ceremony, but his wife, Michelle, informed him very quickly that it wasn't that kind of a Vegas chapel. I chuckled at the look of sincere disappointment on Jason's face. When everyone was finished eating, Carter's parents stood up and began making their way around the table, hugging everyone.

"You're leaving already?" Landon asked. Kathy Greene smiled at her son.

"There's a lot of work to be done in the morning for the reception so I need to get to bed," she replied.

"I thought we were going to check out that big whirlpool bath," her husband, Rick, said as he wrapped an arm around her waist and led her over to the door, waggling his eyebrows at her suggestively.

"Oh, there's time for that still," Kathy told him with a come-hither look. "Besides, I said that we were going to bed, not that we were going to sleep."

A collective groan came from the table and I laughed at the reaction of the couple's children. I watched them as they left the bar, still laughing as they went and I wondered if they said those things on purpose just to get a rise out of their kids. Although, given the looks they'd exchanged with each other throughout dinner, I didn't doubt that they were still completely smitten with each other even after all their years together.

A few of the other couples decided to leave at that point and soon it was just the three Greene brothers, their significant others,

Lachlan, and me. We talked for nearly an hour before Ryan suggested a game of pool so we moved our party out into the main area of the bar. The place was packed so unfortunately there was only one pool table available. Lachlan and I each waved them off and Landon and Micah agreed to wait and play the winning couple.

Several people recognized Carter and myself and stopped to say hello, but overall people were polite and let us enjoy our night out. Although, that may have had more to do with the intimidating looks Micah gave anyone who got too close.

We grabbed some bar stools and sat down to watch the game, laughing at the antics of the couples as they tried to outdo each other. They were surprisingly evenly matched and it finally came down to Carter who sunk the ball into the corner pocket, making it look effortless. I laughed as he and Ryan started a victory dance which had everyone cheering and Caleb and Giovanni rolling their eyes. They were soon laughing along with the rest of us when someone in the back of the crowd screamed "Team Cryan Forever!" Carter and Ryan stopped dancing and narrowed their eyes at the awful name the press had dubbed them, but soon they were laughing too.

I had just taken a drink of my water when I felt a hand on my shoulder. I glanced behind me, surprised to see a man I didn't recognize. He was tall with a curly mop of dirty blond hair, blue eyes, and an easy smile. He was dressed in jeans and a blue tank top which drew attention to his massive biceps.

"Would you like to dance?" he asked. I looked at Lachlan out of the corner of my eye and found him watching us closely so I smiled back at the handsome man.

"Sure," I told him.

"Great, I'm Cody, by the way," he said.

"Rocko," I replied.

"Yeah, I know who you are already," he admitted. His smile grew, showing off a cute pair of dimples as I stood up from my stool. I followed him onto the dance floor where he turned and began swaying to the music. He was a good dancer and before long, we were moving in perfect sync with each other.

The song changed and Cody spun me around so that my back was to his front. His fingers curved around my hips, holding me close against his body as we began a slow rolling motion in response to the pulsating beat of the music. I looked in the direction of the pool tables and saw Lachlan staring at us with his arms crossed and an angry expression on his face. I didn't understand why he'd be pissed though when he'd made it perfectly clear that the only thing between us was business.

I shook it off and let Cody lead us in a sensual grind. My head fell back onto his broad shoulder and his hands slid around the front of my body so that one was on my chest and the other was across my stomach. I closed my eyes and tried to let the tantalizing beat of the music and the feel of a warm body pressed against my own carry me away. It didn't work though and I reached up to brush the hair out of my face with a frustrated sigh. When I opened my eyes, I saw the retreating form of Lachlan as he left the bar. I finished the dance with Cody, but begged off when he asked for more, telling him that I needed to go. The truth was that the only body I wanted to have pressed against mine was Lachlan's.

I told my friends goodnight and made my way through the crowd and out the front door. Instead of hailing a cab, I decided to walk the few blocks back to the hotel. Maybe the fresh air would be enough to help clear my head.

CHAPTER
Twelve

Lachlan

I SLAMMED THE DOOR BEHIND ME AND THREW MY WALLET AND keycard onto the round table in the entryway. My head was pounding so I didn't bother to turn on any lights as I made my way into the living room. There were enough lights from the Vegas strip shining through the window to keep me from falling. I could've used a scotch right then, but the hotel staff had been instructed to remove all alcohol from the room before our arrival. I hadn't wanted to make Rylie's weekend any more difficult by having bottles of alcohol in the same room as him.

Anger thrummed through my veins, but I couldn't tell if I was angrier with the guy dancing with Rylie or myself. Seeing that guy's hands all over Rylie's body as they ground against each other out on the dance floor had made my blood boil. I didn't want to see anyone's hands on Rylie but my own and it had taken everything in me not to storm over there and pull them apart.

I couldn't do that though because Rylie didn't even know how I felt about him. Instead of being honest with him, I'd let him continue to believe that he was nothing more than a client to me. I had no idea if he would ever reciprocate my feelings, but by not telling him, I'd never even given him the chance to decide. I had only myself to blame for the fact that I was in a lonely hotel room while the man I was in love with was off doing God knows what with another man.

My heart constricted painfully in my chest with that thought and I sunk down onto the couch and leaned forward with my face in my hands. I'd seen all of the media footage of Rylie with other men and women and even though it had bothered me then because I'd been infatuated with him, the experience was completely different once I fell in love with him. I yanked at my hair as agonizing images of what Rylie and that man were most likely doing, flashed through my mind.

I shook my head to clear it of the torturous thoughts and leaned back on the couch, releasing a deep breath. I was tired of letting my fear of rejection control me. My whole life, I'd always fought for everything I'd ever wanted. I'd created my business based off of something that Spencer and I had enjoyed as kids and started at the ground level, fighting my way through industry giants until it became one of the biggest record labels in the entire world. Then when Spencer was killed, I had experienced depression so deep that I'd had to fight my way out of the darkness just to stay alive.

So why had I stood by and let fear rule my decisions when it came to Rylie? I should have been fighting for him and for what I thought we could be together all along instead of acting like a coward. I knew I stood the chance of being rejected, but I was tired of running. I needed to know one way or another if Rylie and me being together was even a possibility and I needed to know right away.

As if my thoughts had conjured him, the door opened and Rylie stepped in. He saw me sitting there and froze a second before shutting the door behind him. The sound of the lock clicking into place echoed loudly in the quiet room. I watched silently as Rylie tossed his keycard onto the table beside mine and walked into the kitchen. The light from the refrigerator lit up the entire room as he opened its door and pulled out a bottle of water.

I continued to study him as he leaned against the counter and took a long pull from the bottle. I could make out the movement of his throat as he swallowed and my cock twitched in my jeans. It was then that I noticed he was staring at me too, but the distance between us kept me from getting a good read on his mood.

"Why are you sitting here in the dark?" he questioned, breaking the silence.

"My head was hurting so I didn't want the lights on," I told him. He set the bottle of water on the counter and crossed his arms over his chest.

"Is that why you took off from the bar so fast?" he asked. His voice held a hint of challenge and I felt myself bristle.

"I'm surprised you even noticed, what with you basically having sex with that guy on the dance floor," I hissed, my earlier anger resurfacing. "Why are you back so soon. Didn't you enjoy yourself?" Rylie stood up straight when he heard my tone and I saw a flash of something in his eyes.

"As a matter of fact, I did. It was nice to be with someone that actually *wanted* to touch me," he shot back. My breathing increased and my heart thumped wildly in my chest as I stared at him. He'd basically thrown down the gauntlet and it was up to me to decide whether I was going to walk away or finally admit the truth.

"You think that I don't want to touch you?" I asked. My voice was steady as I stood up from the couch and began walking over to him. "That's *all* I've been able to think about." His eyes widened in surprise.

"Then, why haven't you? I told you it didn't have to mean anything," he said as I stopped in front of him. I was standing close enough to see the vulnerability in his eyes.

"That's the problem, Rylie. I want it to mean something." I drew in a deep breath and forced myself to continue. "Things could never be meaningless between us because *you* mean something to me." It felt freeing to finally confess my feelings and I watched the emotions that played over his face as my words sank in.

"But I thought I was just an investment to you," he whispered shakily. I shook my head sadly.

"I'm sorry that I ever said that to you; it was a complete lie."

"Why would you lie about that?" he pressed.

"I know it's a pitiful excuse, but I was afraid," I whispered. "I was afraid that if I told you how I felt that it would send you running in the other direction and as much as I wanted to be with you, I was more afraid of losing your friendship if you found out the truth."

"And what is the truth?" he asked so quietly I wouldn't have been able to hear him if I hadn't been standing so close. I saw a mixture of curiosity and hope in his eyes, but I also saw fear and I was worried that if I said too much, he would bolt.

"The truth is that I've grown to care about you very much. You are important to me and I would never hurt you." I watched as his shoulders relaxed and I knew I'd made the right decision in not telling him how desperately in love with him I was. I could tell that I was going to have to go slowly with him.

"It's also true that I think you're the sexiest man I've ever met." His eyes grew heavy as I reached out and ran my fingers along his jaw, the short bristly hairs tickling my hand. I leaned forward until I could feel his quick breaths blowing across my lips. "I want you," I said as my thumb grazed his bottom lip.

"You can take anything you want from me," he responded. His tongue darted out to lick the pad of my thumb and I gasped. I stared, transfixed as his mouth opened and he pulled my thumb into his wet heat, sucking it the same way he had sucked my cock.

I pulled my thumb from his mouth and slanted my lips over his.

As soon as our mouths touched, I felt the passion between us flaring like a bright white heat, threatening to consume us both. My tongue reveled in the taste of his mouth as my hands reached up to tangle in his hair. His hands gripped my hips roughly as he matched my kisses with a fervor of his own. I felt his hands move to the buttons of my jeans, but I grabbed his wrist gently, stilling his movements. He pulled away, looking at me curiously as I shook my head.

"It's my turn to taste you," I informed him.

A naughty grin lifted the corners of his mouth and I wanted to eat him alive. I slid my hand around his, lacing our fingers together and pulled him towards my bedroom. We couldn't seem to keep our hands or mouths off of each other as we made our way down the hallway, bumping into walls and nearly toppling a few of the pictures that were hanging there. We left a trail of socks and shoes behind us as we kicked them off as quickly as possible.

When we reached the bedroom, I backed him up until his knees hit the edge of the bed. I quickly pulled his shirt over his head, exposing his tattooed arms and his pierced nipples that I couldn't resist flicking my tongue over, before sinking to my knees in front of him. I wanted to take my time with him and savor the moment, but that feeling was at war with the overpowering need to taste him, touch him, and lay claim to him all at once.

My hands shook with desire as they worked to unbutton his pants. I forced myself to slow down as I slid the material over his hips and down his legs. He kicked them off to the side then leaned forward, grabbing the hem of my shirt and yanking it up over my head. He ran his hands gently over my shoulders and up the back of my neck, feathering his fingers through my hair.

I leaned my face into the juncture of his thigh and breathed him in deeply. He smelled like soap, musk, and one hundred percent man. My head spun with the heady scent and my cock hardened painfully. I reached for the waistband of his sexy black briefs and slid them down his hips slowly, as if I were unwrapping a precious gift and my eyes fell on the mysterious tattoo along his hip, the one that had taunted me through those skimpy little blue swim trunks. I smiled when I saw the beautiful design of a treble clef with a red drum set in front of it. As I pulled his briefs down the rest of the way, my mouth watered at the sight of his Prince Albert piercing and I had to lean forward and flick my tongue over the cool metal. Rylie's hips jerked in reaction and I peered up at him.

"I take it you're sensitive," I said, tilting my head innocently. He nodded, swallowing hard as he continued to stare down at me with wide eyes. "That's very good to know," I murmured.

I wrapped my hand around the base of his shaft and stroked him a few times, letting my thumb glide over the tip, spreading the moisture that had formed there. His cock was long and thick and his dark hair was trimmed, exposing the fullness of his sac which felt heavy when I cupped it in my hand. My tongue moved along the side of his shaft in a gentle glide, memorizing the taste and the feel of him before my lips finally closed over the bulbous head.

His fingers gripped my hair and he groaned loudly as I began to bob up and down on his thick rod. I took him to the back of my throat, swallowing around his length. I began sucking harder as the salty flavor of his pre-cum burst over my tongue, teasing my senses and leaving me desperate for more. I reached down and yanked at the buttons of my jeans, never stopping my ministrations on him as I freed my aching cock and wrapped my hand around it, working it in a steady glide and feeling my own juices coating my fingers.

Soon, I had to stop or risk ending things much too soon. I pulled off of him reluctantly and stood on shaky legs. He grasped my arms to help steady me and leaned forward, sliding his tongue into my mouth and I wondered if he enjoyed tasting the flavor of himself on my lips. After a few minutes, I pushed against his chest, forcing him onto the bed. He scooted back along the mattress until he rested comfortably, his long black hair splayed across the pillow. He was exquisite.

"Stay there," I instructed, my voice sounding strained to my own ears. I strode quickly into the bathroom and retrieved the lube and condoms from my bag then returned to the bedroom. My footsteps halted when I saw him lying on the bed, the colorful tattoos that ran the length of his left arm bunching and twisting with the movement of his muscles as he stroked himself lazily.

"You said I had to stay, you never said I couldn't keep myself entertained," Rylie said with a wicked grin. I dropped the supplies beside him on the bed and he spread his legs further apart as I crawled up the mattress towards him trailing my fingers up his legs as I went. His fingers stilled as I neared his cock.

"Don't stop on my account," I purred. "In fact, why don't you feed it to me."

I kept my eyes on him as I lowered my head, my mouth opening in invitation. Rylie tilted his cock towards my mouth and then held the back of my head as he slipped it between my waiting lips, feeding it to me just as I'd wanted. I let him take control of the situation and soon I could feel the smooth metal of his piercing as it hit the back of my throat.

His hands gripped the back of my head as his hips lifted, pushing himself farther down my throat. His movements were restrained though and I could tell he was holding himself back so as not to hurt me. I wanted more though, I wanted all of him so I increased my efforts and sucked him with wild abandon, getting lost in the smell, the taste, and the sounds of him until he let out a guttural cry and I felt his seed coating my tongue and spilling down my throat. I moaned at the delicious salty flavor of his cum and I continued to drink him in until he collapsed against the mattress. My tongue flicked over him, lapping up his juices that had spilled over the sides of him and dripped onto his stomach. When he was clean, I sat back on my heels between his splayed legs and grinned down at him, licking the corner of my mouth for show. He opened his eyes and chuckled wearily.

"You look like the cat that got the cream," he said. His voice was husky and my cock twitched in answer to the sound.

"I happen to fancy the flavor of your cream," I teased. He laughed and it was such a sweet, carefree sound that I could only stare at him in wonder. *God, how I love this man.* His laughter died out as he caught and held my gaze and I wondered if my thoughts were evident in my eyes.

"Let me take care of you," he whispered. He reached for me, but I shook my head.

"I'm not done with you yet," I informed him and he quirked his brow at me.

"Oh really? What did you have in mind?" I smiled at him, as the teasing lilt returned to his voice.

"Will you let me top you?" I asked. He hesitated for a fraction of a second. "It's okay if you don't want to. I'm a switch so I'm fine either way, I just want to be with you," I rushed to assure him.

"No, it's alright," he whispered shakily. "I'm a switch too and I want to feel you inside me. It's just that it's been a while so…" His words trailed off and I smiled gently at him, my hands smoothing over his hips.

"I'll take care of you," I promised solemnly.

I took my time exploring his body, letting my hands glide across the ridges of his abs and over his pounding heart. He had a light smattering of hair on his chest which I ran my fingers through before landing on the metal hoops in his nipples. I tugged on one, thrilling at the way his body responded as his torso lifted off of the bed and a loud moan rumbled up from his throat.

Rylie's breathing was heavy as my fingers continued their journey up over his pecs to the tips of his shoulders. I studied the beautiful designs on his skin and then began tracing the lines with my fingertips. After a few seconds my hands stilled and my eyes shot to his face. He was looking at me warily and I could feel his muscles tense into tightly coiled springs.

"What is this, Rylie?" I whispered. I could feel the raised scars underneath the colorful artwork; some were circular in shape while others were straight lines. My eyes darted back to his face, but he had moved his stare to the ceiling, avoiding my gaze.

"Some foster homes were rougher than others," he responded hoarsely and I could hear the emotion in his voice.

I had a feeling that I didn't even know half of the ways in which this man had been hurt throughout his life and I knew that trust didn't come easily for him. The fact that he trusted me was humbling to say the least and I vowed to myself that I would never give him any reason to doubt that trust.

Tears filled my eyes as I bent down and pressed my lips over one of the scars. He flinched slightly but didn't push me away so I continued kissing each scar along both arms as if I could erase them from existence with my touch. When I was finished, I cupped his face with one hand and looked down at him. His eyes were squeezed shut and his lips were pressed so tightly together that the skin around them had turned white.

"I want to be inside of you, Rylie, but only if you look at me. If we're going to do this, then you're going to know that it's me you're with." I held my breath as I waited on his reaction for what seemed like an eternity. Finally, he relaxed beneath me and his eyes opened slowly.

"There's those incredible blue eyes," I murmured right before I pulled his bottom lip between my teeth.

It didn't take long for our passion to reignite and soon we were swaying our hips back and forth, our cocks sliding against each other in a perfect dance. I sat up on my heels and grabbed the bottle of lube, pouring a liberal amount onto my fingers and rubbing them together to warm the liquid. Rylie bent his legs, holding them to his chest and opening himself up to me.

"You're perfect," I told him, my eyes darting between his face and where I was circling his pink hole with my fingers.

Carefully, I let one finger dip inside and I had to bite back a moan at the tightness that gripped my digit. *He is going to fit my cock so beautifully.* My head swirled at the thought as I slid another finger in, slowly working him open until I felt his muscles begin to relax around me.

"Please, Lachlan, I'm ready. I need you." A small smile played at my lips when I heard him say my name because it proved to me that he was in the moment with me.

I removed my fingers and quickly ripped open the condom packet and slid the thin latex down my shaft. I grabbed the lube and poured some into the palm of my hand, slicking myself then I lined up the tip of my cock with his hole and glanced up at him. He held my gaze steadily that time.

"Are you ready, Rylie?" I asked. I waited for his nod of consent and then I pressed forward gently until the head of my cock popped through the first ring of muscle.

Rylie gasped and I could see the tightness around his eyes. I leaned down and brushed my lips back and forth over his in gentle, soothing strokes. When he began to kiss me back, I knew he was ready for more and I began rocking back and forth slowly, going a little bit deeper with every stroke. His ass was even tighter than I had imagined and the heat from inside of him burned me in the most blissful of ways. Soon, I felt his legs encircling my waist and his ankles hooked together behind my back.

My tongue dipped in and out of his mouth to the same rhythm as the lower half of our bodies. His hands slid over my back, his short nails scraping at my skin and I prayed that they would leave their mark behind. I sat up, changing the angle of my thrusts and he cried out as I found that perfect place inside him that I knew would bring him the most pleasure.

Sweat dripped down my back and I could feel the telltale burning at the base of my spine that signaled my release was near. The sexy sounds that Rylie made each time I hit his prostate spurred me on and my movements became increasingly frantic. His cock was bobbing between us in response to my thrusts and pearly liquid leaked from the tip, coating his stomach and pooling in his navel. I reached down and gripped his thick shaft in my fist and began stroking him up and down, giving my wrist a little twist whenever my palm reached the head of his cock.

Rylie's moans were coming so close together that they all blended until suddenly his body went rigid and he let out a loud shout. The sight of the white ribbons of cum shooting from his cock and landing on his chin, combined with the strangle hold his arse held on my cock, was enough to put me over the edge and I threw my head back, releasing my own shout as I flooded the condom.

I collapsed on top of him, unable to hold myself up any longer. I lay my head in the crook of his neck and closed my eyes as I gasped for air. Slowly, almost as if he were unsure if he had the right, I felt his arms close around me. I doubted that there was a more perfect place in the world than right there, wrapped up in Rylie's strong arms.

We lay like that until I was forced to get up and dispose of the condom. I tied it off quickly and tossed it into the trash then pulled several tissues from the box by the bed and cleaned us both up. When I was finished, I pulled the covers back and we climbed underneath. I was surprised when he didn't argue about sleeping in my bed, but instead reached for me and pulled my back against him so that he was spooning me. The heat from his body and the sound of his breathing soon lulled me into a peaceful dream-like state.

"It wasn't meaningless for me either," I thought I heard him whisper, but I couldn't be sure because I was already falling asleep.

CHAPTER
Thirteen

Rylie/Rocko

I STOOD IN FRONT OF THE MIRROR, TRYING TO FIX MY TIE AND failing miserably. Not surprisingly, I was not a suit and tie wearing type of guy, but certain situations called for it, such as the wedding of one of your best friends. In fact, I hadn't even owned a suit until Lachlan had his tailor make one for me. I had argued with him at first, I saw no reason to spend a fortune on something that I would probably never wear again, but he'd insisted that I needed something special to wear for such a special occasion and it was just easier to give in; he could be very persuasive sometimes.

My thoughts drifted back to the night before. Finding out that Lachlan cared about me had come as a surprise. I'd felt certain that he cared about me as his client or he never would have gone to such lengths to help me once I left rehab. I also was aware of the chemistry between us and the fact that we had formed a friendship in the time that I'd been at his house. I never would have dreamt that he could care for me as a partner and a lover though and that was what had my head still spinning.

The way he'd kissed me and touched me was unlike anything I'd ever experienced before. The people I'd been with in the past had always shied away from my scars once they'd found them. Most of them pretended they weren't there and avoided touching them. A few had looked at me with a mixture of disgust and pity, but not Lachlan.

I'd watched him as he'd first discovered them, bracing myself for his distain, but the look in his eyes was filled with such pain, as if he could feel the torment I'd been subjected to and I had to look away to try to stop the tears that were burning the backs of my eyes. I'd provided him with a much-edited version of how the scars had gotten there, telling him simply that foster care had been rough. Lachlan was a good and kind man and there was no reason to subject him to all of the horrors I'd been through as a child.

I'd been stunned when instead of avoiding the scars, he'd begun kissing each and every one of them. I could feel his tears as they dripped onto my arms, but I lay still and let him continue. I wondered if he had any idea how powerful that moment had been for me. No one had ever shown me so much care and tenderness and it was as if he were healing each scar with his touch.

The sex was out of this world, but it was so much more than our two bodies coming together. Lachlan had insisted that I keep my eyes open and so I'd seen the emotions playing out in his features. He'd been gentle and attentive and I'd seen how much he cared about me in his eyes. It had left me speechless, shaken, and afraid to hope for more.

I could feel myself falling for Lachlan and it terrified me. Other than the band, I'd had very little good happen in my life so I knew that as amazing as things were between Lachlan and me, eventually it would come to an end. If I allowed myself to fall in love with him, it would just hurt that much more when it ended. That didn't mean I wasn't planning on enjoying him as much as possible until that happened though, I'd just have to be careful to protect my heart.

Satisfied that my tie was as good as it was going to get, I grabbed my comb off of the sink and ran it through my hair. The shoes that Lachlan had picked out to go with the suit had pinched my feet, so I was wearing my black biker boots instead. I completed the ensemble with my favorite black leather wrist straps and a matching leather strap which I used to tie my hair back. I may be celebrating Carter's special day, but I was still going to be me underneath the formal getup.

I checked myself one more time. I had to admit that the tailor had done an incredible job. The black suit and light blue dress shirt fit me perfectly with just the right amount of give in the shoulders so it wasn't too tight. The tie on the other hand was a lost cause.

"Rylie, we need to leave soon if we don't want to be late. Are you almost ready?" The sound of Lachlan's accent sent a delicious chill down my spine and my unruly cock perked up and took notice. *Not now, buddy. We don't have enough time.*

"Yeah, I'm ready. All except for this stupid tie," I grumbled. I could hear Lachlan's deep chuckle as he came around the corner into the bathroom.

My mouth went dry at the sight of him. He was dressed in a light gray suit with a pale lavender dress shirt and a dark purple vest and matching tie. His dark brown hair was styled perfectly and my fingers itched to slide through the soft waves. His warm honey-colored eyes roamed over me and I hoped that he liked what he saw. The smile that spread on his face told me that he did.

"I picked that tie out myself because it reminded me of your eyes," he told me.

He stepped towards me and the smell of his spicy cologne filled my senses as he began fixing my tie. The hairs on my neck stood up as he slid his fingers under my collar to straighten the material before adjusting the knot and smoothing it down over my chest with the palm of his hand. I stared at his mouth as the tip of his tongue darted out to wet his lips and I wanted nothing more than to rip both of our clothes off and fuck him against the bathroom counter while we both watched our reflection in the mirror.

"You look very…" His words were breathy and I wondered if he was sharing the same thoughts as me.

"Edible?" I interrupted, waggling my brows at him playfully. He rewarded me with a bright smile, showing off his perfectly straight teeth.

"I was going to say debonair, but yes, I suppose edible fits too." I leaned forward and kissed him, still somewhat shocked that I was allowed to and sighed when I tasted the minty goodness of his mouth. We kissed for several minutes until, with a frustrated groan, Lachlan pulled back. I was happy to see the pink flush to his skin and the bulge in his suit pants that proved I wasn't the only one completely affected by our kisses.

"We need to go…now," he said hoarsely.

I didn't say anything as I followed him out of my room and to the front entryway, but I stopped him from opening the door when I placed my hand on it over his shoulder. Pressing up against him, I ran my nose up the back of his neck, breathing in the scent of cologne, shampoo, and Lachlan Edwards. I reached down with my other hand and cupped his ass through the thin suit, squeezing one taught globe in my palm and I heard him moan as his head fell back on my shoulder.

"Every time you catch me staring at you, every time I smile and you wonder what it is I'm smiling about, just know that my thoughts are of peeling that suit off of you and feasting on every delectable inch of your body I expose," I whispered into his ear. I heard his swift intake of air and felt his body shiver against me and I smiled, quite pleased with myself.

The wedding was held in a tiny chapel on the outskirts of the city. Micah had brought in his own security team which consisted of elite ex-military special ops members and they'd proven to be excellent at their jobs because not one fan or member of the press was there to disrupt the special day.

Caleb and Landon each stood up for Carter while Ryan had his friends and co-workers from his former fire department, Joe and Kevin, standing with him. Everyone smiled adoringly at Caleb and Giovanni's little girl, Sarah, as she entered the room. She froze when she caught sight of some unfamiliar faces in the audience and her face scrunched up like she was going to cry, but Caleb saw his daughter's distress and knelt down at the end of the aisle with his arms wide open. As soon as she saw him, her face lit up in an angelic smile and she made her way to her daddy's waiting arms, dropping handfuls of rose petals as she went. I watched as he scooped her up in his arms and kissed her neck, making her squeal with delight, before passing her off to his husband and rejoining Landon up front.

Sarah was one of the lucky ones who made it out of the system and into a loving family and I was so happy for her. She couldn't have ended up with two more devoted and caring parents. If I were ever fortunate enough to be a parent, I would make sure that my child always knew how much they were loved and that they could count on me for anything.

For just a moment, I allowed myself to imagine what kind of parent Lachlan would be. I could picture him being there when they got home from school, eager to hear about their day and willing to lend advice when needed. I was sure he'd be patient and kind and maybe a tad over-indulgent, but then I'd be there to rein him in so he didn't spoil them too much. I stopped myself when I realized the direction my thoughts had taken. I glanced at Lachlan and saw him staring at me with his head tilted to the side. He gave me a gentle smile as if he knew what I'd been thinking so I quickly turned my attention to the rear of the chapel. I had to remember to take things one day at a time and not expect too much; that was the only way I could protect myself from getting hurt.

The music grew louder and everyone stood in preparation of the grooms, but after several long seconds there was still no sign of them. I could hear the hushed voices of the others as they wondered if something was wrong. After being nudged by his wife's elbow, Carter's brother-in-law Mark made his way up the aisle and out the doors; presumably to find out what had happened. He came back a moment later, his entire body shaking as he tried to hold in his laughter and motioned for the attendant to start the music over.

The music swelled and this time both grooms appeared in the doorway. It didn't take a genius to figure out what had caused their delay, given their flushed cheeks and swollen lips as they made their way down the aisle to the sound of muffled laughter from the audience. Neither man looked ashamed though, in fact, they seemed quite satisfied with whatever they'd been up to and I smiled when I saw Ryan wink at his groom when they reached the front and faced each other.

Everyone grew serious though as the men took turns exchanging their vows, speaking from their hearts about everything that the other man had brought into their lives and how they were stronger together than apart. I could hear Kathy Greene's gentle sobs when Carter spoke about Ryan saving his life in more ways than one and then again when Ryan talked about how Carter had given him a family.

"Hang in there, Mom. We're almost done," Ryan said, turning and smiling at his new mother-in-law. The rest of the family laughed at that and I chuckled. Carter had told us on more than one occasion how easily his mom cried and I'd witnessed it firsthand when she'd come to tell him goodbye as we were leaving to go on tour. Kathy Greene was a sweet lady with a big heart and I'd told him then that there were a lot worse things than to have a mom who cried over you.

By the time they got to the kissing part, there was barely a dry eye in the place and I even thought I saw Caleb and Landon wiping at the corners of their eyes. The minister announced them as Mr. and Mr. Marshall-Greene and they didn't even get a chance to make it down the aisle before the rest of their family converged on them, offering their congratulations. I stood, clapping with a broad smile stretched across my lips.

"It must be wonderful to be a part of something like that," I heard Lachlan say beside me.

I turned to look at him and saw that he was watching the Greene family with a wistful smile on his face. I realized in that moment that we really weren't all that different in some aspects of our lives. I may have had no parents growing up, but maybe it was just as hard on Lachlan to have had parents around who simply chose to ignore him.

I reached for his hand, squeezing it gently and he turned to me with a smile. I tugged on his hand and began side stepping out from between the pews and into the aisle. I looked up as I reached the end of the long wooden seat and stopped when I saw Steve standing directly across from me. His eyes darted down to where my hand was joined with Lachlan's and then shot back up to mine in surprise. There was a mixture of hurt and anger etched on his face and then he narrowed his eyes and turned, storming out of the chapel and leaving a bewildered Lindsay to chase after him.

I wasn't sure why he had been so angry, but I was tired of Steve avoiding me whenever there was a problem. We were supposed to be friends for fuck's sake so we should be able to talk things out. I turned to Lachlan with an apology on my lips, but he beat me to it.

"Go," he ordered. I didn't waste another second as I let go of his hand and ran out the doors in search of Steve. I found him storming across the grass to a nearby tree where he stopped, linking his hands behind his head and glared up at the sky.

"He's usually so calm all of the time, but he's been on edge ever since we got in town," Lindsay said from beside me. I hadn't even noticed her standing there. She was watching Steve with a look of concern. "He said he wanted to be alone, but I don't know…"

"It's my fault that he's so upset, I'll go talk to him," I explained. She looked like she still wasn't sure and then I heard Lachlan's voice from behind me.

"I agree, the two of them have a lot to work out. Why don't I give you a ride to the reception in the car I have and then Steve and Rocko can join us there when they're finished talking," he offered. Lindsay smirked at each of us, seeing that she was obviously outnumbered.

"Thank you," she said to Lachlan as he offered her his arm. I gave him a grateful look as they passed and my heart warmed when he winked at me.

I watched them walk down the steps and across the parking lot to the car that Lachlan had rented for the day and waited for them to climb in before I turned back to Steve. He was still standing near the tree, but he had shoved his hands into his pockets and was staring at me. I took a deep breath to steady my nerves and then started walking down the steps and across the yard towards him. I slowed down when I was still a few feet away.

"Lachlan gave Lindsay a ride to the reception so we could talk," I explained.

"You'll never fucking change, will you?" he said, his eyes focused on the ground between us. His voice was low, but it whipped through me as if he had shouted it. His anger was so out of character for him and I felt for the first time that maybe I really had pushed him too far.

"What do you mean?" I asked cautiously.

"They all tried to convinced me that you'd changed, that things would be different this time," he muttered, shaking his head. His head shot up suddenly and the look on his face nearly brought me to my knees because my best friend was standing in front of me looking completely shattered. I stepped forward with my hands out, wanting to help him if I could, but he backed away, holding his hand up in a stop gesture. My arms fell to my sides uselessly and I waited for him to finish. I deserved everything he was about to say and I knew he needed to get everything out in the open so we could see if there were any pieces worth putting back together afterward.

"I was almost convinced when I saw you at dinner," he continued. "I saw you looking over at the bar and I could tell how difficult it was for you to be around all of that alcohol, in Vegas of all places. I watched you to see what you would do and when you turned away from it and took a drink of your water, I felt something I hadn't felt in a long time when it came to you; I felt hope." He looked at me with a sad smile.

"I felt hope that I might finally get my best friend back. The one who would come to my place and hang out all night watching movies and eating every last bit of my food. I miss that guy." He swallowed hard and I had to brush away the tears that were streaming down my cheeks.

"I've missed you too, Steve. I'm so sor…" I tried to say, but he cut me off.

"Just stop it, okay?" he yelled, making me flinch. He glared at me through watery eyes and when he blinked they splashed over. "I can tell that it was all just another lie. Unfortunately, you were able to con the others into believing that you'd changed, but it's clear that you've already gone back to your old ways."

"Wait a minute, I *have* changed," I interjected. "I haven't had any drugs or alcohol since I wound up in the hospital that night. So how exactly have I gone back to my old ways?" I was willing to stand there and take whatever I had coming to me for the pain I had caused him, but I wasn't going to listen to him yell at me for something I hadn't done.

"Well, it's clear that you're still fucking around, which for you always went hand in hand with your addictions. It's only a matter of time before you slide back into your old habits, except this time it looks like you'll be taking the rest of us down with you since your new boy toy happens to be our boss!" Steve spit out angrily. That time when I moved forward I didn't stop until I was right up in his face and my body was vibrating with just as much anger as his.

"Don't you dare talk about what's going on between Lachlan and me like that," I yelled. "Lachlan is a good man and he's shown me nothing but kindness and friendship. He took me into his home and set me up with a therapist and he's been there any time I've need-ed him, no matter how much I've fucked up; so don't you dare talk about him that way."

"Holy shit," Steve breathed out. He cocked his head and looked at me like he was trying to work out a difficult puzzle. "You really care about him, don't you?" he asked incredulously.

"Yeah, I do," I admitted quietly, my shoulders slumping.

"I never thought I'd see the day when you'd let yourself fall for someone." The beginnings of a smile played at his lips and I felt my-self relax as I realized the worst of the argument was behind us.

"Look, I'm sorry about what I said before and for doubting you. Carter told me you'd really changed and I wanted to believe it, but then I saw you holding hands with Lachlan and it all just came rush-ing back, you know? But that wasn't fair to you and I'm sorry," he said sincerely.

"Nah, I'm the one who should be apologizing to you," I told him. "I've never given you a reason to believe in me and even though I've changed and I don't ever want to go back to the way I was before, I also understand that it's going to take a lot of time before you guys trust me again. I'm willing to put that time in though because you mean the world to me. You're my best friends and you're also my family."

"You're my best friend too. That's why it hurt so bad when I found you in that hotel room," Steve said quietly. "I've never felt so helpless in my entire life and all I could think about was that maybe

I could have done more or tried harder and none of that would've happened. Then at the hospital, I overheard the EMTs say they'd lost you twice on the way there and I just shut down because it was easier than facing the pain of watching my best friend die."

I heard the sob tear from his chest and I reached for him. That time he let me and I pulled him towards me and wrapped my arms around him tightly. We stood that way for several minutes, each of us crying out our fear and our sorrow and our regrets. When we'd finished, I pulled back so I could look him in the eyes.

"I need to tell you something and I want you to really listen, okay?" I waited for him to nod his head before I continued. "There was nothing you could have done or said to stop that from happening. I had a really rough start in life, not that that's any excuse for my behavior, but it definitely played a large part in how I ended up with my addictions. I've been working with a therapist and he's helping me to open up more and work through some of my old issues, but I realize that if I hadn't hit rock bottom then I never would have gotten the help I truly needed. I will always regret the pain I caused everyone, especially you, but I hope you'll give me the chance to prove that I can change."

"Of course, I'll give you a chance. You're my best friend and I can already see big changes in you, Rocko," he told me.

"Rylie," I responded.

"What?" Steve asked, his brow wrinkling in confusion. I cleared my throat.

"My real name is Rylie." I watched as realization sank in and Steve's eyes softened.

"Thank you for telling me that…Rylie," he said and a warm grin spread across his face. It didn't feel strange to hear him call me by my real name, it felt good.

"Come on," I said. "We better get to the reception before all the food's gone." We turned and started heading back towards the parking lot. Steve's rental car was the only one left in the lot and I was surprised that I hadn't noticed everyone leaving. I cringed as I wondered if they'd heard us yelling.

"I've got to say, if this is what being with Lachlan has done for you then I approve." Steve gestured to my suit and waggled his brows.

"Yeah, well don't get used to it. I won't be trading in my jeans and concert t-shirts anytime soon," I assured him.

"It's not just the suit though," Steve said as we climbed in the car. He started it up and watched me as I leaned forward to angle the AC vents in my direction. It was hotter than hell out there and I didn't want to sweat through my brand-new suit.

"What exactly is going on between you and Lachlan?" Steve asked, trying the more direct approach when I didn't immediately offer the information. I shrugged my shoulders and gestured for him to get going. He sighed and began driving. I wasn't ready to pour my heart out yet, but maybe it would help to have someone I could talk to that could help me sort through my feelings. I rolled my eyes when I thought of how pleased Hudson would be if he'd heard that.

So, I spent the rest of the ride telling Steve how Lachlan and I had become friends and the way I felt when I was around him, how I looked forward to the end of each day when he'd be finished with his work and we'd spend time together. I didn't tell him about the night before because that was private between Lachlan and myself and I didn't want to share it with anyone else. He pulled into the reception hall and parked the car but left it running as he turned to face me in his seat.

"It sounds to me like the start of something incredible. Rylie, I know there's a lot you still haven't told me about your past, but I believe I know you pretty well; probably better than almost anyone else in the world. I know that you've had to deal with shit all by yourself for a long time and I've seen you hold people at arm's length, never letting them get too close as a means of protecting yourself." I looked up at him, surprised that he'd picked up on a lot more than I'd realized. He blew out a puff of air.

"Look, what I'm trying to say is, give this thing with Lachlan a chance. Maybe it'll work out for the two of you and maybe it won't, but at least give it a chance. Who knows, maybe you'll find that you don't have to handle everything all on your own anymore." I stared at him for several seconds, sifting his words through my mind.

"Thanks, Steve."

"No problem. Now let's get in there before that rich boyfriend of yours sends out a search party," he teased.

I punched his shoulder and climbed out of the car. As we walked into the building, I ran that word through my brain. *Boyfriend.* I wasn't sure that's what I would call Lachlan. Of course, that was unchartered territory for me, I'd never had a boyfriend before. Somehow it didn't seem to adequately explain who he was in my life though, but I wasn't sure what word did. The only things I knew for certain was that he was significant, he made me happier than I'd ever been and I hoped it didn't end anytime soon.

CHAPTER
Fourteen

Lachlan

I woke up and smiled when I saw Rylie sleeping soundly beside me. He was lying on his stomach with his face turned towards me on the pillow, his long black lashes fanned out over his cheekbones as he slept and his hair was spread out all around him in wild disarray, probably from where my hands had pulled it the night before as I'd taken him from behind.

We'd been back from Las Vegas for a couple of weeks and not one night since our return had we slept alone. I'd been thrilled to discover that under the rough exterior that Rylie exposed to the rest of the world, lay a warm, sweet man who loved to cuddle. I suspected that he hadn't received much affection growing up and I could relate. Even when my parents bothered to come home, they were never the affectionate type.

I'd never realized how much I craved being touched by someone until Rylie began doing it. I wasn't sure he was even aware he was doing it most of the time. It was often just the brush of his hand over my lower back as we walked together, or the way he'd lean against my side as we watched a movie together. I cherished his touches and more than that, I cherished the fact that he had finally begun to feel close enough to me to let his guard down.

That wasn't to say that he had completely opened up to me, in fact, I could tell that there was still something weighing heavily on his mind, but I trusted that Hudson would be there to help him whenever he was ready to talk and so would I, if he'd let me. Rylie hadn't said how he felt about me and as much as I was dying to know, I refused to push him. Although, there were times when I thought I saw something resembling affection in his eyes, but perhaps that was just wishful thinking on my part. I chose instead to enjoy every moment I had with him and kept my own feelings for him under wraps so I wouldn't scare him off.

"Morning," Rylie said, startling me from my thoughts. My heart did a backflip when I saw those piercing blue eyes staring back at me and he blessed me with a lazy smile.

"Good morning, sleepyhead," I teased, smiling back at him.

"I couldn't have slept that long, it's barely light out," he complained.

"Yes, but it's getting late for our morning run," I explained. I leaned over and kissed his shoulder in a few areas. I'd spent so much time lavishing attention on his scars that he didn't even flinch anymore, which made me extremely happy. I knew I couldn't erase their existence in his life, but maybe I could at least show him that he was worthy of love with or without the scars of his past.

"No." I chuckled at his pitiful whimper. He was so adorable first thing in the morning when he was still all sleepy and a bit grumpy. I burrowed my nose into his neck and breathed in his sleep-warmed scent. My hand slid underneath the covers and smoothed down the silky length of his back to the rounded globes of his arse where I gave him a firm squeeze. He moaned, lifting his arse up into my hand for more. I gave him a firm slap instead and he yelped.

"Hey! What was that for?" He glared at me as he reached down and rubbed the offended flesh.

"I couldn't help it, it was just out there, begging to be spanked," I explained, laughing at his bottom lip sticking out in a pout.

Kicking the covers off he flipped me onto my back and climbed over me so that he was straddling my waist. I leaned up and tried to capture that beautiful lip with my mouth, but he pulled back just out of reach as he held my wrists firmly in place above my head. He smirked at me devilishly and began a slow and steady grind of his hips against mine. Neither one of us were wearing any clothes and my eyes rolled back in my head at the first touch of his cock against my own. He leaned down and I could feel his hot breath against my ear.

"When I hear words like *spank* come out of that proper British mouth, do you know what it makes me want to do to you?" he purred. I warbled an incoherent response, too overwhelmed by the purposeful sway of his hips to make any sort of sense.

"It makes me want to do very, very naughty things to you." I moaned as he licked the outer shell of my ear. "Unfortunately, those things will have to wait." *Huh?* My eyes sprang open when I felt a gust of cool air against my skin and saw him climbing off of the bed.

"Wait! Where are you going?" I cried out. He stopped at the foot of the bed and tilted his head at me.

"What? I thought you wanted to go for an early morning run," he said with mock innocence. I growled and lunged for him, but he sprang back with a laugh. "Do try and hurry, dear, it's nearly light out already," he said in a terrible imitation of a British accent.

I threw a pillow at his retreating form and he laughed, tossing me a saucy wink over one shoulder. With a little extra sway to his hips he disappeared into the bathroom. My cock was frustrated at the turn of events, but I couldn't help the smile that spread across my face. *God, how I love that man.*

Rylie ran alongside me, keeping pace. As much as he complained about having to get up at what he humorously referred to as the ass crack of dawn, he was getting stronger each day and I no longer needed to hold back and wait for him to catch up, not that I'd minded that in the least. We'd been running for about fifteen minutes when he suddenly slowed.

"Are you alright?" I asked, slowing my pace as well.

"Yeah, I need a drink," he explained. We stopped and I handed him a bottle of water from my pack.

I eyed him around my own bottle of water as I took a long sip. His hair was pulled up in a bun on top of his head and sweat ran down his neck, soaking the front of his shirt. My eyes zeroed in on his mouth as he poured water into it, his throat working to swallow the liquid and I wanted to lean forward and lick the sweat from his body. I was still worked up from his little prank that morning and I didn't know how I was going to make it through the entire day before I would finally have him back in my bed and could do something about it.

"We've been running for quite a while, are we still on your property?" he asked.

"Yes," I answered, wondering how he could talk about property lines when all I wanted to do was strip him down and maul him. His next move answered my question.

"Good, then we shouldn't get in any trouble for what I'm about to do to you," he growled, tossing his bottle aside and pulling his shirt up over his head as he stalked towards me. I backed up instinctively until a tree stopped my progress.

"It looks like you have nowhere to go," Rylie said with a wolfish grin.

I didn't bother to tell him that I wasn't really trying to escape because I was sure that my rapid breathing and the look in my eyes had already given me away. If not, then the fact that I was peeling my shirt off too should have done the trick. His eyes devoured me and I shivered when he reached a finger out and let it trail a line down my chest. I sucked in a breath as he reached the waistband of my shorts and then his mouth descended onto mine.

His tongue swept through my waiting mouth, dipping and swirling in a sensual pattern that made my head spin and I grabbed onto his hips to keep from falling. I was forced to break the kiss when the need for air became too great and he moved his attention onto my neck. His wet tongue trailed a path down the side of my neck, lapping at my sweat and his hands reached behind to cup my arse roughly, kneading it in his large palms.

His mouth continued its sensual assault and when he reached the spot at the curve between my neck and shoulder, he bit down, sucking the tender flesh mercilessly. Stars burst behind my eyelids and I threw my arms around his neck and clung to him, pleading with him to mark me. When he was finished, he backed away to admire his handiwork. His pupils were blown wide and he touched the bruise he'd left behind with his fingertip, giving me a predatory grin that curled my toes.

"Please," I whispered and his eyes shot to mine at the sound of my urgency. It was a plea for him to take me, love me, mark me as his own so the world would have no doubt that I was his. He stared at me for a long moment and it felt as if he could see directly into my soul. I stared back, unblinking, offering myself to him in every way possible.

"Take your shorts off and turn around," he instructed and I released a breath I hadn't realized I'd been holding. I quickly followed his command, tossing my shorts and briefs on top of my shirt and turning to face away from him. I heard the crinkling of a foil package and I shivered in anticipation. I wondered briefly if he'd planned the whole thing out, but then decided I didn't care as his body pressed up against my back.

"I'm going to fuck you," he whispered into my ear, flicking the tip of his tongue inside. "But first, I want to eat your ass." I nearly came from his words alone and I bit my lip, trying to pull myself back from the edge. He reached around and took my hands, bending my body in half and placing my hands on either side of the tree. "You're going to want to hold on," he informed me.

My head dropped down between my shoulders at the first swipe of his flattened tongue. Wet heat tickled over my hole, awakening the nerve endings and making me moan embarrassingly. I loved to get rimmed, but had never found a partner that went at it with as much enthusiasm as Rylie. He buried his whole face between my spread cheeks and feasted on me like he was a starving man and I was his last meal.

He alternated between tracing the outer rim of my hole with the tip of his tongue and sliding a wet finger inside to coax the muscles open. When he speared his tongue and began dipping it inside of me over and over, I cried out, afraid that I was going to lose control. I let out a shaky sigh when I felt him move to a standing position behind me, giving me a momentary reprieve. Rylie's hand smoothed over my sweat-soaked back and then I felt his erection press against my entrance.

I took a deep breath and forced myself to relax as he spread my hole bigger and wider around the broad head of his cock. When the mushroomed tip finally popped through the tight ring of muscle, we both moaned. Rylie curled his body over mine and licked a straight line up my spine.

"So fucking perfect," he whispered.

He moved slowly at first, easing me into it with gentle glides. That proved to not be enough for either one of us though and soon he was using punctuated thrusts which hit my prostate with perfect accuracy. I'd never been much of an exhibitionist, but there was something deliciously sinful about having sex outdoors and even though we were on private property, it was still a rush to imagine that someone could walk along the same path and catch us in the act.

The rough bark of the tree tore into my palms, but I registered only pleasure as he continued to fill me. Rylie halted his movements as he bent down and dribbled more spit onto his cock to help lubricate our movements then his hands gripped my hips roughly, urging me to move. I began rocking back and forth, using the tree to push off of.

"God, you feel so good, baby. I wish you could see us from this angle, so sexy the way your hole grips onto me like it doesn't want to let go." Rylie continued his dirty talk, creating images in my mind that spurred me on and soon, I could feel my orgasm closing in around me.

I felt his movements falter and he reached forward, gripping my shoulders in his hands and began pounding into me with a renewed vengeance. I fought to hold myself steady, but then I was caught in an orgasm so powerful that it blurred the edges of my vision. The world around us disappeared and all that existed was the feel of Rylie's body pressed to mine. I was aware of his strong arms wrapping around me and his breath in my ear.

"I've got you, I won't let you fall," he promised. I lowered my head, trusting him to keep me safe as I drifted.

When everything had stopped spinning, I blinked my eyes open and found that we were on the ground and Rylie had me cradled in his lap. He kept smoothing a hand over my cheek and his eyes were filled with what could best be described as awe. We didn't say anything for the longest time as we stared into each other's eyes, but then we didn't need to. It felt as if an entire conversation was taking place with just that one look. A conversation that spoke of connection, trust, and happiness.

"I love you," I whispered, before my brain could catch up with my mouth.

"What?" Rylie stiffened and his jaw dropped open as he stared down at me in shock. I scrambled to sit up then I grabbed onto his hands, my eyes pleading with him not to run away.

"I'm sorry, I didn't mean to spring it on you that way," I rushed to explain. Rylie's eyes widened even further and he sucked in a breath.

"Wait, so…you weren't…you weren't just saying that because of some leftover orgasmic bliss or something?" he stuttered.

I took a deep breath. The moment I had agonized over for so long was finally right there in front of me. The fear that he would turn away from me had me wanting to grab on to his excuse and run with it, citing it as just a post-orgasmic response brought on by a surge of pheromones, but then I looked at him. His bright blue eyes that even in their shock were filled with trust, his chest which housed one of the kindest and purest hearts I knew, and finally his arms that while decorated in bright splashes of colors, covered scars which not only marred his skin, but had left an indelible mark on his soul. There was no way I could deny him the love I felt, it was time to be honest. I reached up and cradled his face in my hands and I could feel him trembling. I held his gaze, hoping he could see the sincerity in my eyes.

"No, Rylie, I wasn't just saying that. I love you. I am so deeply, passionately, and unconditionally in love with you," I told him. I watched silently as a series of emotions flashed through his eyes.

"Since when?" he asked. It wasn't exactly the response I'd been hoping for, but at least he wasn't running away.

"I'm not really sure when it happened. I've been attracted to you since the first time I saw you, but I was as surprised as you to find that we had so much chemistry between us. Then we started to become friends and my feelings grew from there."

"I don't know what to say. No one has ever told me they loved me before," he admitted and I sent out a silent curse to everyone in his past that had hurt him or made him feel as if he weren't worthy of their love.

"You don't have to say anything. I don't want to put any pressure on you or scare you away, I just needed to tell you how I felt. I still want you to stay, if you..." Rylie cut off my nervous rambling with a press of his lips to mine and my body sagged against his. It was a gentle kiss, but it knocked my socks off just the same. He ended the kiss and leaned his forehead to mine.

"I have no idea what I'm doing and frankly I'm scared to death that I'm going to make a mistake and you'll change your mind, but you should know that I love you too, Lachlan," he whispered. My heart swelled with his words and I slid my hand around the back of his neck.

"I have never felt about anyone else, the way I feel about you. There is nothing you could do or say that would make me quit loving you," I promised. I pulled him towards me and kissed him so soundly that there couldn't possibly be any doubt in his mind how I felt about him. When I pulled back he smiled at me.

"What do we do now?" he asked shyly.

"I say we take it one day at a time and just see where this goes," I suggested.

"Yeah, that sounds good." Rylie's smile was so sweet; I couldn't resist pulling him in for another kiss.

"However, I think we should get dressed first because I'm starting to feel a little strange sitting naked in the middle of the woods," I joked.

He laughed as we both stood and began retrieving our clothes and pulling them back on, sharing glances every few seconds. Once we were dressed, we started walking towards the cut in the woods that would lead us back to the house. I couldn't wipe the smile off my face, especially when he allowed me to reach down and hold his hand. He looked down in surprise at first, but then threaded his fingers through mine, giving me a shy grin. It seemed almost comical given the fact that he had just ravaged me in the middle of the woods, but it was sweet and pure and felt like a new beginning. When we reached the opening to the back yard, I started to walk out, but he grabbed my arm to stop me.

"When did you decide to buy this house, Lachlan? You said it was a recent purchase, but I wasn't the only one surprised to find out that you were living in Chicago. My friends said that you never mentioned it when you talked about taking me somewhere after I got out of rehab." His head was tilted curiously and I could feel heat rising to my face as he stared at me.

"I had my realtor begin looking for something as soon as I heard you were in the hospital," I admitted quietly.

"So, you bought a house, moved across the country, and began working out of your home office all for me?" Rylie's tone was incredulous. It was my turn to back him up to a tree and I did, spreading my hands across his chest.

"You should know that there is nothing in this world that I wouldn't do for you," I told him. I wanted to say more, to promise him that I would show him a love like he had never known if only he would give me the chance, but he looked so shell shocked that I was afraid to push my luck. Instead, I pressed my lips to his and let them speak for me. We were both breathless when we finally broke apart, but I saw him smile as we turned and continued walking towards the house. The morning had definitely been full of surprises.

CHAPTER
Fifteen

Rylie/Rocko

I T HAD BEEN A WEEK SINCE LACHLAN AND I HAD ADMITTED HOW we felt about each other and we'd continued to grow closer every day. On the surface, nothing had really changed, we still enjoyed spending our evenings together when he was finished working for the day and we continued to spend every night wrapped around each other. Below the surface however, I could sense a deeper connection between the two of us and the feeling that I wasn't alone in the world anymore.

I was still shocked that anyone, especially a man as amazing as Lachlan, could fall in love with me and there was a small voice inside that kept telling me that it would all come to an end once he found out what I'd done. Guilt had washed over me when he'd said that he'd begun falling in love with me as he'd gotten to know the real Rylie

Anderson because I knew that I was hiding a big part of who I was. I loved Lachlan more than I ever thought I could possibly love someone else and even though the thought of losing him terrified me, I knew that I would have to eventually be honest with him.

I shook off my thoughts as I turned onto a new street and began searching for a place to park. I'd been surprised when Lachlan had offered to let me take one of his cars because that would be the first time I would be going anywhere on my own. He explained that Hudson had cautioned him in the beginning to set up boundaries for me which would give me a sense of security as I recovered. However, after talking with Hudson about my progress they'd agreed that I was strong enough to set my own boundaries. I'd felt a sense of pride that they recognized the changes I'd made and I felt renewed in my own efforts to keep getting stronger.

I pulled up alongside the curb and turned the car off. I'd tried to choose the least flashy car Lachlan owned for the trip, not wanting to stand out like a sore thumb in the run-down neighborhood, but that was nearly impossible with his collection of vintage muscle cars and sleek sports cars. I'd finally settled on a black 1968 Shelby Mustang and had immediately fallen in love with it. I was quickly beginning to understand Lachlan's fascination with old cars.

I locked the car and then stared up at the tall building in front of me. On the outside, it was unimpressive and blended in with all of the other buildings in the neighborhood, but what was happening on the inside was nothing short of miraculous. Hudson had suggested that I start volunteering somewhere a few days a week as part of my recovery program. He said that most addicts felt like they'd been a drain on their loved ones and that volunteer work often gave them a way to give back and to feel like a contributing member of society once again.

I'd talked with Carter about Hudson's idea while we were in Vegas and explained that I wanted to find a place that helped LGBTQ youth and he'd told me about Agape House. When he'd described how the center helped teens who were often living on the streets after their parents became abusive or kicked them out when they found out they weren't straight, I knew that it was exactly the kind of place I'd been looking for. As soon as I'd gotten back from Las Vegas, I'd gotten in touch with Matt, the owner of the center who had sounded very excited about my offer to volunteer, stating that he would love for me to come in and have a look around and see if it was the right fit for me. I did and before I'd left that day, I'd signed up to volunteer three days a week.

The staff there were very friendly and appreciative of the volunteers, making me feel at ease as I tried to find what role I could fill. I wasn't handy with tools and I didn't feel like I was smart enough to help them with their math homework, but I could proofread their papers, help out in the kitchen, and teach them to play the drums. It felt good to be useful to someone and to be helping to make a difference in those kids' lives. I was happy to help out however I was needed, but my favorite times were right after they'd finished their homework for the day and were free to choose their own activities. That was when they'd break apart into smaller groups and play games or watch TV and it was the best time to just talk and get to know them better.

At first, the kids were a little standoffish with me. I was sure they'd heard many stories about me in the news and how I used to be a wild party animal and some of them were wary, particularly the ones who had grown up with parents who were addicts. I'd used my vices as a way to shield myself from the pain of my past, but I didn't want to hide with those kids. I wanted them to see the real me and just maybe some of them would be able to put down their own shields and stay true to themselves instead of making the same mistakes I had. Once I'd started talking to them and they could see that I wasn't the same person they'd seen in the headlines, they began opening up to me.

I was surprised to find out that most of them had stories similar to mine. Many of them had been in the foster care system for years, getting bounced from one home to the next and never feeling like they really fit in anywhere. Agape House was the one place they could go to where people looked forward to seeing them and accepted them exactly as they were. I smiled at Isaac, the front desk manager, as I walked in. He was a vibrant young man who always had a cheery smile on his face and that time was no different.

"Hey, Rocko, how are you?" he asked in his soft voice. So far, only Lachlan, Hudson, and my bandmates knew my real name and I wasn't sure if I'd ever tell anyone else. Lachlan had assured me that it was up to me when and who I told and that if I never wanted to tell anyone else, I didn't have to.

"I'm great, how's everything here?" I responded.

"Well, today is special because it's Jenn's birthday. The kids all wanted to make cupcakes so Matt told them that as soon as they finished their homework they could start."

"Sounds like fun," I said, but Isaac shook his head and snickered which had me questioning my answer.

"Sounds like a mess and you know how Gladys is about keeping her kitchen clean," he said. "Do them all a favor and keep an eye on things, would you?"

"No problem." I understood what had caused his laughter. Gladys was a sweet lady who loved all of the kids as if they were her own, but she ran her kitchen with a military precision. Rumor had it that she'd even made Caleb and Giovanni scrub the pots until they could see their reflections in them after they helped cook the Thanksgiving feast the year before. Whatever had made Matt decide to unleash over twenty-five teenagers into the kitchen was beyond me.

I wandered through the hallway, smiling when the kids' voices got louder as I approached the rec room where they all gathered after school. The building was old and needed a lot of work done to it, but I could see how much effort the staff had put into making it seem as homey as possible for the kids. There were cozy area rugs on the floors, colorful throw pillows on the various furniture throughout the rooms, and framed pictures of the center's kids hanging on the walls.

The thing that had struck me the most the first time I'd volunteered there was the genuine care the staff showed the kids beyond the walls of the center. Not only did the staff help the older kids find jobs and apply for funding so they could attend college if they wanted to, but it wasn't uncommon for them to spend their evenings attending parent teacher conferences, plays, or art shows that the kids were involved in. The staff there treated the kids like their parents should have treated them in the first place and I wished that more of society would do the same.

"Hey! Rocko's here!" I heard shouted across the room as I walked in and nearly every head swiveled in my direction.

"Hey, guys! How's it going?" I responded with a big smile. It felt good to be back there. Several of the kids came over and gave me a high-five or a hug and others waved excitedly from where they were sitting. I noticed the pretty raven-haired girl sitting on the floor and narrowed my eyes at her. She looked up at me curiously.

"I heard something, but it had to be wrong," I said, scratching my jaw and continuing to study her.

"What did you hear?" she asked with a small smile.

"I heard that today was your birthday, but it can't be because you don't look old to me," I teased.

"That's because I'm only fifteen, not old like you," she joked back, covering her mouth to hide a giggle.

"Old? You think I'm old?" I cried, clutching my chest melodramatically. "You wound me, Jenn. You really do." She couldn't contain her peals of laughter any more, especially when the others joined in with their own jokes about how old I was. I pretended to be hurt by each new joke that was lobbed my way, but inside I was just thrilled to hear them laughing and being kids. I couldn't help but wonder how different things may have been for me if I'd had a place like Agape House to go to when I was growing up.

I was whistling as I walked in the front door of Lachlan's home. I'd had a great time making cupcakes with the kids and had stayed longer than usual to help clean up the mess they'd left behind. It had been hard not to laugh when Matt had walked in and Gladys had turned a full glare on him. He'd kissed her on the cheek and then joined in, good naturedly scrubbing the countertops until they passed her inspection.

I didn't know Matt all that well, he had always seemed very quiet and kept to himself most of the times I had been there, but he was completely different when he was with the kids. He smiled and laughed with them and gave them his full attention when they were speaking to him. I could see why he was so adored by everyone there, although there were times when he thought that no one was looking when he'd get a faraway, almost sad look in his eyes and I wondered what he was thinking about. I set down the box of cupcakes that the kids had insisted I take home with me, still whistling when a voice startled me from behind.

"It sounds like someone had a good day." I smiled when I heard the British accent that made my heart race every time and then I felt his arms circle around my waist.

"I had a great day, actually, but it just got even better," I told him, letting my head drop back onto his shoulder and wrapping my arms securely over his. He nuzzled his nose into my hair and I heard him take a deep breath as we began swaying back and forth to a song only we heard.

"I missed you while you were gone," he whispered and my heart squeezed in my chest, no one had ever missed me before.

I turned my head, offering him my lips. His mouth slid over mine and I licked at the seam of his lips until he opened then I slid my tongue into his mouth, reacquainting myself with his flavor. It had surprised me at how easy it had been for me to show him how I felt for him, considering the fact that I had no experience with that kind of thing whatsoever, but then again, loving Lachlan felt as easy as breathing. It was almost hard to imagine a time when I didn't have him in my life, in my arms like he was right then.

"Why don't you take me upstairs and show me how much you missed me," I whispered. Lachlan groaned and laid his forehead against mine. I turned in his arms so I could see him, wrapping my arms around his waist so we were still connected.

"What's wrong, baby?" I asked.

"Nothing's wrong," he assured me quickly. "I'm just trying to be good and you're making it very difficult for me." He thrust his hips against mine and I could feel his rigid erection, emphasizing his meaning. I reached between our bodies and cupped his groin in my hand then gave him a wicked grin.

"Why would you want to be good when you know how much I love it when you're very, very bad?" I teased, smiling when he whimpered.

"Because," he said. My eyes widened when he stepped just out of my reach. Lachlan had never turned down sex before and I was curious to know why he was doing so when he obviously wanted it as much as I did. He ran his fingers through his hair and took a deep breath, trying to calm himself then he looked at me with a shy smile.

"I know we've gone about things a bit backward, but I was wondering if you'd like to have dinner with me. Somewhere outside of my home," he tacked on nervously. A warm feeling washed over me as I realized what was going on.

"Are you asking me to go out on a date with you, Lachlan?" I asked.

"Yes, that's exactly what I'm asking," he answered quietly. "I want to take you out, do something special for you the way you deserve." *Just when I thought I couldn't love him more, he goes and proves me wrong.* I reached out and grabbed onto his hips, pulling him closer to me.

"I would be happy to go anywhere with you," I whispered, brushing my lips across his. "Thank you for asking me." Lachlan kissed me back gently and then backed away, biting his bottom lip like he was very pleased with himself.

"Alright then, I'm going to go get ready and we'll leave in say... an hour?"

"I'll be ready," I told him with a grin. I watched him, admiring the view of his perky ass as he climbed the stairs. He looked over his shoulder and gave me a wink and I laughed. He knew me so well.

"May I have a word please, Rocko?" The smile slid off my face and my shoulders slumped. *It had been such a nice day.*

"Are you sure you'll be satisfied with just one word, Benji?" I pivoted to where he was standing, not bothering to hide my sarcasm. "I have a feeling you've got a lot more than one word you've been saving for me." I paused when I saw the worried expression on his face. I'd become used to the scowl that always seemed to appear on his face whenever I was around, so to see the look of concern marring his features was disconcerting.

"Is something wrong?" I asked.

"That depends on your answer to my question." I narrowed my eyes at him and crossed my arms over my chest.

"Okay, Benji, I'll take the bait. What's your question?"

"What are your intentions toward Lachlan?" he demanded.

"My what?" I sputtered. Benjamin straightened when he heard my laughter and the familiar frown lines appeared between his eyes.

"This is not a laughing matter, I assure you," he stated firmly. "Now, are you quite finished?" I chuckled a few more times and then nodded once I'd gotten myself under control.

"Sorry, please continue," I said. It was funny seeing him get all parental, but I could tell that he was completely serious about what he had to say and if it had to do with Lachlan then it was important to me too.

"I don't know if you are aware of this, but Lachlan means a great deal to me. His parents were never around when he was growing up," he shook his head as if remembering something unpleasant. "I used to beg them to come home and spend some time with their boys. I tried to reason with them that their children needed them, but they were too caught up in their own lives." Benjamin rolled his eyes. "Oh, they would pop in at Christmas and their birthdays and lavish the boys with expensive gifts, but that was more about easing their own guilt than about wanting to spend quality time with their sons."

I pictured the photo that I had seen of Lachlan and Spencer when they were little boys and I rubbed my chest. My heart hurt for the pain that their parents must have caused them. I knew what it was like to ache for a parent that wasn't there and I hated that Lachlan had gone through that. My protective instincts kicked in and I wanted to race up the stairs and take him in my arms.

"Kerry and I tried to step in and fill the void their parents had left behind. I know it wasn't the same, but Lachlan and Spencer never complained." Benjamin smiled ruefully. "That's not to say they were perfect angels, mind you. They were typical boys, I lost count of how many things ended up broken because they were wrestling inside the house or the number of times they made Kerry shriek because they had decided to bring some live, squirmy thing into the kitchen." He laughed at the memories and I smiled. I was seeing Benjamin in a new light and I could tell how much he cared about Lachlan.

"Those boys were each other's best friend. They preferred spending time together instead of inviting their friends over from school. Even when Spencer enlisted with the Royal Air Force, they wrote each other and talked on the phone as much as possible." I watched as his face crumpled. "Then the unthinkable happened and Spencer was killed. We were all devastated, but Lachlan was hit the hardest. He withdrew from everyone, he quit going out with friends, barely slept, and we had to force him to eat just to keep his strength up." My heart ached for the man I loved as I listened to Benjamin's story and I wished I would have known Lachlan then so I could have tried to help him through that painful time.

"He told me how Spencer died and that Micah was there." My voice was strained and I swallowed hard around the lump in my throat. "He told me that's how he met Hudson." Benjamin nodded his head.

"Yes, Micah has been a good friend to Lachlan and Hudson helped bring him out of his depression," he said. "We were finally starting to see signs of the old Lachlan again, but not quite. He would smile on occasion and join in on conversations, but it was like the light in him had burned out forever. He had always been a hard worker, but suddenly that was *all* he did." Benjamin cocked his head and narrowed his eyes as he stared at me and I fidgeted, feeling like a bug under a microscope.

"Then one day, out of the blue Lachlan announced that we were moving to Chicago. When I asked him why the rush, all he would tell me was that someone needed help and he was going to be there for them." Warmth spread throughout my body. I still couldn't believe that Lachlan had gone to such lengths to help me and that was before we even became friends. I was reminded yet again what an incredible man I was in love with.

"He's been different ever since you arrived here," Benjamin said. "At first, I think he was just determined to help you, but then I started noticing that he was smiling more and joining us for dinner instead of eating in his office while he worked. He laughed for the first time in over a year and it was all because of you."

My head was spinning as I wondered if everything he was saying was true. I knew all of the ways that Lachlan had helped me and made my life better, but could I really have had that much of an impact on Lachlan's life? Was it possible that he needed me as much as I needed him? I looked at Benjamin and wondered why he was frowning at me.

"I've kept my eye on you since you arrived, first because I was curious as to why Lachlan was so determined to help you and especially when I noticed you and Lachlan becoming closer." He held his hand up in front of him. "Please understand that I am beyond thrilled that Lachlan seems to have found happiness and I will forever be grateful to you for being the reason for that happiness, but I worry what will happen if you leave. So, that brings me back to my original question. What are your intentions with Lachlan?"

That time I didn't laugh, because there was nothing funny about his question. I finally understood why Benjamin had always seemed cold to me. He had basically raised Lachlan as if he were his own son. He'd watched helplessly as Lachlan's world had crumbled around him and then he'd felt as if he may never get his son back as Lachlan had been swallowed up by his misery. Benjamin had been happy when Lachlan began to return to who he'd been before he lost Spencer so it just made sense that he would be worried that I was going to do something to send Lachlan back to that dark void. He was simply a father trying to protect his son and I had more respect for that than he would ever know.

"Benjamin." His eyes widened just a fraction and I wasn't sure if it was because of my serious tone or the fact that I had used his proper name. "I understand why you would be worried. I was a complete disaster when I first came here. I was rude and flippant to you and I'm sorry." His jaw dropped, but he nodded at me.

"I've had to work through a lot of issues and I'm still working through them. I'm sarcastic, obnoxious sometimes, and I still fight my cravings for drugs and alcohol every day. You have every reason to doubt me." Benjamin's lips were pinched tightly as he glared down at the floor. "But, I have never had anyone love me before." Benjamin's head shot back up at that and I took a deep breath.

"It's not just that no one's ever loved me as much as Lachlan has or loved me as well as Lachlan has; it's that no one has. Ever. Loved. Me." I smiled at him, hoping he'd understand. "Yet somehow, my first try, I ended up with the most kind and loving and selfless man I've ever met in my life. I feel like I've won the lottery and it doesn't have a damn thing to do with money." I paused to take a breath and Benjamin waited patiently. I couldn't get a good read on what he was thinking and that made me nervous, but I pushed on.

"I understand why you're worried, I worry all the time that I'm going to do something stupid and Lachlan will realize that he made a mistake in choosing me, but the one thing you will never have to worry about is me deliberately hurting him or deciding I don't want him anymore. I can promise you that will never happen. I am happier and more whole than I have ever been in my entire life and it's all because of that man up there," I said, pointing towards Lachlan's room at the top of the stairs. "He is my whole world and all I want to do is make him as happy as he has made me." I was shaking by the time I was finished. I had never offered up so many of my feelings at one time and it had to happen with Benjamin of all people. He stared at me for a few moments and then he stepped forward and stuck his hand out towards me. I looked down at it in shock, but I managed to reach out and shake his hand.

"Thank you, Rocko. I know there are no guarantees in life, but I can see the honesty in your eyes and I can tell how much you love Lachlan. That's good enough for me." Relief swelled over me and I opened my mouth before I could stop myself.

"Does that mean you don't hate me anymore, Benji?" I wished I could take the words back as soon as they left my mouth, so I was surprised when he threw his head back and laughed.

"I suppose I will learn to tolerate you," he answered.

"I'll get you to like me someday," I promised.

"You stick around and I suppose I will." He patted me on the shoulder as he walked past me. I stood there smiling at the fact that everything seemed to finally be falling into place in my life, but Benjamin's voice interrupted my thoughts.

"Shouldn't you hurry and get ready? You don't want to keep your date waiting." I sucked in a breath. I'd almost forgotten that Lachlan wanted to take me out on my very first date. I could hear Benjamin's laughter as I raced up the stairs to get ready.

I stood in front of the mirror, making sure I looked alright. I'd taken a quick shower and washed my hair, then dried it, deciding to let it hang down my back the way I knew Lachlan preferred it. I hadn't thought to ask him where we were going so I had no idea how to dress. I hoped that my dark blue jeans and black polo shirt would be alright, but I supposed I could change into my suit from the wedding if I needed something fancier. A knock at my bedroom door drew my attention and I walked across the room and opened it, a smile spreading across my face when I saw who was on the other side.

Lachlan was dressed in a pair of jeans and a white linen button-up shirt and he was holding a bouquet of fire and ice roses. "These are for you." He smiled as he handed them to me and I smiled back, feeling strangely shy.

"Thank you. You look amazing," I told him, running my eyes over his thick dark hair, warm golden eyes, and perfectly plump lips. He was beautiful to me in every way and I couldn't believe that I was the one he wanted.

"You're perfect," he whispered. My eyes shot to his and I realized he was looking at me the same way I had been looking at him.

"I thought we were going to meet downstairs. Was I taking too long?"

"No," he said, stepping closer. I breathed in, enjoying the spicy scent of his aftershave and my favorite smell of all, Lachlan. "This is our first date so I wanted to do it right and pick you up at your door."

"Since it's our first date, does that mean I'm not going to get lucky later?" I teased.

"What kind of guy do you take me for?" he joked back. I heard his swift intake of breath as I leaned in and bit gently at his bottom lip.

"You're my guy so I'll take you or you can take me, but either way one of us is going to be buried inside the other by the end of the night," I promised. I stepped back, pleased with the dazed look on his face and the slight flush to his skin. "Are you ready to go?"

Lachlan mumbled an incoherent reply and I smirked as we left my room and made our way down the steps. Kerry was waiting at the bottom of the stairs with a big smile on her face and I elbowed Lachlan in the side when I heard him sigh. I knew he wasn't really frustrated with her, but after everything Benjamin had told me, I understood why Kerry was so excited to see Lachlan being happy.

"Let me take those flowers, Rocko. I'll put them in water for you." I handed her the roses and she giggled when I gave her a kiss on the cheek.

We stepped outside and I saw that Lachlan already had a car waiting for us at the bottom of the steps. It was my favorite out of Lachlan's collection, the same Koenigsegg that I had taken the day I went out with Hudson. I smiled when he held the door open for me like a true gentleman. I turned to him with a smile when he climbed into the driver's seat.

"So where are you taking me?" I asked.

"You'll have to wait and see, it's a surprise," he explained.

"Lucky for you, I happen to like surprises," I informed him.

"And I happen to like you, a lot." Lachlan leaned over and kissed me, just a gentle press of his lips to mine, but it was enough to leave me breathless. He made me feel so damn special with everything, not only our date, but also in the way he looked at me or spoke to me. He showed me with his actions that I was the most important person in the world to him.

I knew that it was time to tell him the disgusting truth about my past. I owed it to him to be completely honest and let him decide if I was still the person he wanted to be with. My blood turned to ice in my veins at the thought of him sending me away, but I did my best to push the fear to the back of my mind. I wasn't going to let anything spoil the perfect night Lachlan had planned for us.

CHAPTER
Sixteen

Rylie/Rocko

I woke the next morning and smiled when I saw Lachlan still sleeping beside me, his hair messy and his jaw pink from rubbing against my stubble, both evidence of the passionate end to our date. Lachlan had planned everything out perfectly for our date. We stopped at Romero's, the restaurant that Caleb and Giovanni owned together, but when I started to get out, Lachlan winked at me and told me to wait in the car. Afterwards he'd driven us to Grant Park where we enjoyed a picnic dinner while we watched the light show on Buckingham Fountain. I had never realized how much of a sucker I was for romance until Lachlan Edwards decided to romance me.

We'd ended the evening with a candlelit bubble bath where we talked until the water turned too cool for our liking and then we'd climbed into bed and made love. It was sensual and erotic as we took our time memorizing each other's bodies and then fell asleep wrapped around one another. I'd woken in the middle of the night, reaching for him before I was even fully awake, but he'd met my demands eagerly and we'd enjoyed a round of sheet-clawing, name-screaming, sweat-dripping sex. It was the most intense sex I'd ever had in my life and I knew it had very little to do with the physical act and everything to do with the man I was with. The slightest touch of his hand could light my body on fire.

"What are you thinking about?" I looked up at him, smiling when I heard the accent I loved so much. He was wearing a soft smile and the sunlight streaming through the window showed off his natural highlights and made his eyes turn to liquid gold.

"Good morning." I leaned in for a kiss and he met me with lips still soft from sleep. My fingers traced the firm line of his jaw. "I was just thinking about what an amazing time I had last night, it was by far the best night of my life."

"It was for me too. Of course, I cherish any time I have with you, even if all we're doing is talking." Lachlan played with the ends of my hair, absentmindedly wrapping the strands around his finger and his eyes were filled with adoration as he gazed at me.

With a contented sigh, I laid my head on his chest and listened to the gentle thrumming of his heart. When I'd first arrived at Lachlan's home, I never would have imagined that I'd end up in his arms, feeling more love and security than I'd ever known. I'd heard couples, like Carter and Ryan or Tyler and Kalia, talking about how they'd found their soulmate and I always wondered if that was a real thing or something thought up by the greeting card companies. But, lying in bed with Lachlan and feeling the way our bodies and our thoughts seemed to fit together like two puzzle pieces was enough to convince me that soulmates were in fact a real thing and I'd been lucky enough to find mine.

We dozed for a while longer until our stomachs reminded us

that it was time for breakfast. With one last kiss, I made my way down the hall and began getting ready for the day. I smiled when I remembered that Lachlan had asked me to move my things into his room. It shouldn't have been such a big deal, considering I was already staying in his house and sleeping in his bed every night, but it was a big deal to me because it signified my role in his life.

I hurried through my morning bathroom ritual and pulled a pair of soft jeans and my favorite band t-shirt on. I didn't feel like messing with my hair, so I yanked a brush through it and pulled it up into a simple ponytail. Lachlan was waiting for me when I stepped out of my room and we walked downstairs together, holding hands.

We walked into the kitchen and stopped dead in our tracks. Benjamin had Kerry backed up against the refrigerator and was kissing the daylights out of her. By the way she was gripping his arms I could only assume that the old boy still had game. Lachlan winked at me and then cleared his throat loudly. They turned and looked at us with surprise. Kerry's face turned a pretty shade of red as she tried to fix the hair that had come loose from her bun. Benjamin on the other hand wrapped his arm around her proudly and faced us head on.

"If you thought that you two were the only ones permitted to woo your true love, then you were sadly mistaken." His words were spoken stiffly, but he gave us a quick wink.

"True love?" Lachlan asked. He looked back and forth between them as Kerry fidgeted and Benjamin eyed him warily. Lachlan turned to me. "Honey, it appears that my parents have fallen in love with each other."

He said it jokingly, but I could see the impact it had on the two older people when Lachlan referred to them as his parents. Then Lachlan squeezed my hand and I realized that he knew, of course he knew. He was the most sensitive and caring man in the world. He walked over to them and gave Kerry a hug and shook hands with Benjamin.

"Are you sure you're alright with us being together, dear?" Kerry asked worriedly.

"I couldn't be happier," he told them. "I'm just glad Benjamin finally took a chance, I was getting tired of watching the moony eyes he was always making when you weren't looking."

Kerry slapped Lachlan's chest playfully and gave him a look like he was crazy. "I was well aware of his moony eyes, but he was taking forever to make his move. That's why *I* took the initiative." I laughed loudly at the smug look on her face and the way Lachlan's jaw dropped. She winked at me and turned to finish getting breakfast ready. I poured drinks for everyone and then took a seat next to Lachlan who was still watching the two as they moved around the kitchen with a faraway look in his eyes.

"Are you okay?" I covered his hand with mine on the table and he turned to me.

"Yes, I was just thinking how happy Spencer would've been to have seen them together. He always worried that their devotion to the two of us caused them to miss out on having a life of their own. I think he'd be relieved to know that they're not alone anymore." He smiled at me. "And that I'm not either." He reached up and cupped my face and I grabbed his wrist, placing a kiss on the palm of his hand.

Kerry had outdone herself with a wonderful breakfast of homemade bread, fresh fruits, and warm crepes. I'm sure it was delicious, but I'd lost my appetite just thinking about what I needed to do.

As much as I dreaded telling him about my past, I couldn't put it off any longer. It would gut me if the loving look in his eyes changed to disgust, but I'd understand. After all, I'd spent years being ashamed of myself. All I could do was be honest with him and hope that my honesty didn't cost me the love of my life. When we'd finished eating, Kerry and Benjamin busied themselves with cleaning the kitchen so I took a deep breath and turned to Lachlan.

"Lachlan, I know you're probably very busy today with a lot of meetings, but I was wondering…" I trailed off as my nerves started to get the better of me.

"What is it, Rylie?" He looked at me with concern. He must have seen the panic in my eyes because he grabbed my hand and quickly pulled me out of the room. When the door shut behind us, he wrapped his arms around me and hugged me tight. "You can tell me. Whatever it is, I'll help you."

I squeezed my eyes shut and pulled him closer, my hands fisting in the material of his shirt. I was shaking, but he held me together, rubbing his hands in soothing circles over my back and giving me time to speak. There was nowhere safer in the entire world than in his arms and I had no idea what I was going to do if I lost the right to hold him like that.

"I need to tell you the truth." My voice was muffled from where I'd buried my face against his shoulder, but I could tell he'd heard me because he stiffened slightly in my arms. "I need to tell you and Hudson, but I don't think I can do it more than once. Would you please be there with me when I talk to Hudson? I need to tell you everything and then you can decide if you want me to leave." Lachlan pulled back quickly and looked at me. I was having a difficult time making eye contact with him so he lifted my chin, forcing me to look into his eyes.

"I will be there, if you're sure you're ready, but nothing you say is going to make me change my mind about you. I love you." He leaned forward and kissed me and even though I knew he believed what he had just said, there was that small voice inside of me that kept whispering that he'd be a fool to want me after he heard the truth.

Lachlan excused himself to make a phone call that would clear his schedule for the entire day. I felt guilty, knowing that many of them were probably multi-million-dollar meetings, but he kept insisting that I was more important than anything on his agenda and he wanted to spend the day with me. Hudson arrived a few minutes later and I explained to him what I wanted to do. He was happy that I was ready to talk, but he wanted to make sure I was positive that I wanted Lachlan in the room when it happened.

"I know you two care about each other, but most of the time it's very overwhelming for clients to open up about the painful parts of their past. Are you sure you want him here for all of that?" His brown eyes were gentle as he waited for my answer. I took a deep breath and blew it out.

"Yeah, I'm sure. I know Lachlan may hate me when he hears what I have to say, but I need to do this, you know? Otherwise, it's just going to stay there in the back of my mind and it'll be this *thing* between us. I love him, Hudson, and I don't want anything to come between us. If he can't handle what I have to tell him, then it's better that I find out now rather than five years from now." I looked down at my arms which were crossed protectively over my chest. I could see the raised scars underneath the colorful tattoos and I clenched my jaw then looked back up at Hudson.

"Besides, I'm tired of letting this thing control me. I tried to push it down and bury it, but instead it festered and grew into this sickness that became so painful that the only thing that helped was numbing myself with drugs and alcohol. I can't live like that anymore; I don't *want* to live like that anymore. I know that the only way to really make that happen is to tell the truth and then hopefully you'll still be willing to help me and I can begin to move past all of it." Hudson smiled at me warmly.

"Not to sound condescending or anything, but I'm proud of you. You've come a long way from when we first met and I believe you are finally on the right track to being able to heal the pain inside of you. No matter what you have to tell us, I will continue to be there for you and I'm not going anywhere until we both agree that you don't need me anymore." My eyes burned and I swallowed around the lump in my throat. All I could manage was a slight nod.

Lachlan walked back into his office and we all sat down, Lachlan beside me on the couch and Hudson in the chair across from us. Usually, I preferred to have our sessions outside, but that time, I'd decided I needed the security of having four walls around me. I had never told anyone about my past and something about being outside seemed too open and exposed for what I had to say.

"So, Rylie, you said you wanted to tell us about your past. Would you like me to help guide you through it or would you like to just tell us in your own way?" Hudson asked.

"I think it would be easier if I just talked, if that's okay," I said.

"We can do this however you're most comfortable. You're in control, Rylie. You decide what and how much you want to say and if at any time it gets to be too much, we'll stop, no questions asked," Hudson assured me.

I glanced over at Lachlan who nodded his agreement with what Hudson had said and then as if he couldn't help himself, he leaned over and kissed me. It was a brief kiss, but it was enough to bolster my courage. *God, please don't let that be our last kiss.* I gave him a slight smile as he pulled back and then I began to talk.

"I never knew my parents. From what I was told, I was born to a drug addicted mother who gave me away as soon as she had me and never looked back. I spent the first three weeks of my life going through withdrawal from all of the shit she took while she was pregnant with me." I let out a humorless laugh. "I guess that might be one thing my mother and I had in common, our weakness for drugs." My fingers began tapping out a nervous rhythm along the arm of the couch.

"She didn't even bother to give me a name before she signed me over as a ward of the state. Apparently, the social worker assigned to my case felt sorry for me so she named me after her late grandfather, Rylie Anderson. Not such a bad name I suppose, all things considered. Anyway, she put me on a list for potential adoption, but most young couples looking to adopt wanted a healthy newborn, not one that was underdeveloped and cried for hours on end, so I ended up in the foster care system and never made it out of there." I paused to take a breath.

"I got moved around so much that eventually I quit bothering to unpack my stuff and just left everything in the garbage bags I carried them in. I learned the rules of foster care pretty quick after getting beat up too many times, usually by the other kids living in the house, but occasionally by the adults. Keep your head down, do what you're told, and don't ever tell the social workers what happened behind closed doors." I ticked the rules off with my fingers as I recited them.

"This one kid that I shared a room with for about a month told me about a home he'd been in that was really nice. He said that the mom would help him with his homework and they would all have dinner together every night when the dad got home from work. Then the mom found out she was pregnant with twins and they couldn't afford to keep him there anymore." I closed my eyes, lost in the memory. "I used to hear him crying himself to sleep every night because he missed them and I wondered if maybe I wasn't the luckiest of the two of us because it was hard to miss what you'd never had."

Lachlan made a choking noise and I turned to look at him. His face was pinched and he looked like he was in pain. I reached over and offered him my hand, sorry to be putting him through this. He gave me a look of disbelief, but grabbed onto my hand. I could feel him trembling or maybe it was me, it was hard to tell at that point. All I knew was that holding his hand helped keep me in the present and I held onto that tether like it was my lifeline.

"When I was fifteen, I was placed in a home with a married couple. Dave, the husband, was a truck driver so he was gone for long stretches at a time. Trina, his wife, stayed home and took care of the little ones during the day while Dave was away. There were a couple little girls in the home too, but they weren't theirs. They said they weren't able to have kids of their own and that's why they'd started doing foster care." I was getting to the hardest part of the story and I wouldn't be able to handle it if I felt Lachlan pull away from me, so I pulled away from him first and shifted in my seat.

"I had been at their place for over a month, when Trina came to my room one night. I'd been so excited when I'd been given my own room because I'd always had to share, but in that home I got a room all to myself." I pulled my legs up on the couch and wrapped my arms around my knees. Hudson asked me if I needed to take a break, but I just shook my head and stared at my knees, too ashamed to look at either of them as I continued.

"At first nothing happened. She just slept beside me and I didn't mind it because I was used to having to share my space. Other nights, there were a few touches that she said were accidental and then there was one night where everything changed. She'd just gotten off the phone with Dave and she was crying. She told me that they'd had a big fight and that she didn't feel like Dave wanted her anymore. She said she needed me because I understood what it was like to not be wanted, but that if we were together then neither one of us would have to feel that way again." My hands were shaking as I swiped at the tears that were streaming down my cheeks, but I didn't look up, I couldn't. I knew the shame and disgust that I would find in their eyes and I couldn't face it until I'd gotten everything out.

"When we were together she would tell me how much she loved me and how special I was. At first, I told her that it felt wrong, but she convinced me that all moms did that kind of thing with their sons and I had nothing to compare it to, so I took her word for it. I remember feeling so relieved to finally be someone's son, to finally have a mom that wanted me and loved me. For the next several months she slept in my bed every night, except on the nights when Dave was home. Then one night, he decided to come home early and surprise her." I drew in a shaky breath and wrapped my arms around my legs tighter, trying to hold myself together. *Just a little bit longer.*

"Dave walked in and found us together and he went into a rage. I couldn't understand why he was so upset at first if that was the way all moms and sons behaved, but then he started screaming that I was sick and that I had brought my sickness into his house. I looked to Trina for help, hoping she would explain it to him, but she just stood there crying and saying that she hadn't wanted any of it and that I was a pervert. Dave was a big guy and it only took one punch to knock me out cold." I bit back a sob, forcing myself to finish.

"When I came to, I was locked in a dark closet. They told me that I was bad and that I deserved to stay in there until I could be sent to a new home. I stayed locked in that closet for over a week, long enough for the bruises to heal. No one spoke to me the entire time, the only contact I had was when they would shove food and water in the door and then slam it shut again. Finally, I was let out and Dave warned me not to tell anyone what had happened. I was so relieved to be getting out of there and so ashamed for what I'd done that I never said another word until right now." I swiped at my tears angrily.

"After that, I went to another home where I stayed until I aged out of the system. For most kids in my situation, aging out is a scary thing. Suddenly you have no money and nowhere to go, but for me it meant freedom; freedom to move on and reinvent myself. I could become a whole other person and no one would ever have to know the horrible thing that had happened." I let out a deep breath, knowing I'd made it through the worst of it.

"The dad from the last house I lived in played in a garage band. He used to let me tag along for their practices. The drummer was a nice guy, he showed me all the parts of the drum and let me mess around on his set during their breaks. They all were surprised when they heard me play and they said I was a natural. When I turned eighteen, I packed my things, and headed out. I filled in on the drums for a few bands when their drummer was sick and that helped put enough money in my pocket to keep me fed. It wasn't very hard for me to find people who were willing to let me crash at their place for a night or two, even though it usually came with a price. At first I felt numb when they would touch me, but eventually, I began to enjoy the attention and the feeling of connecting with another human being."

"Then one night, someone told me about a guy that was looking to start his own band. He gave me his number so I texted him and we agreed to meet the next day." I felt myself smiling for the first time since I began telling my story. "He was cute, with a friendly smile and the brightest green eyes I'd ever seen. He introduced himself as Carter and I told him my name was Rocko. I'd made it up in the spur of the moment, but he told me it was a cool name and seemed fitting for a drummer in a rock band. Things took off from there and I found a family within the band. I pushed what had happened out of my mind and just focused on the music and having fun, but there were times when the darkness would creep back in and it would all get to be too much, so I began to drink or smoke marijuana to help me forget. Eventually that wasn't enough and a guy I knew told me about the effects of coke. I tried it and found that he was right, I didn't feel any pain when I had that in my system. Before long, though, the drugs had taken over and you know what happened from there."

The room was quiet. I let out a long breath and laid my head down on my knees. I felt completely drained and I didn't have the strength to look at their reactions. I needed just a few minutes to regroup. I wasn't sure if they sensed that or if they were so disgusted that they were speechless, but either way, they let me have some time to myself.

Finally, I picked my head up. My eyes were sore and itchy from crying and I rubbed them with the heels of my hands before turning to face Hudson. I would find out his reaction first because even if it was bad, it wasn't the reaction that had the power to destroy me. Hudson gave me a small smile and told me that he was so proud of me and that he knew what courage it had taken to share all of that with them. He said that he wanted to begin working right away on rebuilding my perception of myself and of what had happened, but that it could wait until the next day.

"You've been through a lot and I don't want you to get overwhelmed. I think you should take it easy the rest of the day and I'll be back in the morning, alright?" Hudson said.

"Yeah, thanks," I responded quietly. Lachlan stood and shook Hudson's hand.

"Thank you." His voice sounded gravely when he spoke. I was still too afraid to look at Lachlan, but I heard Hudson encouraging him to talk to me. He told Lachlan to call him if we needed anything, no matter what time it was and then he left.

As he shut the door behind him, fear swept through me, fear of seeing hatred on Lachlan's face and fear that I had just destroyed the only chance I had ever had at real love. My eyes filled with fresh tears and I found myself unable to move. I closed my eyes and willed the tears not to spill as I forced myself to speak.

"You're a wonderful man, Lachlan. The finest man I've ever known and I'll understand if you want me to leave." My heart was breaking, but there was no way I would let him feel bad about wanting me to leave after everything he had done for me. I felt the cushions sag beside me as he sat down.

"Why would I want you to leave?" he asked. The catch I heard in his voice had me turning to look at him and I was surprised to see tears streaming down his beautiful face. He reached up and cupped my cheek with his hand and I automatically leaned into his touch.

"I'm not going to lie, it hurt hearing everything you had been through, but that's only because I love you so much. Rylie, you mean the world to me and when you're hurting, I hurt too. I'm also so angry that the people who were supposed to take care of you treated you so terribly and I wish like hell I would have been there so that I could have put a stop to it somehow. I know you blame yourself for a lot of what happened, but none of it was your fault. You were just a child." He bit back a sob and the tears I'd been holding back started to flow down my cheeks. I couldn't believe that he still wanted me there after everything he'd learned about me.

"Hearing your story just reinforced what I already knew about you. Rylie, you are the strongest, bravest, most incredible person I know. There aren't many people who would've had the strength to keep going after everything you'd been through and certainly not at such a young age. You are my soulmate and the whole time you were talking there wasn't one second in which I thought of letting you go."

He cupped his hand around the back of my neck and pulled me into his arms. I went willingly, so thankful that he wasn't pushing me away, and buried my face into the crook of his neck. He rocked me back and forth as we both cried. I cried for the little boy who had never been loved, for the teenager whose trust and innocence had been shattered, and I cried for the man who had been so lost that he nearly lost his life. I cried for each of those parts of myself until there were no tears left. When I'd calmed down, I sat back and wiped my eyes.

"What can I do, baby?" Lachlan asked.

I looked at him for several moments. I was worn out both physically and mentally from reliving my past and I knew that I had a lot of work left to do with Hudson before I could begin to move past what had happened, but like Hudson had said, all of that could wait. All I wanted was to spend the rest of the day wrapped up in the arms of the man I loved. To have his love erase the pain and misery of my life before him.

"Make love to me?" I whispered. I saw the hesitation in his eyes and I didn't want any of that so I leaned forward and brushed my lips against his. "Please, Lachlan," I begged.

His soft breath fanned out over my lips and then he kissed me. I sank into that kiss and everything else disappeared as I focused on the feel of his lips against mine. He grabbed my hand and pulled me from the couch and I followed him as he led us out of the office and up the stairs, not stopping until we had made it to the safety of his room.

Our movements were unhurried as we undressed each other. We'd had sex many times, but in some ways, it felt like the very first time since there was nothing I was keeping hidden anymore. I had spent so many years running from my past and not letting anyone in for fear that they would find out and hate me, but Lachlan knew every dark corner of my soul and still, he had called me his soulmate. I knew I probably didn't deserve his love, but it was the most precious thing in the world to me and I was going to fight like hell to keep it.

When we were both naked, we collapsed onto the bed. Lachlan proceeded to kiss me until my thoughts had all scattered and nothing remained except for the two of us in that moment. His lips grazed down my neck and I tilted my head to give him better access. He bit down on the tender flesh at the curve of my neck and began sucking on it, marking me as his. He leaned back to look at his handiwork and the look on his face was pure satisfaction. A primal growl rumbled up from his chest, the sound filling me with joy and wiping out all of the darkness from before. He was letting me know, in no uncertain terms, that I belonged to him and he wasn't letting me go.

Suddenly, I was filled with the need to stake my claim on him as well, to show him that he was mine and that I wasn't going to just roll over and let my past control me anymore, I would fight to keep what we had because it was the most precious thing in the world to me. I turned us so that I was on top of him and he went willingly, letting me have control of the situation.

I sat up, straddling his waist and gazed down at him. His eyes were filled with so much love and adoration that it left me stunned for a moment and I wondered if my heart could withstand all of the emotions I felt for this man. He had been there for me, before I even knew it, watching over me and putting a plan in place that would keep me safe. He had welcomed me into his home and protected me from my own demons, all without expecting anything in return. The fact that he loved me on top of everything else was something that I would never take for granted because it was the rarest gift I'd ever received.

"I love you, Rylie," Lachlan whispered. "I hope you know now, that there is nothing that you could ever say or do that would make me stop loving you. I know you don't trust easily, but if you'll let me, I'll spend the rest of my life proving it to you."

"No," I said, shaking my head at him. "You don't need to prove anything because I already believe you. When you stayed, and held me as I cried, despite everything I had just told you, I knew that you would be mine and that I would be yours for the rest of our lives."

He gasped. "That's all I've ever wanted."

I leaned down and covered his mouth with mine. Our kiss spoke of love and devotion and a promise of forever. When the need for air grew too great, I broke the kiss and let my tongue trail down the long column of his neck. Our chests rubbed together and I could feel the rigid nubs of his nipples brushing against my own and it sent a shockwave of desire through my body. I slid lower and captured one of those teasing nubs in my mouth, sucking on it until Lachlan was writhing on the bed and begging me for more.

Moving lower still, I let the tip of my tongue circle his navel, dipping inside and teasing him. I kissed my way down his body, nipping him gently with my teeth along the way. He spread his legs for me and I settled between them on my stomach. I nuzzled my face into the crease of his leg and breathed deeply, taking in the heady masculine scent of him. I looked up and our eyes met. He had his head tilted up and he was gazing down at me, his bottom lip pulled in between his teeth. Heat blazed in his eyes as he nodded at me, he wanted me to claim him.

No further urging was required as I bent and licked at the tender skin there. Lachlan's hips shot off the bed and he cried out as I began to suck hard, but I locked my arms over him, forcing him to accept what I was doing. His hand went to the back of my head, but instead of pushing me away, he pressed me closer to him. I didn't let up until a nice reddish-purple bruise had formed just under the surface of his skin then I flattened my tongue and licked over the mark, satisfied. It was a very primal act, but it left me feeling invincible. I had just claimed my mate and nothing could tear us apart.

I was shaking with need and desire as I climbed back up his body and took his mouth in a blistering kiss. Our tongues swirled around each other in a ritual dance as old as time and our hands touched and explored everything within reach. I broke the kiss long enough to reach into his bedside drawer and pulled out a bottle of lube. When I went for a condom, Lachlan stopped me by grabbing onto my wrist and I swiveled my head to look down at him.

"No," he said, shaking his head. "I got tested after my last relationship ended and I haven't been with anyone since. I already know you're clean because the hospital did a full workup on you when you were there. I don't want anything between us anymore, but only if you want that too." I was humbled by the trust he was putting in me and there was nothing I wanted more than to be bonded to him in that way.

"I don't want anything between us either," I told him, shutting the drawer.

I sat back up over his hips and opened the bottle of lube, pouring some of the cool liquid into his waiting hand before coating my own fingertips. I rubbed it around to warm it and then leaned up on my knees and reached around to rub my hole.

"God, that's so fucking sexy," Lachlan groaned and my eyes shot to his. I could tell that he was enjoying the show so I played it up a bit by arching my back and moaning loudly.

He must have decided to get even because he grasped both of our cocks together in his slick fist and began stroking up and down until we were both panting and shaking with need. I slid two fingers into my hole, preparing myself for him. It felt good, but it wasn't what I needed; I needed to feel him. I slid my body up so that I was hovering right over his thick cock and he held his stiff rod straight up in his hand, holding it steady as he entered me.

Our eyes stayed locked on each other, watching the myriad of emotions that were flickering between us as our bodies joined together. When I was fully seated, we both sighed and I held still as I waited for my body to adjust to his size. Lachlan's hands went to my hips, holding me steady.

"You feel amazing," he whispered. I reached up and pulled out the band that was holding my hair back, letting it fall down over my shoulders. I leaned over him, my lips inches from his and my hair curtaining us, protecting us from the rest of the world as it created our own private bubble.

"I love you," I breathed out.

We kissed as our bodies began to rock together. I thought we'd made love before, but it had all been a prelude leading up to that moment, because in that moment, we ceased to exist as two separate entities and our souls merged into one. Our movements were slow at first and then became more frenzied as we each raced towards our release.

I clenched my muscles, squeezing him from the inside and milking his pleasure. Lachlan canted his hips and began thrusting upward so that the head of his cock hit my prostate with perfect accuracy. My cock was pressed between us and it rubbed over his firm abs, creating just enough friction until it was too much and I cried out. My teeth latched onto his shoulder as my cum spilled over his stomach and chest, coating us both as we continued to move.

A few seconds later, I felt Lachlan stiffen under me and he arched his neck, his head pressing into the pillow as he came with a loud shout. I shuddered as I felt his warm cum filling me. He sank into the bed, drained from his powerful orgasm, and I let my weight fall on him as my own limbs gave out. His arms circled around me and he held me tight as we both drifted, neither of us willing to be separated.

CHAPTER
Seventeen

Lachlan

I T HAD BEEN A MONTH SINCE RYLIE HAD TOLD US ABOUT HIS PAST and things were going very well. At his request, I'd sat in on several of his sessions with Hudson. It was difficult to sit there and not say a word, when all I wanted to do was take him in my arms and protect him from the world, but I knew Hudson would handle the situation in a way that was best for Rylie so I kept quiet and let Hudson take the lead. However, that hadn't stopped me from doing some digging on my own. I needed to find out where Trina and Dave were and if they still had access to any children; the thought of them doing to anyone else what they'd done to Rylie, made my blood boil. What I found out seemed to be poetic justice if you asked me. Trina had been killed in a car accident about a year after Rylie left their home and Dave was in the end stages of colon cancer. At least I didn't need to worry that they could hurt anyone else.

Hudson continued to work with Rylie, trying to get him to understand that what had happened to him was not his fault, Rylie looked ashamed as he confessed that he'd enjoyed parts of it. I'd wondered if that was at the root of his guilt, but I was afraid to push him before he was ready so I was relieved when he finally said it out loud. Hudson explained that many people who are abused feel a physical reaction to stimuli, but that it didn't mean they were enjoying the act itself. That coupled with his need to feel loved and his feelings of abandonment, had unfortunately made him a prime target for someone like Trina.

I could finally see that Rylie was beginning to accept what Hudson was telling him and it was as if a cloud had been lifted and the real Rylie Anderson began to emerge. I was the only person who he had shown that part of himself to, but it was still different to see him without the darkness that had surrounded him before. It was as if the light that I always knew existed inside of him was finally able to burst through and it refused to be contained again. He laughed more easily, he was very playful and he was beginning to spend more time playing the drums and not just using them to escape his pain.

I had never been happier either. There had been a period of time after Spencer died where I had to force myself to get out of bed for the day. With Rylie though, every day was like a brand-new adventure and I woke each morning excited to see what the day had in store for us. I realized that I had merely been existing before he came along and breathed fresh air into my life. I made it my mission to keep him as happy as possible for the rest of his life.

My phone rang, pulling me from my thoughts. I'd been trying to get some work done while Rylie was volunteering at Agape House. He'd told me a lot about the center and the good things they were doing to help local LGBTQ youth. Rylie was very impressed with the staff and had grown quite fond of several of the kids so I'd made a mental note to check it out for myself soon. If it made Rylie that happy, then I wanted to be a part of it.

"Hello?" I said into the phone.

"Hi, Mr. Edwards, I'm so sorry to bother you," my assistant, Carolyn, said. No matter how many times I'd asked her to call me Lachlan, she always insisted on using a formal way of addressing me. "I know you wanted to handle all of your business from Chicago, but a problem has popped up that needs immediate attention and unfortunately Mr. Danvers is in Japan on business at the moment."

"That's okay, Carolyn. Tell me what's going on." I gave her my full attention as she explained the situation. Apparently, there had been a big mix-up in the scheduling of one of our world tours and several of the venue managers were irate, with good reason because if we had to cancel, they stood to lose hundreds of thousands of dollars. "Alright, call and make arrangements for the plane to be ready first thing in the morning, please," I said.

I hung up the phone and pinched the bridge of my nose. I dreaded the thought of leaving Rylie for even one day, but I knew that he needed to stay and continue working with Hudson. I didn't want him to lose the forward progress he'd been making and unfortunately, I knew that the mix-up wasn't going to be an easy fix, I would probably be gone at least a week if not more. I looked up as someone knocked on the door and then opened it slowly and I smiled when I saw Rylie's head peek in around the corner. My heart gave a flip when I saw him and I wondered if it would always react that way to his presence, I had a good feeling it would.

He strode towards me with a sexy smirk and I let my eyes soak him in. He was dressed in his usual jeans and t-shirt, but he'd begun filling them out better. Once he'd had his breakthrough session, it was like something inside of him clicked and he'd started taking better care of himself without me having to coax him into it. His appetite was much healthier and most mornings he was the one pulling me from our bed to go running. He'd also started using the home gym and lifting weights several days a week and his efforts were paying off as witnessed by the tight pull of the material across his chest. I backed my chair away from the desk as he neared and opened my arms to him in invitation. His smile widened as he accepted and slid onto my lap, throwing his arms around my neck.

"How are you?" He brushed his nose over mine as I wrapped my arms around his waist.

"I'm better now that you're here," I answered. I tilted my head up and sighed into his mouth as he kissed me. By the time we'd finished we were both panting and the room spun around me. He leaned his forehead against mine as we both caught our breath.

"Tell me what's wrong," he said softly.

"What do you mean?" I asked, surprised that he'd read my mood so easily. He leaned back so he could look at my face.

"Lachlan, I can read your moods just by your body language," he responded sassily.

"Oh really? Care to enlighten me?" I teased.

"Sure, when you're happy, your eyes sparkle like they're lit up from the inside. When you're sad, your bottom lip juts out in the prettiest little pout." Rylie reached down and cupped the bulge in the front of my pants with his hand and I made a sound in the back of my throat. He bent towards me and licked the shell of my ear, whispering his next words. "When you're turned on, you purr." I watched him through hooded eyes as he reached a finger up and rubbed gently between my eyes. "And when you're worried, you get a little crease right between your eyes, kind of like you had when I first walked in. So, are you going to tell me what's wrong or are you going to keep deflecting?" I chuckled, but I was a little surprised that he'd picked up so much about me already. Although, I'd studied him just as closely because I had trouble looking at anything else when he was in the room.

"I have to leave," I explained. "There's a problem with a tour line-up and they need me to fly to Los Angeles and take care of it."

"Oh." Rylie stiffened slightly in my arms. I could see the

uncertainty that crept into his eyes and I wasn't having any of that.

"I want you to go with me more than anything because the thought of being away from you for even one day seems like too much," I told him, hugging him tighter. "But I know that you need to keep working with Hudson. I may be gone a week or more and I don't want you to get behind on your sessions when you've come so far."

"When do you have to leave?" he asked quietly.

"First thing in the morning," I told him. I watched him closely for any signs of worry or doubt, but he only nodded thoughtfully. He circled his arms around my neck and took a deep breath.

"Well, Hudson and I were just talking about how far I'd come, but I've had someone with me every step of the way. We both agreed that it would be good if I had some time to myself out in the real world to see how I handle situations." Rylie shrugged his shoulders. "I guess with you leaving it would be as good a time as any to test things out. What do you think?" He gave me a pensive look, worrying his bottom lip between his teeth. I reached up and pulled the abused lip free and kissed it before answering him.

"Do I think you can handle being on your own and still resist temptation?" I asked and he nodded. "You have had to fight like hell your whole life and I know you're going to continue fighting to stay clean. I believe in you and I don't have one single doubt in my mind that you can make it on your own. Although, I'd still prefer that I get to be with you, but I understand that you need the time and I respect that. Will you stay here at least?"

"No," he said, shaking his head. "I think if I'm going to prove to myself that I can make it, then I need to really stand on my own. I'm going to move back into my place," he said quietly.

I dropped my head onto his chest, I didn't want him to see how badly those words hurt to hear. The rational side of myself knew that what he was saying made sense, but the other side of me, the one that wanted to hold onto him and never let him go, was struggling not to kick the rational side's arse.

"I don't want you to leave," I whispered. I felt his fingers sifting through my hair and he kissed the top of my head. Then he lifted my chin so he could see my face.

"Lachlan, you've given me so much. You've given me shelter, safety, understanding, and best of all, your love. I trust you completely, but it's time I learn to trust myself again. Once I've done that, then we can talk about where we go from there, if you want that too, that is."

"Of course, I want to. I want you to be in my life forever," I answered quickly and without question. He must have liked that answer because he gave me a beautiful smile and bent down to kiss me. I met him halfway and we shared a lingering kiss. "I'll miss you while I'm gone."

"I'll miss you too, but I expect you to call or text me as much as you can and you better come see me the minute you get home." He poked his finger into my chest sternly, making me laugh.

"I promise," I said capturing his wrist and moving his hand back down to my groin with a devilish smile. "Now, why don't you show me again how you make me purr, I wasn't aware I did that." He smiled and pressed his hand against my growing erection.

"Oh, I'll make you purr alright," he answered seductively. "But first, we need to get ready. Our company will be here soon and I don't think you want them walking in on us while I'm sucking you off."

I moaned pitifully. I'd forgotten that we had invited Micah and Landon over for dinner. I hadn't seen Micah since we were in Las Vegas and I'd missed him. Plus, I wanted him to get to know Rylie better since it was obvious that he was going to be a permanent fixture in my life. Although, I was seriously considering cancelling since the offer of Rylie's mouth on my cock had come into play. As if he read my thoughts, Rylie began scooting off my lap. I tried to pull him back, but he slipped from my grasp with a laugh.

"Oh no, mister. If I have to have dinner with your best friend who has seen me at my absolute worst and try and somehow convince him that I'm not out to ruin your life, the least you can do is keep your hands to yourself while I do it." He gave me a playful look, but I could see the anxiety that lie just beneath the surface. I caught up to him and grabbed his hand, lifting it and kissing each finger.

"You don't have to prove anything to anyone. Just be yourself and Micah will see all of the good inside of you that I see. Besides, it doesn't matter what he thinks because I'm head over heels in love with you and that's never going to change." I kissed him. "But we do need to hurry because they'll be here in less than twenty minutes."

Rylie yelped when I slapped him on the arse and then laughed as I chased him through the house and up the stairs. If that was going to be my last night with him for a while, then I was going to make the most of it.

Kerry had outdone herself with dinner. The London broil was grilled to perfection and the herbed potatoes and roasted asparagus made delicious side dishes. She'd also prepared a decadent chocolate cheesecake with a raspberry sauce drizzled over the top. She'd insisted on setting the dining room table for our guests and then she and Benjamin had left. When I'd told them that Rylie and I would both be gone for the next week, they'd decided that it would be the perfect time to visit Kerry's sister in England so I'd arranged for them to fly there on my company's private jet. I would use the smaller plane the next day for my own flight.

Conversation flowed easily while we ate and I could feel the tension ebbing out of Rylie as he and Landon began discussing the new album Carter's Creed was working on. Carter had called the day before to let Rylie know that he had finished writing all of the songs for the album and was ready to begin practicing. The band members had been excited to learn that they wouldn't have to fly out to Los Angeles to begin recording and could use my home studio instead to lay down their tracks. I was just happy to see Rylie so excited at the prospect of getting back to doing what he loved to do, playing the drums.

I caught Micah staring at Rylie on more than one occasion throughout dinner, a thoughtful look on his face, but he remained quiet and I wished I knew what my friend was thinking. Micah was an ex-Navy SEAL who had been trained to read a person's body language. He could determine just from the inflections in their voices or the way they held themselves if they were a threat or not, and I had a feeling that he was studying Rylie for what his body was saying. Micah was a level-headed, fair man who gathered all of the facts in a situation before making a judgement, but he was also fiercely protective of those he loved and I wondered how much that would factor into his decision of whether or not to give Rylie a chance. It wasn't until we were enjoying coffee and dessert that he finally spoke.

"You seem to be doing well, Rocko," Micah said. His tone was kind, but cautious and I felt Rylie straighten in his seat. I reached for his hand under the table and twined our fingers together in a show of support.

"I am, thank you." Rylie gave my hand a gentle squeeze as he glanced over at me. "I owe most of my progress to Lachlan and Hudson of course, but I'm better than I've ever been."

"No, the work was all yours," I insisted. "I was just there to lend support along the way." Rylie smiled at me lovingly then turned back to face Landon and Micah.

"I can only imagine what the two of you must think of me, considering what I was like before." Landon looked like he wanted to argue and he opened his mouth, but Micah stopped him by placing his hand over Landon's. He wanted to hear what Rylie had to say.

"I didn't have the easiest time growing up," Rylie began, downplaying everything he'd been through. "There were certain events in my childhood that affected me so deeply that I found it easier to numb myself with drugs and alcohol rather than dealing with the pain they'd left behind. I didn't even realize how out of control things had become until I ended up in the hospital, fighting for my life." I clasped his hand tightly when he said that, the thought of losing him too painful to even thing about.

"Lachlan gave me a second chance though, by taking me into his home and hiring Hudson to help me work through the things in my past that I had tried to bury. I love Lachlan with all of my heart and I know that you're like a brother to him so I hope that you'll give me a chance to prove how much I've changed." I stared at Rylie, so proud of the confidence and determination he'd just shown.

"You don't need to convince me of anything, Rocko," Micah said. "I can see how much you love Lachlan and I know that's the reason why he's happier than I've ever seen him. As long as he's happy then I'll be happy." Rylie looked stunned by Micah's easy acceptance, but he turned his attention to Landon who smiled at him kindly.

"We all have our own demons from the past, Rocko. I'm just glad you've found a way to put them to rest. You mean a great deal to my brother and we all want to see you succeed, that's all we've ever want-ed," Landon said. I put my arm around the back of Rylie's chair and he sagged against me in relief.

"Thank you both, you have no idea how much your acceptance means to me. Since we seem to be getting off to a fresh start though, I'd like it if you'd call me by my real name, Rylie Anderson." Micah and Landon both smiled and told him they would like that very much and I leaned over, planting a kiss on the side of his head and whispering in his ear that I loved him.

"Okay, now that that's settled, Landon and I have some news," Micah announced. We turned our attention to our friends who were both wearing matching dopey smiles. "We've set a date for the wedding."

"That's fantastic! When? Where?" I smiled excitedly.

"Two months. We're going to get married at my family's cabin in Tennessee," Landon answered. "Caleb and Giovanni were married there as well, it's always been a very special place for my family."

"That's wonderful, but two months? Does that give you enough time to prepare everything?" I asked. Micah looked at Landon for a moment before turning a serious face to me.

"I think each of us here understands how quickly life can change. We know we love each other and that we don't want anyone else, so there's no sense in wasting time. Besides, I can't wait to make Landon my husband." I smiled when Landon covered Micah's hand with his own. He had brought the light back into my friend's eyes and I couldn't be happier for them that they were going to have their happily ever after.

"I'm so happy for both of you," I said sincerely. "What can I do to help?"

"Well, my mom and sisters took over planning the wedding the minute Micah dropped down on one knee," Landon said, rolling his eyes. I knew he was just joking though because I'd never met a family that was closer than the Greenes.

"There is something you could do for me though," Micah told me.

"Of course, whatever you need," I said, wondering at the suddenly serious tone to his voice.

"Landon has asked his two brothers to stand up with him as his best men during the ceremony and I want my brothers to stand with me. I'd like it if you and Giovanni would be my best men," Micah said quietly. His eyes turned watery when he saw me blinking back my own tears. We had met under the most horrible of circumstances, but somehow, we managed to form a lasting bond. I would never get to stand up at Spencer's wedding, but standing up with Micah would be the next best thing.

"I'd be honored, thank you for asking me." My voice was raspy as I answered him. We smiled at each other and I was pretty sure we both could feel Spencer in the room with us in that moment.

After Micah and Landon left, we cleaned up the dishes and then decided to go for a swim. It was a warm night and the cool water would feel good. We didn't bother with swimwear since we had the place to ourselves. We swam for a while, laughing and splashing each other and enjoying the relaxing pool, but after a while of watching Rylie's beautifully naked form skimming through the water, I'd had enough and pulled him towards me.

He read my change in mood easily and wrapped his arms and legs around my frame, kissing me deeply. His tongue teased me, darting in and out of my mouth until I captured it and sucked hard. He tasted like a mixture of chocolate, raspberry, and Rylie and I wished I could somehow bottle that flavor forever. I carried him over to the side of the pool where the waterfall was and slipped between the two, letting the flowing water shield us from the rest of the world.

I put my arms on either side of him, holding onto the ledge and trapping his body between myself and the side of the pool. I tilted my head as he licked at the side of my neck, crying out as he bit down and sucked hard at the tender skin. It drove me crazy when he marked me and he knew it.

"More," I growled when he started to ease off. I needed his mark to last while we were apart so I wanted him to keep going. He sucked harder and my hips bucked against his in response. Then he moved across my chest to the spot right over my heart and marked me there as well. I could feel him claiming me all the way to the depths of my soul and I reveled in the feeling of completely belonging to someone else.

I growled as I lifted him from the water and set him on the edge of the pool in one swift motion. Rylie leaned back on his hands and stared down at me, his mouth hanging open as I took his thick cock in my hand and licked up the entire length of it with the flat of my tongue. I circled the tip with my tongue, tugging gently on his Prince Albert before dipping it into his slit and tasting a mixture of chlorine and his salty goodness.

He moaned in response and I eyed him as I drew the mushroomed head in my mouth and began alternating between short sucks and flicking my tongue over the bundle of nerves just under the cap. Finally, I wrapped my lips around him and swallowed him down until my nose was buried against the short hairs that surrounded the base of his cock. I loved the feeling of cool metal from his piercing at the back of my throat and I swallowed around him. He bucked his hips, pushing further down my throat and I felt my eyes water, but I didn't stop. My head bobbed up and down on him at an even pace and he laid back along the side of the pool, completely at the mercy of my mouth.

I slid my hands up his thighs, and over the hard ripples of his abs until they reached their destination where I tugged on each of the metal rings in his nipples. His cock grew incredibly big in my mouth, stretching my lips even more and Rylie screamed. His seed shot down my throat and coated my tongue and I continued sucking until I'd gotten every last delicious drop. Then I moved from between his bent knees and lifted myself from the pool.

I grabbed a couple of cushions from a nearby lounge chair and tossed them onto the concrete beside him then I stood above him, taking my still hard cock in my hand and stroking it lazily. He was still breathing heavily as he opened one eye and peered up at me, a sated smile on his lips.

"Whatcha doin' there, Lachlan?" he drawled.

"I'm not done with you," I answered huskily. I smirked when I saw his cock twitch in response. Perhaps I could convince it to come out and play again after all.

"I don't know if I can move," he teased. "I'm pretty sure you just sucked the life right out of me, literally."

"Aww! I hate to hear that because I was hoping to fuck you on these cushions until I made you scream again," I told him. I watched as his whole body shuddered then laughed when he rolled over and climbed onto his hands and knees in the middle of the cushions, wiggling his arse back and forth teasingly.

"Fine," he said saucily. "But don't be gentle, I'm in the mood for rough."

"Good thing," I replied as I got on my knees behind him. "The only thing we have out here is spit and I don't feel like running all the way in the house to get lube." Rylie moaned and lowered his head onto his forearms, obviously pleased with the situation.

He may have wanted it rough, but I refused to hurt him. I bent down and spit on his quivering hole then proceeded to tongue him until he was relaxed and begging me to get on with it. Satisfied that he was wet enough, I straightened and spit into my hand, coating my aching cock until it was slick. Rylie leaned up on his hands and arched his back while I held the base of my cock and lined it up with his entrance.

We both moaned as I slid inside in one long thrust, his slick walls gripping my cock like a warm vise. When his arse was cradled against my groin and I couldn't go any deeper, I bent over him and licked a line up his back while my fingers reached under to twist his nipples. After a few seconds, he wriggled his arse, letting me know that he was ready for more and I knelt up and placed my hands on his hips. Rylie looked over his shoulder and the look of need in his eyes filled my body with molten lava.

"Don't you dare take it easy on me," he growled. "I want to be able to feel you long after we're apart. I need that, Lachlan."

I clenched my jaw, understanding exactly what it was my man needed and I had every intention of giving it to him. I slowly withdrew from his body almost to the tip, his tight channel awakening every nerve ending as it rippled over my cock and then I slammed back into him.

"Again," he demanded, so I repeated my thrusts again and again until he was whimpering incoherently.

I could feel sweat dripping down my back as I tried to hold off my release, wanting him to come again before I found my own pleasure. I pulled back and let a thick strand of saliva drip down on my cock, slicking it once again and then I tilted my angle and began pounding into him, nailing his prostate with precision. I didn't hold back, just as he'd asked. Instead, I unleashed all of my passion onto him that would have to be withheld during our separation.

Finally, when I'd begun to feel the fire at the base of my spine and I knew I wouldn't be able to hold off any longer, Rylie threw his head back and screamed, louder than I'd ever heard. Seconds later, my own orgasm barreled through me, choking me with its power and leaving me dizzy with exhaustion. I moved back unsteadily and my cock slipped from his arse with a wet sound.

I leaned back for a second, mesmerized by the sight of my cum dripping out of his hole and down his thighs and then we both collapsed side by side onto the cushions. Rylie managed to turn his head in my direction and we lay there staring into each other's eyes as we breathed in tandem. I would breathe him in and then he would breathe me, back and forth until our heart rates had slowed.

So much was said in those silent moments right before we drifted off to sleep; sadness over our impending separation, promises made to each other, and hope for the future we both wanted to see happen. I had no idea it was possible to feel that perfectly in sync with another human being and it was like I could feel my soul vibrating with happiness over finding its mate. As difficult as our time apart would be on each of us, I harbored no doubts that we would find our way back to each other.

CHAPTER
Eighteen

Rylie/Rocko

I WATCHED THE LIMO AS IT PULLED AWAY FROM THE HOUSE, taking Lachlan with it and I felt a heaviness in my heart that I hadn't experienced since I'd first arrived there. I had to keep reminding myself that I needed the time to prove that I could make it without having someone around at all hours of the day or else it would have been too tempting to call Lachlan back and beg him to take me with him. The house seemed too dark and lonely with no one inside since even Kerry and Benjamin were away on vacation, so I didn't look back as I picked up my bags and headed towards the garage.

Lachlan had insisted that I have a car to use while he was away and I'd agreed just to make him happy. I could have argued that I'd made it my whole life without having a car, but I could tell that it was already difficult enough on him to be away from me; if my using one of his vehicles would ease his mind, then I would do it.

I went to the garage and grabbed the keys to the Shelby Mustang off of the rack on the wall, figuring I was at least already familiar with that one since I'd driven it to Agape House a few times. I climbed in and started the engine, loving the roar as it came to life. I pulled out of the garage and hit the button to shut the door behind me, then drove down the long driveway, forcing myself not to look at Lachlan's house in the rearview mirror.

I stopped at the grocery store on the way home and picked up some essentials I knew I would need at my place and was shocked when a few people stopped me to ask for an autograph. I had spent enough time out of the limelight that I'd begun to forget that there was an entire world out there who thought they knew who I was, but they didn't know. Only a select few had ever gotten close to knowing and only one man had ever cared enough to tear down my walls brick by brick. My heart twisted painfully as I pictured Lachlan's perfect face and I sighed, the time away from the man I loved was going to be harder than I thought.

I parked in front of my building and rode the elevator up to my floor. I unlocked my door and stepped in and then just stood there, the bags of groceries growing heavy in my arms as I looked around. I felt like I had stepped into a stranger's home, somewhere I didn't belong because that wasn't home to me anymore. My home was on a flight to Los Angeles at the moment. *It's only for a week, you can do this.*

I carried the bags into the kitchen and set them on the counter then busied myself with putting them away. I looked around at the mess I'd left behind. There were empty bottles of alcohol, dirty dishes in the sink, and something sticky all over the top of the stove. If the kitchen was that bad, I didn't even want to look at the rest of the place. I could have easily hired a cleaning service to come in and get everything back in order, but I felt like I was the one who had made the mess so I needed to be the one to clean it up. I cranked some music on my sound system then I tied my hair up into a messy knot, pulled on some gloves, and got to work.

I poured out the contents of the various whiskey and vodka bottles, without blinking an eye and when I found my hidden stash of marijuana, I flushed it down the toilet with a laugh, thinking of how good it felt to finally be stronger than the drugs that used to own me. Three hours later, I ran the last of the garbage to the trash chute then walked back into my condo and stopped, smiling at what I saw; the place was spotless. Granted, it still didn't feel like home to me, but at least it no longer looked like an animal had been living there.

I was filled with satisfaction at a job well done, but I was also exhausted and grimy. I jumped in the shower and let the scalding water wash the last of my old life off of me then I pulled on a comfy pair of sweats and a threadbare t-shirt. I padded out to the kitchen and heated up the frozen meal I'd bought at the store. I almost sat at the table to eat because I'd grown so accustomed to having meals as a family, but then I realized that would be too depressing without Lachlan, Kerry, and Benji there.

God help me, I was even beginning to miss Benji. I smiled as I thought about the older man, the talk we'd had right before my date with Lachlan seemed to have broken down whatever wall there was between us and he'd been much more accepting of me. Although, I still liked to mess with him every chance I got because it amused me to get him riled up.

I ended up lounging on the couch, eating my tasteless meal and binge watching The Walking Dead on Netflix, picking up where I'd left off. I had just watched a beloved character get beheaded and was yelling at my TV when I heard "Pour Some Sugar on Me," my ringtone for Lachlan, playing from somewhere in the distance. I looked around franticly for my phone and finally realized I'd left it on the kitchen counter when I was heating up my dinner. I stubbed my toe on the couch and sent a vase teetering on the edge of the table as I rushed to get to my phone before he hung up. I snatched it up at the last possible second and hit the green button.

"Lachlan?" I shouted as I jumped up and down on one foot while holding the abused toe of my other foot in my hand. "Shit!" I said as the wobbling vase behind me fell to the floor and smashed into a million pieces.

"Rylie? What's wrong? What happened?" Lachlan shouted through the phone and I immediately felt bad for causing him worry.

"I'm fine, I didn't mean to worry you. I just crashed a vase and severed a toe trying to answer the phone," I explained. I sat down on one of the bar stools along the island counter and lifted my leg onto the stool beside me so I could inspect the damage to my toe. I was surprised to see that it was just a little red, but otherwise still intact. *How can something hurt that badly yet show no outward signs of mutilation?*

"You severed a toe?" I heard him gasp through the phone. "That's it, I'm coming home."

"No, no, no," I said in a rush. "I'm fine and my toe is fine, I promise. It hurts like a son of a bitch, but nothing's broken and it's still attached. Stay there and get everything figured out."

"Okay," he grumbled. He sounded disappointed that he wasn't going to be turning around and coming back right away and it made me feel warm inside to know that he was missing me as much as I was missing him.

"So, where are you?" I asked.

"I just got off the plane and I'm heading to the beach house I own," he answered.

We talked until he was pulling into the driveway of his house, but he sounded exhausted and I knew he was going to have a lot of work ahead of him so I told him to get some rest and to call me whenever he had time the next day. We exchanged a few whispered I love you's and then hung up. I cleaned up the remnants of the vase then wandered through the condo, making sure the doors were locked and turning off lights as I went.

I brushed my teeth and slipped out of my clothes then climbed between the clean sheets that I had put on my bed earlier and re-played our conversation in my head. I noticed that he hadn't referred to his property in Los Angeles as home. I thought both of us consid-ered his place in Chicago our home base since that's where we first connected and fell in love. Each of our jobs required that we trav-el all around the world throughout the year, but I could picture the Chicago house being our main home, the one that we'd live in after we got married and raise our children in.

My body stilled in the bed. I was surprised at the direction my thoughts had taken and I waited for panic to take over at the men-tal image of me getting married or becoming a father, but it never came. Instead, a warm feeling flowed through my veins and my heart filled with hope for something that, just a few months before, I never would have thought could be an option. Falling in love with Lachlan had opened my eyes to a whole new world, a world in which possi-bilities were endless. I rolled over, burrowing down in the covers and fell asleep with a smile on my face.

"So, there we were enjoying a nice family dinner and Michelle asked Landon where he and Micah were planning on going on their honey-moon," Carter said. "Next thing I knew Mom and Dad were talking about their own honeymoon and how they never even saw the is-land they were on because they were too busy exploring each other in their room." We all laughed as Carter made fake gagging sounds at the memory. The five of us were all sitting around talking as we took a break from practicing the new songs that Carter had written. I'd missed spending time with my friends and it felt good to be playing music with them and hanging out again.

"I think it's sweet," Kalia said. Carter looked at her like she was crazy and she rolled her eyes at him. "I get why you don't want to hear about it since they're your parents, but if you think about how they've been married so many years and raised five kids and they're still that crazy in love with each other? That's romantic to me." She sighed with a dreamy look in her eyes that we rarely saw out of the pink-haired, tattoo-covered, rock girl. Tyler pulled her closer to him and kissed her hair then whispered something in her ear that made her blush.

"Yeah, I guess you're right," Carter conceded. "If Ryan can put up with me for that long and still look at me the way my dad looks at my mom then I'll consider myself lucky."

"I don't think you have to worry about that," I told him. "Your husband still looks at you with the same puppy dog eyes he wore the first time I saw him. I can't picture a devotion like that ever going away." I stopped talking when I noticed everyone's eyes trained on me. Some were just studying me while others looked downright shocked.

"What?" I asked, suddenly feeling self-conscious.

"Nothing," Steve answered since he was the first to recover. "It's just going to take some time getting used to the new you."

"Yeah, we were used to you being a whore," Tyler jumped in with a smirk to let me know he was teasing.

"And an asshole," Carter interjected with a playful wink. I flipped them both off as Kalia started talking.

"I think what the boys were trying to say," she said, glaring at Carter and Tyler. "Is that while we're still getting used to the changes in you, we realize that the changes are all for the better and we couldn't be happier for you."

"Yeah, what she said," Tyler said sweetly, earning him an eye roll from his girlfriend.

"Ditto." Carter smiled at me. "Now, if the lovefest is over can we get back to work, please?" We all laughed and got up to head back over to our instruments. We played for another hour or two before calling it a day, it was getting late and Kalia and Tyler had to get moving if they were going to meet Tyler's parents at the restaurant in time to have dinner.

"Yeah, Ryan just texted that he's got dinner in the oven so I'm heading out too. You guys have a great night," he called over his shoulder as he hurried out the door. I smiled after him, but I felt a heaviness in my chest as I pictured heading back to my condo for another frozen dinner which I would eat all alone.

"You feel like getting a burger or something?" I turned around, surprised to see Steve standing there looking at me, a nervous expression on his face. Things between us had been better since our come to Jesus moment in Las Vegas and we laughed and talked when we were together with the rest of the band, but we hadn't spent any time alone since before I'd ended up in the hospital.

"Sure, that sounds good," I told him.

We had each driven ourselves to practice so I followed him to the place that made our favorite hamburgers. It was the local bar that Carter's Creed used to play at and they had the best burgers in all of Illinois. I parked beside him and climbed out, meeting Steve's gaze over the hood of the car. His face was red and he wore an apologetic frown.

"I'm sorry, I was just thinking how much we love the burgers here and that the people are used to us so they'll probably leave us alone, but if you'd rather go somewhere else, that's fine," he stammered. I tilted my head in confusion, trying to figure out what I'd missed. Then it hit me, Steve was worried about making me uncomfortable because the place was a bar. I smiled at him, so thankful to have a best friend like him that would always look out for me.

"Nah, man, I'm fine." I looked him in the eye so he'd see how serious I was. "I haven't even wanted a drink in several months and if I do, my therapist has given me a long list of tricks I can use to get me through until the craving passes. Besides, it's been forever since I've had one of their burgers and it sounds so good." Steve smiled at me and then nodded his head.

"Nice wheels, by the way," he said with a low whistle as he glanced over Lachlan's Mustang. "You must suck cock like a vacuum cleaner." I laughed loudly at his teasing and bumped him hard with my shoulder as we walked towards the front door.

"Aww, you need me to give Lindsay some pointers?" I joked back.

"Nope, I have no complaints there," Steve quipped as I held the door open for him.

We were still laughing as we walked into the loud bar and were met with a chorus of hellos. Steve was right, the people there had known us before anyone else did, we weren't famous rock stars to them, we were just Steve and Rocko. They were happy to see us, but after a few slaps on the backs and how are you's they left us alone to enjoy our dinner.

We settled into a booth and ordered burgers and fries along with an order of fried pickles. I asked for a Coke with mine and even though I told him that it was fine if he wanted to have a beer, Steve insisted on having the same as me. We spent a long time reminiscing about the good old days of playing in that same establishment as well as swapping memories of our time on the road.

As we ate, talk turned to how things were going for each of us since the tour had ended. Steve had done a lot of travelling with Lindsay and he said he liked helping her out with the photo shoots for the magazine she worked for. After their second trip, they'd decided that they were ready to move in together so Lindsay had sold her house and moved in with him. He seemed happier than I'd ever seen him and I told him as much.

"I am," he said with a shy grin. "I don't know what it is, but I just feel happier when I'm around her, you know? Like she makes everything better and brighter." Steve caught me smiling at him and his shoulders slumped. "Go ahead and say it, you think I'm crazy, right?"

"No, I get it," I assured him. "I feel the same way about Lachlan.

It's like when he walks into the room, I can finally breathe again."

"Yeah," Steve said, staring at me as he leaned back into his seat. "It's exactly like that." He shook his head at me and grinned. "I'm really happy you're here, Rylie," he said quietly so no one could overhear his use of my real name. I knew he wasn't just referring to the bar we were in.

"Me too," I told him sincerely. "Me too."

When we finished eating, I excused myself to go to the restroom. I had just finished washing my hands when I heard the door open. I glanced up in the mirror and fought back a groan when I saw Brad, one of my old party buddies, standing behind me wearing a broad grin.

"Hey, man, I heard you guys got back in town months ago, but I haven't seen you around. Where've you been?" I turned to face him as I scrambled to come up with an excuse about where I'd been. Somehow, we'd managed to keep my stint in rehab out of the public eye and I wanted to keep it that way. Before I could up with anything, Brad started talking again.

"It doesn't matter because you're here now. Look what I just scored today," he exclaimed, holding up a clear baggie with an all too familiar white powder in it. My heart pounded in my chest wildly and my mouth suddenly felt as dry as the Sahara. "So, where should we start this party?"

"Ummm…I don't…" It was the first time I'd been faced with my drug of choice and my stomach roiled. I closed my eyes, took a deep breath, clenching my hands into fists to stop them from shaking. After a few seconds, I opened my eyes and saw Brad looking at me expectantly.

"I don't do that anymore," I told him and the more I spoke, the stronger I felt. "I don't *need* it anymore. I got clean and I am never going back to that way of life." Brad studied me for a few seconds as if he were waiting for the punchline to some joke.

"But this is some grade A shit. You'll be missing out, dude." He waved the bag in the air as if to accentuate his point, but I shook my head at him.

"I'm not missing out on anything," I told him firmly.

"You can't be serious." Brad looked at me in shock, but I ignored him and moved towards the door. I'd said everything I wanted to say and I just wanted to get out of there. I was about to reach for the handle when the door swung open and I came face to face with Steve. He looked over my shoulder and his eyes narrowed when he saw the baggie Brad was holding up in the air. He glanced back and forth between the two of us, but I couldn't speak around the lump in my throat.

"He already said no, so I suggest you get out of here with that shit before I call the police," Steve snarled. I stared at my friend, wide eyed as Brad stuffed the bag back into his pocket and slipped out the door.

"Steve, I can explain," I finally managed to get out. Steve's shoulders slumped as he blew out a long breath.

"Are you okay? I saw him follow you in here and decided to wait outside the door in case you needed any help." I must not have hidden my surprise very well because he smirked at me, knowingly. "I knew who he was because he used to lurk around backstage when we played here. Even as bad off as you were, I knew you weren't hooking up with a guy like that." My lip curled up in disgust at the thought of doing anything sexual with Brad. "I'm proud of you though, I knew you'd tell him no," Steve said. My jaw dropped as I stared at him.

"How did you know I would turn him down?" I asked him incredulously.

"Because, you're not a stupid guy. You died twice the last time you used drugs and were lucky enough to get another chance. You're not going to go down that road again, not when you've got so much to live for. You just needed an opportunity to prove it to yourself." Steve smiled at me and I felt warm all over when I saw the proud look in his eyes.

"You're right, I do have a lot to live for." A wave of relief mixed with pride washed over me as I realized what had just happened. I'd come face to face with one of my demons and I'd laughed in its face. Sure, I'd been tempted for a fraction of a second, but that was the nature of the beast known as drugs. The thing that mattered was that I had chosen my life over a life of drugs.

"How about we go back to my place and play some video games," Steve suggested.

"Now, that is the best offer I've had all night," I said with a laugh then I threw my arm over his shoulder as we walked out of the bathroom.

"How's everything been going?" Hudson asked. It was my second session in his new office since I'd moved back into my condo and I loved it there. It was decorated beautifully in plush, oversized furniture that made me feel as comfortable and as at home as the doctor himself.

It had been seven days since Lachlan had left for L.A. and I was growing increasingly anxious to have him back in my arms. When I'd spoken to him the night before, they still hadn't reached an agreement with the owners of the concert venues and they seemed to be at a standstill. He'd sounded tired and frustrated and I wished I was there with him.

"Good, practice is going well and we should be heading into the studio soon to lay down some tracks," I told him with a smile.

"That's terrific," he said with a smile. "I'm sure you're excited to get back to doing what you love."

"I am, but the best part is being with my friends," I told him.

"They sound like an incredible group of people and I'm so happy that you've got so much support in your life."

"Yeah, I'm really lucky," I agreed.

"I think they're just as lucky to have you," Hudson said and I smiled at him. I was finally learning to accept compliments and not just brush them off with self-deprecating humor like I used to. Hudson smiled widely when I thanked him.

"Are you still doing alright, living on your own? Have you had any challenges?" Hudson asked. My cheeks puffed as I blew out a breath then I told him all about my night out with Steve and about Brad's cocaine offer. Hudson listened quietly as I told him the entire story.

"So, what stopped you from taking him up on his offer?" Hudson shrugged his shoulders. "I mean, it was a guy you knew, you had the opportunity, and it might have helped you forget how much you were missing Lachlan. Why not just do a line?" I stared at him, wondering if he'd lost his mind.

"Because I don't want that life anymore," I said, sounding exasperated. "You know as well as I do how hard I've had to work to move past everything that happened to me, but I've done it. I'm stronger than I've ever been, not only physically, but also mentally and emotionally. I've also found someone who loves me and I want a future with him, I'm not going to pour all of that down the drain for some white powder." I was out of breath by the time I'd finished my impassioned speech and I was surprised to see Hudson's eyes twinkling and a broad smile splitting his face.

"Rylie, do you remember what I told you the three stages of your therapy would be?" Hudson asked. I furrowed my brow as I tried to remember his words from long ago.

"Yeah, they were Recover, Redeem, and Renew," I said, ticking them off with my fingers.

"Exactly. The first stage was Recover which you passed through as the drugs and alcohol left your system and you began to exercise and take better care of yourself physically. Then you moved on to the Redeem stage which was one of the hardest stages for you because it required you to face what had happened to you in your past and to come to terms with it. It was in that stage that you rediscovered the boy inside of you that had gotten lost along the way and you found value in him again." I listened to him carefully, feeling a flush of pride at all that I had already accomplished.

"The third stage was Renew," Hudson continued. "I told you that in that final stage you would take all of the things you'd learned about yourself and decide where you wanted to go from there. That your life would be a blank canvas that you could use to create whatever life you chose. Rylie, when you were offered a prime opportunity to use your drug of choice and you chose your future instead, you were renewed. I don't expect you to answer this right away, in fact I'd like you to take time and really think it over." Hudson leaned forward and looked directly at me with a serious expression. "Rylie, the canvas is in front of you and the brush is in your hand, what type of picture will you create?"

I swallowed hard with the weight of his question and I was glad he didn't expect an immediate answer. I stood, ready to leave and shook his hand before heading for the door. Hudson stopped me right before I opened it though.

"One more thing before you go." I turned back around to face him and cocked my head to the side. "I asked you when we first met if you liked who you were and you told me no. So, I'm asking you again, do you like yourself, Rylie?"

I was quiet for several moments as I considered his question and I thought about all the ways in which I had changed and grown over the last several months. I had shown up at Lachlan's door, broken and lost and hiding behind a mask I called Rocko. Somewhere along the way and without even realizing it had happened, I had rediscovered Rylie Anderson and I like who I was when I was him.

"Yes."

CHAPTER
Nineteen

Lachlan

I SLAMMED THE DOOR BEHIND ME SO HARD THAT IT RATTLED IN its frame then stomped through the entryway and threw my keys onto the round table, not caring when they slid across the slick marble and crashed onto the floor. I was so frustrated; I could hardly see straight. I'd been in Los Angeles for nine days already and had barely scratched the surface of being able to resolve the issues with the tour schedule.

The venue owners were all angry because they didn't want to give up their allotted time in the lineup even though I had added more dates to the already packed schedule to try and appease everyone. The conference call I had arranged that morning had started out civilly, but soon turned childish and petty and their bickering had wound up giving me a crashing headache. I'd spent the rest of the day trying to calm everyone down when all I really wanted to do was tell them to grow up and be thankful I hadn't cut them from the lineup completely.

I walked into the kitchen and grabbed a bottle of water out of the fridge, downing half of it before I shut the door hard; enjoying the satisfying sound of clanking of bottles. My day had been terrible, but the hardest part was yet to come, I still had to call Rylie and explain that I wouldn't be coming home the next day.

I'd hated every minute that I'd had to spend without him and that was why I'd hired two new operations officers to serve under Tyrone. They would have the authority to make executive decisions in the absence of both Tyrone and myself. Unfortunately, they would need extensive training before I could just hand over the reins to them and with Tyrone still out of the country, that left me to do the training.

I'd spent years working myself into the ground as I built my company into the recording giant it had become and then when Spencer died, I'd dug deep and worked even harder because it was all I had left. Things had changed though the minute Rylie walked into my life and I found myself wanting to work less and spend more time enjoying the fruits of my labor with the man I loved.

Carter's Creed was getting ready to start recording their songs which meant they'd be headlining another world tour to promote the new album. I would need to discuss things with Rylie, but I'd come to some decisions while I'd been away from him. I'd grown up always waiting for my parents to decide that they were ready to come home and spend time with Spencer and me. They never had and it had made for a lonely childhood, but at least I'd had Spencer. Then when he'd died, I'd been lucky to have Kerry, Benjamin, and Micah there to watch after me, but it wasn't the same as having my brother and so I'd felt lonelier than ever.

Then Rylie had walked into my life and I'd felt more happiness and more sense of belonging than I'd felt in a long time. It was a precious feeling to have and I wasn't going to stand on the sidelines and watch it get snatched away from me. When Rylie went on tour next time with the band, I planned on going with him. I just needed to make sure that was alright with him, but first, I needed to call him and tell him I couldn't come home yet.

I pulled my phone out of my pocket and headed out on the balcony of the house which overlooked the ocean. Perhaps the smell of the salty air and the sound of Rylie's voice would soothe my frazzled nerves. I slid the door shut behind me and closed my eyes for a few seconds as I took a deep breath. As usual, I began to relax when I heard the sounds of the waves crashing.

I walked over to the balcony and leaned my forearms on the railing as I peered out at the darkness. A light flickering off to my left caught my eye and I turned, noticing a fire not too far off from where my house sat. My property spanned a half mile on either side of the house so whoever was out there was definitely on my property. I sighed tiredly and pocketed my phone as I made my way down the steps.

I kicked my shoes and socks off when I reached the bottom and left them there so they wouldn't get filled with sand then began walking towards the fire. I could hear music playing and I wondered if it wasn't some teenagers who'd decided to have a beach party. Even more reason for me to tell them to move along, I didn't need to get in trouble for having underage kids drinking on my property. As I got closer, I scanned the area, but didn't see anyone else around other than the lone shape of a man who was bent down, tending the fire.

"Excuse me," I called out, not wanting to startle him. "I'm afraid you're on private property, sir." He was dressed in tan cargo shorts and a white tank top and he stood quickly at the sound of my voice, his long hair flowing around his shoulders as he turned. I stopped, drawing in a quick breath and my pulse started racing franticly. "Rylie?"

"Lachlan!" He ran towards me and pulled me into his arms, hugging me tightly. My eyes burned as I buried my face into his hair, filling my senses with the familiar scent of his shampoo. My arms circled around his waist, drawing him closer to me until there wasn't even a breath between us. He felt so damn good in my arms and I hoped that his being there wasn't all just a figment of my imagination.

I pulled back and placed my hands on the side of his face, letting my fingertips reacquaint themselves as they moved over his perfect cheekbones and the scruff along his jaw that I loved to feel against my skin, over his brows, and down his sculpted nose until they reached his lips where he pressed a gentle kiss on the tips of each finger.

"How? When?" I whispered. My thoughts were all jumbled, but luckily Rylie understood.

"I got here a few hours ago, and you weren't here so I decided to take a walk along the beach and I found this old fire pit on my way back, along with the radio I swiped from your back deck," he said with a cheeky grin. "I started the fire once it got dark and I've just been hanging out here, waiting for you to get back," he explained.

"Why didn't you call me? I could've flown you in on one of the company planes and then..." My words cut off as he tilted his head and covered my lips with his. I sagged against him as he proceeded to kiss the breath right out of me. We broke the kiss, each of us gasping for air and I was proud of the heated look in his eyes. I was the one who had put that look there.

"I missed you and I was tired of waiting," he confessed. He turned his head and kissed the palm of my hand. "Plus, I wanted to surprise you."

"I'm definitely surprised," I chuckled and then sighed. "It has been just miserable being away from you and I still don't have everything figured out yet. I was just about to call and tell you that I couldn't return home yet, but here you are instead."

"Here I am," he whispered.

Rylie circled his arms around my waist and buried his nose in the crook of my neck as we began swaying to the music coming from the radio. I slid my hands around his neck and let my fingers sift through his silky hair as we danced. The rest of the world disappeared as we soaked each other in, our hearts welcoming each other home.

The music changed and Rylie lifted his head, nuzzling his cheek against mine. "This song is how I feel about you," he whispered into my ear and I shivered when I recognized "Tangled Up in You" by Aaron Lewis. My eyes burned as Rylie began to sing the beautiful words to me then he kissed me as the last few bars of the song played. "I love you, Lachlan."

"I love you too, more than you could ever know," I told him.

"I'm counting on that," he murmured as he stepped out of my arms and sank down on one knee. My brain was still trying to make sense of what was happening when he pulled a small black box out of his pocket. Rylie gazed up at me and I thought that I had never seen him look more beautiful than he did at that moment, with the firelight glowing on his skin and his eyes full of love as he prepared to ask me the most important question of my life.

"Lachlan, you have given me everything. When I was lost, you gave me a home, when I was shattered, you held me in your arms until I was put back together, and when my heart called out to you, you answered back with the purest love I've ever known." My eyes swam with tears and I reached up and brushed them away so I could see him clearly. That was when I noticed that Rylie had tears streaming down his face too and a sob tore from my chest.

"I've never been in love until I met you and I may mess up at times, but I promise that if you let me, I will love you more than anyone has ever been loved before. Lachlan Edwards, I want to spend the rest of my life with you. Will you please be my husband?"

Tears flowed freely down my cheeks as I dropped to my knees in the sand and took his face in my hands. "Rylie, you have brought laughter and love back into my world. You made me start to live again and there is nothing in this world that I want more than to live my life with you, as your husband. Yes, I will marry you."

Rylie's hands were shaking as he pulled the beautiful gunmetal ring out of the box and slipped it onto my finger. When he lifted his head, he was wearing a smile so glorious that I just had to grab him and kiss him. He tugged on my bottom lip with his teeth and I experienced a jolt of electricity that travelled all the way from my lip to my groin and I moaned with need.

"Let's go to the house, I need to feel you inside of me," I told him.

His blue eyes blazed with heat and the air around us grew thick with tension. Without a word, he stood and began kicking sand onto the fire until the flames were completely snuffed out. Suddenly, we were shrouded in darkness with only the light of the moon to guide us. Rylie reached for my hand and we began walking towards the house, but neither one of us seemed capable of making it more than a few steps without stopping to taste the other. It was as if our bodies had had enough and they weren't willing to wait the few minutes it would take to get inside the house.

By the time we'd made it to the bottom step of the deck, the only clothing we had left on was our boxer briefs. A trail of clothes littered the beach behind us, but we couldn't be bothered to care. We shared another passionate kiss then I turned and began making my way up the stairs, but I stopped, grabbing onto the railing as he slid my briefs down my legs. A cool breeze blew across my overheated skin and I cried out as I felt Rylie's teeth against the tender flesh of my arse. His hand pressed against my back and I bent over, placing my hands on the step above my head.

Rylie parted my cheeks and I felt the wet slide of his tongue through my crease, swirling around my pucker and teasing the nerves into an anxious frenzy. He blew a cool breath against my skin and I felt my hole contract. Rylie must have enjoyed the view because he let out a loud groan and then pressed his face into my crease, licking and sucking at my entrance. It felt so good that I reached behind and pressed the back of his head with my hand, holding him to me. He continued to eat me with complete abandon, giving me exactly what I needed. When he pressed a finger into my wet hole, I had to grip the step or risk falling. He added another finger and I began to buck against him.

"That's it, fuck yourself on my fingers," Rylie growled. I thrust back and forth on his fingers, moaning at the delicious sensations he was causing inside me and then his fingers curled, pressing against my prostate and I saw stars dancing behind my closed lids. I felt the warmth of his body as he moved up to stand right behind me.

"Get up on the deck and hold onto the railing," he murmured into my ear and I rushed to follow his instructions, grabbing onto the wooden rail in front of me.

I looked out over the ocean and shivered when I heard him spit and then the wet sound of him slicking his cock. He slid into me, stretching me around his thickness and it felt so good, so right. I had missed that so much, the feeling of completeness in body and spirit that I felt whenever Rylie and I came together. His hands gripped my hips as he thrust inside me and the burn inside me began to build.

I pushed back, meeting each of his thrusts with a rhythm of my own, and soon we were rocking back and forth in perfect sync. My breathing increased as our passion built and I could hear Rylie groan behind me.

"I love you so much," he whispered, his speech broken by his heavy panting. He slid his arm around my waist and his hand wrapped around my cock as he increased his pace. My head dropped back onto his shoulder and I stared up at the stars as he continued working his magic on my body. The dual sensation of his hand stroking me and his cock thrusting into my arse was too much and I began to see flashes of colors and lights before my eyes.

"Rylie!" I shouted as my body bowed inward with the force of my release. His body followed, bending over mine and his thrusts began to falter. Seconds later he yelled and I felt his hot seed filling me up.

I recovered first and went inside to grab a blanket off the back of the couch. I walked back outside and we sat together in a lounge chair with the blanket wrapped around us. Rylie leaned back against my chest and sighed contentedly as he picked my hand up and kissed the ring on my finger.

"Before I left Chicago, I met with Hudson. He told me that my life was a blank canvas and that I could decide what kind of picture I wanted to paint on it," Rylie said quietly. "I've thought about it for a long time and I think I have a pretty good idea of what it would look like."

"Really? Will you tell me?" I asked. I kissed the side of his head as he twined our fingers together.

"I think it would look kind of like a collage of music and the people who are important to me, like the guys from the band, Hudson, and Kerry...and even Benjamin," he said with fake annoyance and I chuckled in response. "In the center, though, would be your house in Chicago..."

"*Our* house," I interrupted. Rylie turned his head and reached up to cup my cheek in his hand.

"In the center, would be our house with you and me and maybe a few kids one day." His eyes were hopeful as he gazed up at me and my heart filled to overflowing for the man in my arms.

"I've always wanted kids," I said, grinning down at him.

"Not too soon, of course. I want plenty of time with my sexy husband first," he said.

"It has a nice ring to it, husband." I leaned forward and I could feel the smile on his lips as we kissed.

I couldn't believe after all of the loneliness and sorrow we both had been through in our lives that we had been fortunate enough to find our perfect soulmate. With Rylie by my side, the future looked happier and more colorful than I could have ever imagined and if you were to ask me, the picture that he had described sounded like the perfect masterpiece.

EPILOGUE

Akio

I PARKED MY CAR OUTSIDE OF THE BUILDING AND LOOKED UP AT what I was sure had been a productive manufacturing warehouse in its day, but had become nothing more than an empty shell as the years moved on. It wasn't in the best part of Chicago either, which had the hairs on the back of my neck standing up. I pulled my phone from my pocket and double-checked the address that Landon had given me, just to be sure; I was definitely in the right place. Landon had mentioned that Carter and Ryan lived in one of the abandoned buildings and had fixed it up into a beautifully designed living space, but I was having trouble picturing anything beyond the broken windows and graffiti-covered walls.

I was half an hour early for my meeting, but there was no way I was going to wander around the creepy building by myself so I stayed in my car and locked the doors. The fact that I was even there in the first place proved that there wasn't much I wouldn't do for Landon Greene. Not only was he my boss, but he was also my best friend.

We'd met when I was working as a temp at the same agency as him. The two of us had hit it off right away, quickly becoming friends and he'd confided in me that he was unhappy with his job as a talent scout. He'd wanted to not only discover up-and-coming musicians, he also wanted to take them under his wing and help them to navigate their way through the music industry so that they could reach their full potential.

Finally, Landon made the decision to start his own agency that would allow him to do all of the things he wanted and when he asked me if I would be interested in joining him as his office manager, I'd jumped at the chance. It was exactly the kind of job I'd been looking for and Landon was more than generous with my starting salary and benefits package. The best part however was that I would get to continue working with Landon who was a wonderful boss, but an even more incredible friend.

Landon's knack for recognizing raw talent had helped build his reputation and when he took over the management of Carter's Creed, his business skyrocketed. He quickly became one of the most sought after music agents and had ended up having to hire more managers to help oversee the many bands that wanted to be signed on with his agency. Landon would never hand his brother's band over to another manager though, so between preparing them for their second worldwide tour and wanting to spend more time with his fiancé, Micah, he had begun handing more of the responsibility over to me to help carry the load.

Part of that responsibility included a project that was near and dear to all of our hearts, Agape House. Landon's family had always been very involved with the center for LGBTQ youth and he'd gotten me involved as soon as we'd become friends. Recently, Rocko had started volunteering there as part of his recovery program and when he told his music mogul fiancé about it, Lachlan had decided that he needed to check it out for himself.

After meeting with the center's owner, Matt, and seeing the

amazing difference Agape House was making in the lives of local LGBTQ teens, Lachlan had agreed that it was a very special place indeed, but that it needed a lot of updating. Matt explained to him that the center depended on fundraising and the kind donations of others to stay in operation and he'd admitted to Lachlan that it was often a struggle to keep their doors open, which unfortunately, left no funds for upkeep on the building.

Lachlan called a meeting with the band, along with several members of the Greene family and myself, to help come up with a plan to build a new facility for the center. Lachlan was going to pay for the new building, but he also wanted to set up a fund that would keep the center running for years to come without having to struggle to make ends meet. While they had enough money between all of them to fund everything themselves, they agreed that it would be better if the community were also involved in the effort, which would bring attention to the center and what it was they were doing for the youth of Chicago.

Ryan suggested that instead of building a brand-new facility, that they look into renovating one of the old warehouses near where he and Carter lived. He pointed out that space to build was limited in the thriving city. By using one of the old warehouses they would be able to expand the center and therefore help more kids in need. Everyone agreed with Ryan's suggestion and then they began discussing fundraising ideas that would get the community involved.

It was also brought up that with the band preparing for another tour, the time that they could personally devote to the project would be limited. Kathy and Rick Greene had volunteered to head up the fundraising end of things, but they would need someone to oversee the building renovation, including meeting with contractors, electricians, and inspectors.

Landon turned in my direction and said that he didn't know anyone with better organizational skills than me, which made me preen until I realized what he was suggesting. I told him that I had far too much work to do at the office and that I wouldn't know where to start with a project of that magnitude, but he promised to hire extra help in the office so that I could focus solely on the renovation.

Caleb added that they'd really like the person overseeing the project to be someone who was already involved with the center and cared about what happened to it, like he knew I would. I could feel my resolve crumbling and then Landon pulled out the big guns. As my best friend, he knew that flattery was my kryptonite so he reminded me of what an important role I'd played in organizing the band's first worldwide tour and that if I could handle that, then overseeing the Agape House project would be a piece of cake. Then he'd winked at me, making me glare at him in return. He knew he was going to get his way and I did too. Not only because of the flattery, but because I had a soft spot for the kids at the center.

Which was how I had ended up sitting in front of a building that looked like it could be on the set of The Walking Dead and wondering if I should have brought one of Micah's security guys along with me for protection from whatever might be lurking in the shadows. Landon had set up meetings with three different contractors and wanted me to decide which one would be best for the job. He hadn't told me much about any of them because he said he wanted me to make my decision based off of my own impression.

A knock on the glass beside me made me scream and I clutched at my chest, attempting to keep my heart from jumping out. I turned and glared out the window, wanting to know who was responsible for trying to send me to an early grave when I was met with the most amazing pair of sea-green eyes I'd ever seen in my life. I was mesmerized by them for a few seconds, until I realized that they were also accompanied by a laughing mouth. It didn't matter that the mouth had a full bottom lip or that the teeth were perfectly straight and it didn't matter that the skin around it was perfectly golden. I saw red.

Who did that guy think he was, sneaking up on me in that kind of a neighborhood and scaring the bejeezus out of me, only to turn around and laugh about it? I should've stayed in my car because I had no idea who he was or what he might do to me, but I was too pissed off to think logically. I narrowed my eyes, hit the unlock button, and swung my door open, making him jump back or risk getting hit.

"What the hell? I don't know what you're doing in this area, but you have no business sneaking up on people and scaring them half to death," I screeched, poking my finger into his chest. I admired the fact that his t-shirt stretched nicely over his broad chest and the hardness of his pectorals under my finger tip, but that was only because I was very good at multi-tasking. His eyes widened in surprise and he held his hands up in surrender.

"I'm sorry, I didn't mean to scare you. I thought you saw me pull up beside you. I'm here for our meeting," he explained.

His words broke through my anger and it was then that I noticed the bright red Ford F-250 pulled up alongside my car just as he'd said. I'd been so lost in my thoughts that I hadn't even seen him. I could feel my face heating up with embarrassment when I realized that I had just yelled at the man who could possibly end up being our new contractor. *Please don't let me have screwed this project up already.*

"No, I'm the one who should apologize, I should have been paying better attention and then I wouldn't have been so surprised. Let's start over, shall we?" I pasted my most winning smile on my face and offered him my hand to shake. "I'm Akio Forrest."

Luckily, he didn't seem too upset because he smiled at me and slid his hand against mine. A tremor went through my hand and travelled up my arm when our skin made contact and I glanced up at his eyes, startled. He looked shocked and I wondered if he'd felt it too.

"It's nice to meet you, Akio. I'm Morgan Greene."

"Greene?" I asked.

His face lit up with a smile. "Yeah, Landon's my cousin."

The End

ACKNOWLEDGEMENTS

My first thanks always go to my family because without them, I wouldn't have the confidence to try anything new. You three are my strength and my heart and I love you to the depths of my soul.

To Aimee, my evil twin. Thank you for all of your support, encouragement, humor and love. I look forward to all of the crazy adventures ahead of us, because this is a year of celebration.

To Deena, for always being my rock. I'm the luckiest girl in the world to have a friend like you in my corner.

To Kerry and Wes. You are the most incredible siblings anyone could ever ask for. You were my first friends in life and there is literally nothing I wouldn't do for either one of you. I love you both.

To my incredible team: Pam Ebeler, thank you for your patience with me and for knowing how to kick my guy's butts when they need it. I can't wait to spend more time with you this year and to create even more fun memories. Jay Aheer, thank you for finding my Rocko and for your amazing creativity and insight. You are by far the most incredible artist. Judy Zweifel, thank you for your incredible eye for detail and for taking on the impossible task of making me look good. Stacey Blake, thank you for the wonderful work you do and the special touches you add to each story. To my betas, Jodi Temple, Lee Rey, Melissa McIntyre, Lori Greis, N.B.S, Allison Holzapfel, Wendy Maples and Leslie Copeland. Thank you all for being willing to read my book again and for your great input, your enthusiasm and your support. Thank you so much for sticking by my side and for the friendships we have formed along the way. I have the best team in the world.

ABOUT THE AUTHOR

I am married to my high school sweetheart who let's face it, is a saint for putting up with me all of these years. Together we have been blessed with the chance to raise two amazing human beings and so far we haven't screwed it up; I'll let you know for sure later. I am a business owner and spend more time laughing than actually working most days. I love watching movies, cooking, going to the beach and spending time with my family and best friends. I am an obsessive reader who is a complete sucker for a good love story, but loves to feel a broad range of emotions throughout a book. I think real life is hard enough and so my books offer twists and turns, but always with a happy ending.

I love to hear from my readers. You can reach me at:

Twitter – www.twitter.com/annabellamicha1

Facebook – www.facebook.com/profile.php?id=100011438515157

Blog – annabellamichaels.blogspot.com

www.ingramcontent.com/pod-product-compliance
Lightning Source LLC
Chambersburg PA
CBHW051149030726
47504CB00004B/1121